# TAKEN

## ERIN BOWMAN

**HARPER TEEN**

*An Imprint of HarperCollinsPublishers*

HarperTeen is an imprint of HarperCollins Publishers.

Taken

Copyright © 2013 by Erin Bowman

Tree photograph by Alisdair Miller

www.epicreads.com

Library of Congress Cataloging-in-Publication Data

Bowman, Erin.

Taken / Erin Bowman. — 1st ed.

    p.    cm.

Summary: "In the isolated town of Claysoot, every male is mysteriously
'Heisted' on his eighteenth birthday, and seventeen-year-old Gray Weathersby
is determined to figure out why"— Provided by publisher.

ISBN 978-0-06-211727-4

[1. Adventure and adventurers—Fiction. 2. Brothers—Fiction.
3. Government, Resistance to—Fiction. 4. Fantasy—Fiction.] I. Title.

PZ7.B68347Tak 2013                                    2012022150

[Fic]—dc23                                                    CIP

                                                                AC

Typography by Erin Fitzsimmons

14 15 16 17 18  CG/RRDH  10 9 8 7 6 5 4 3 2 1

First paperback edition, 2014

For my mother:
who read to me when I couldn't,
and put a book in my hands when I could.

PART ONE

# OF HEISTS

# ONE

**TODAY IS THE LAST DAY** I will see my brother.

I should be spending these remaining hours with him, but instead I'm in the meadow, watching a crow pick at the carcass of a half-eaten deer. The bird is a filthy thing: slick black feathers, a beak of oiled bone. I could wring its neck if I wanted, sneak up on it and crack its frail frame between my palms before it even heard me coming. It doesn't matter, though. Crushing the life from the bird's small body won't save my brother. Blaine's been damned since the day he was born.

Just like me. Just like all the boys in Claysoot.

I stand abruptly. The crow, startled by my movement, lifts briskly into the early morning light. I send an arrow after it and miss, mostly on purpose. Truthfully, I'm no better than the crow, scavenging what I can, hoarding any bit of meat that will feed our people. If my black hair were feathers, I might outshine even the bird's gleaming darkness.

There's nothing much left of the deer. The corpse is hollowed out, animals having feasted on the belly. A hind leg appears intact, but there are too many flies. I don't want people getting sick. It's not worth the risk. Especially not today. The last thing we need on the eve of a Heist is more stress and worry.

I reshoulder my pack and let my feet carry me back toward the forest. My boots know the way, and as their leather soles press against familiar footpaths, I think about Blaine. I wonder what he's doing right now, if he's sleeping in, clinging to the remnants of a carefree dream. I would guess not. Too much looms before him. He was still in bed when I left for the woods before dawn, but even then he was muttering in his sleep.

I have only two quail from my morning in the woods, which will be more than enough for lunch. Blaine probably won't even have an appetite. The Heist tends to do that to people, especially the boy of age. Eighteen is far from a celebrated milestone, and come midnight, Blaine will unwillingly greet his fate. He'll vanish before our eyes, disappearing the way all the boys do when they turn eighteen, as good as dead.

I'm terrified for him, but I'd be lying if I said I wasn't scared senseless myself. Since Blaine turns eighteen at midnight, it means I turn eighteen just three hundred and sixty-four days later.

It was fun to share a birthday when we were younger. Ma gave us what she could: a whittled boat, a woven hat, a metal pail and shovel. We galloped through town and made everything our playground. Sometimes it was the stairs leading up to the Council building, others the tables of the healing Clinic, at least until Carter Grace shooed us away, hands on her waist and curses escaping her lips. Our antics rendered us well-known throughout town. We were the Weathersby brothers, the boys with too much zest for life in such a gray place. That zest didn't last forever, of course.

You grow up quickly in Claysoot.

By the time I hit the hunting trailhead and make my way from the forest, it is midday. I pass two boys playing near a small fire as their mother hangs laundry on a flimsy line behind their house. One is very young, maybe four or five. The other can't be older than eight. I smile at the mother as I pass by, and though she attempts to return the gesture, her grimace is less than convincing. She looks aged, beaten down, even though I suspect she is no older than twenty-five. I know it's because of the boys. I bet not a day goes by that she doesn't wish they were girls, or at least that one of them was.

I run into Kale outside the Council building. She is playing on the steps, tugging behind her a wooden duck that Blaine and I played with as children. It was a gift from our father, before he was lost. We were both too young to remember the toy being given to us—or even our father, for that matter—but Ma said he carved it himself, whittling the thing from a single piece of wood over the course of three months. The duck is showing signs of age now, a chunk missing from its bill and an uneven chip running the length of its tail. It clunks awkwardly down the steps, never landing right side up as Kale skips to meet me.

"Uncle Gray!" she exclaims. She is a small thing, not even three yet. Her nose is still soft pink, a tiny button stitched into the center of her face. She beams as I approach.

"Hey there, Kale. What are you up to?"

"Taking Ducky for a walk. Mamma said I could." She pulls at the wooden toy behind her and it plunks onto the dirt road. "Where's Pa?" She stares up at me with those bright blue eyes of hers. They look just like Blaine's.

"I'm not sure. Why don't you come with me to the market? Maybe we can find him together." I offer her my hand and she takes it, pudgy fingers wrapping around my thumb.

"I miss Pa," she mumbles as we move along.

I smile at her, but there's nothing else to say. It is moments like this that make me feel lucky. I am not Blaine. I am not turning eighteen. I am not a father. I will not disappear when someone needs me most. If Kale misses Blaine now, when he's merely at work or still asleep, how will she feel tomorrow, after the Heist? How can I explain that to her? How can anyone?

The market is bustling as always. Women and girls are there, trading herbs and cloth and vegetables. There are boys, too, all my age or younger. Some hoist freshly caught game onto tables, others tools and weapons or livestock gear, but everyone is trading for various goods. Kale fidgets behind me as I barter with Tess, an older woman who sells cotton and clothing sewn at the textile shop.

"I know, Tess. I know one bird doesn't amount to a new jacket," I admit as I set one of my quail before her. "But remember two weeks ago, when I gave you rabbit for next to nothing because you were in a bind?"

"Gray, you know I'd be out of business if I made every deal based on kindness alone."

"It's for Blaine," I say, rubbing my thumb over the wooden buttons on the jacket. It's made of heavy cotton, streaks of dark brown and black running through the material. "He's always wanted a good jacket, and I wanted to give him one for his birthday, even if he can only enjoy it for a day." I pretend to admire her handiwork but peer from beneath my bangs to see how she reacts to the thickly laid-on guilt. Tess bites her lip anxiously. She knows as well as anyone that tonight Blaine faces the Heist.

"Oh fine, take it," she says, thrusting the jacket at me. "But we're even now."

"Of course." I take Kale's hand and we leave the market, a new jacket thrown over my shoulder and the remaining bird still dangling from my hip.

Kale continues to pull the wooden duck behind her as I lead the way toward our place—Blaine's and mine. It sits on the southern edge of the village, set back from the other homes where it is quiet and peaceful. I frown, realizing that in less than a day's time it will no longer be *our* place but *mine*.

"Aw, what a precious sight!" Chalice Silverston stands before us, sneering. "Father and daughter, out for one final stroll perhaps?"

I raise my head and glare at her.

"Oh. Hey, Gray. I thought you were your brother." She's seen my eyes at this point, the one thing that differentiates me from Blaine. His eyes are blue and vibrant. Alive. Mine are stormy, so colorless that I was named after their dreary hue.

I grunt audibly but don't feel like arguing. I want to focus my efforts on enjoying this last day—if that's even possible.

"What's the matter, Gray? Feeling a little *under the weather*?" she drawls. Gray Weathersby. Under the weather.

She's been flaunting that play on words since we were children, and now, after hearing it a million times over, I've had enough.

"Chalice, you better shut that hole in your face before I make you," I snap.

"Oh come on, Gray. You're just bummed about your big brother. Sad and moping because he's going to be up and gone in a matter of hours."

That strikes a nerve. Anger rages into my chest, surges against my rib cage. I couldn't care less that we went to school together, spent days sitting in the same classroom. I forget that she's a girl and that I probably shouldn't hit her. I react automatically, dropping Kale's hand and throwing my fist into Chalice's cheek. She deserves it, all of it. I hit her again, this time in the stomach. We end up in the dirt, flailing. A few strikes later someone yanks me off Chalice and pushes me aside.

"Get ahold of yourself, Gray." I roll over and find Blaine standing above me, his eyes filled with disappointment. Sasha Quarters, Kale's mother, stands behind him. I can taste blood on the inside of my lip and my jaw throbs. Well, good for Chalice, having the nerve to actually sock me back.

"You're crazy," Chalice says through a mouthful of blood. "Absolutely crazy."

"But she . . ." I look between her and my brother. "She was

mocking you, Blaine. She doesn't even care about the Heist."

Blaine frowns. "I don't give a crap whether she cares about me or not. I'd rather know why my kid brother is beating up a girl half his size. You okay?" he asks, turning to Chalice.

This is why everyone likes Blaine better than me. This is why they'll all miss him but barely notice when I'm gone. He's calmer and has a better heart, looks at the whole of things. But me, I'm reckless, always reacting to some feeling in my chest.

I sit in the dirt and wipe the blood from my teeth as Kale runs to hide between Sasha's legs. Sasha's older than Blaine but doesn't look it. I think she's nineteen or twenty now, only it's hard to tell because she's so damn pretty. When Blaine had first been slated to her, I'd been jealous. Months later she was pregnant and that jealousy instantly turned to relief. That was when I started being careful with my own slatings, avoiding them when possible. I never want to be a father. Ever.

Sasha helps Chalice hobble off. I watch as they go, wondering how Blaine can stand it: how Kale lives with Sasha while Sasha continues with the slatings. Blaine's left floating on the outskirts of the picture as if he doesn't matter, which is a pretty standard treatment. Boys are important to an extent, but sooner or later we're all gone, so no one bothers getting attached. Children get the father's last name, but that's about it. They live with their mothers; and the boys, well, the boys just drift.

"Where are they going?" I ask.

Blaine offers a hand and pulls me to my feet. "To the Clinic. You need to go, too?"

"Nah, I'll survive."

"Good. You deserve whatever pain follows." He smirks and punches me in the shoulder. It hurts more than it should. And then his face changes, grows stern and parental.

"You can't do stuff like that, Gray," he scolds. He still looks disappointed, which is worse than his being angry. "You're always lashing out before you even attempt to understand others. Chalice has dealt with a lot of pain and suffering. Of course she hates the Heist. And is bitter. And says rude things. She's lost three half brothers in the past two and a half years. That's not an easy burden to carry."

I roll my eyes. "That doesn't give her the right to mock the losses of others."

Blaine sighs and gives me a look. A big brother look. An I know best look. Then he stoops to retrieve the jacket I bought for him. When he straightens up, he looks tired. I don't want to argue with him. Not today. Not on our last day.

"That jacket's for you." I nod to the dirty lump in his arms. "Happy birthday." For a second he looks elated and then somewhat terrified, but he shakes the look of fear from his face and pulls on the jacket.

"Thanks, Gray." His smile is back. The friendly, brotherly one.

"You're welcome."

It's all we say. There are a lot of other things that could fill the silence, but they'd all be meaningless. We both know what's coming and nothing will change it, least of all words.

We walk the rest of the way home together, Blaine wearing his jacket even though the summer sun is quickly warming the land.

"I'm going to miss you," I say, squinting in the light.

"Gray, don't even start with me." His tone is more pained than angry, as if discussing his fate for the hundredth time this week might finally break him.

"Maybe we can run? Hide? We could leave tonight and live in the woods."

"And then what? We can only go as far as the Wall, and the Heist is unavoidable no matter where I am."

"I know. But maybe if we go over the Wall. Maybe there's more."

Blaine shakes his head sternly. "There is no more."

"You don't know that."

"Every person who climbs over the Wall winds up back on this side, dead. If there's anything *more*, we'd see it for two seconds before meeting our own end."

"If the two of us go together, it could be different. Like when we hunt. We're better together, Blaine." I'm practically begging at this point. This can't be it. Life can't really be so short.

Blaine pushes his hair out of his eyes and buttons the jacket high about his neck. "No boy makes it past eighteen, Gray. The Heist is going to happen whether we want it to or not. Don't make this any harder than it has to be."

We both know he's right and we enter the house together, in complete silence, for the very last time.

# TWO

**TODAY IS A SERIES OF** lasts. Our last lunch. Last afternoon tea. Last game of checkers. After tonight it will be over. After tonight, he'll be gone.

Blaine picks up one of his dark, clay tokens and jumps over two of my wooden ones. I finger the lines of the game board carved into our table as he collects my fallen pieces, smirking.

It's hard to believe his Heist is already here. It feels like the years flew by, like I must have missed a bunch of them while blinking. The moments I remember with clarity are the milestones of our childhood. Starting school, learning how to hunt. Xavier Piltess taught us over the course of a muggy summer when I was ten. He was fifteen and had his own bow. He sat in Council meetings and got to vote on important issues, and he knew exactly how much a rabbit could go for in the market compared to a deer or wild turkey. The way we saw it, there was no question Xavier couldn't answer.

Until, of course, he was Heisted as well.

By the time I was thirteen, Blaine and I were selling game regularly in the market and helping Ma in the textile building twice a week. A year after that, Ma caught a chill that even Carter and her medicines couldn't chase away, and the two of us carried on alone.

As customary, we became men at fifteen, attended Council meetings, and were eligible for the slatings. It's strongly encouraged, of course, for the boys to make their rounds in Claysoot and follow through with slatings. I've always felt a little torn about it, though. Not that it isn't enjoyable—it always is—but I've grown to hate the moving around, sleeping with one girl only to be pushed at another. There's a level of comfort that is always missing. Each encounter feels like a formality and one that could far too easily result in fatherhood. While I hate the routine, I understand why the Council shoves us at a different girl each month. If we don't want to die out, there's really no other option.

Blaine was always a year ahead of me in these milestones, always leading the way, setting the example. When I was uncertain or scared or confused he'd set me at ease. And now he's just hours away from being gone forever.

"Gray?" Blaine's voice pulls me from my thoughts.

"Huh?"

"I think I'm going to go to the blacksmith shop. I need to stay busy."

"No, don't go to work. Let's at least finish this game."

Blaine touches one of his game pieces but pulls his hand back without moving it to a new square. "I can't do this 'til midnight, Gray. I'm too anxious."

"I'll come with you," I offer.

He shakes his head and points at my chin. "You should get your jaw checked out. It looks worse compared to this morning."

I notice for the first time it's already late afternoon. Had we really been playing that long, or are all lasts quicker by nature?

"Fine," I say. "I'll stop by the Clinic."

He nods in approval, almost the way our mother used to, and then tosses my pack into my lap. He pulls on his new jacket, even though the air is now oppressive and heavy, and tousles my hair before leaving. I sit there, staring at the game pieces, Blaine's clay tokens far outnumbering my wooden ones. Our last unfinished game.

He would have won.

<hr />

The Clinic has several beds, separated by thin curtains that hang from wooden rods running the width of the building. The curtains aren't being utilized when I arrive and I can see that Carter is not in. Her daughter, Emma, is there though, reorganizing a set of clay jars on the shelves at the far end of the room.

I've known Emma since we were kids. Our mothers had been close, mostly on account of how sick I was as a child. Ma once told me that I'd seen nothing but the inside of our house until I was a year old; and throughout that time Carter visited often, fussing over me and working her magic. Whatever she did, she did it well. Half of Claysoot still stares at me like I'm some sort of miracle, like it should be impossible to be so sick as an infant and still come out on the strong side of healthy.

Ma and Carter remained inseparable through most of my childhood, and as a result, I spent a lot of time with Emma. Sometimes Ma brought Blaine and me to the Clinic and we chased Emma around the wooden tables until she cried mercy. Other days, when Carter had less work, she brought Emma over to our house and we entertained ourselves with games like checkers and Little Lie.

Emma was a scrawny thing back then, but she kept up with us. If we were getting good and dirty in the streets, she tagged right along. If we were climbing trees and scuffing our knees on rocks, she boasted the same battle scars. And even though we spent countless hours together as children, Emma was always closer to Blaine. I've never been able to shake the jealousy, but I suppose I brought it upon myself. When I was six and the two of them seven, I pushed Emma over and stole the wooden toy she was playing with. She favored Blaine from that day forward, and naturally that's when it started. As soon as she favored Blaine, I favored her.

At first it was a childlike thing, but my affection never faded. I watched her change over the years, abandoning her thin frame for the curves that now fill out her dresses. She's become increasingly pretty as she nears eighteen, and for as long as I can remember, I've been interested in no one else. I've made my rounds in the slatings, but I'd be kidding myself if I said I didn't want just Emma. I guess it's fitting that I've never been paired with her. I probably don't deserve it.

"Is Carter in?" I call out.

"She's making a house call," Emma replies, answering my hopes without even looking at me. "Give me a moment and I'll be right over."

I sit on an empty bed and rub my jaw, wincing as my hands find an open gash. Blaine was right. I definitely need to have it looked at.

I watch Emma as I wait, admiring how her steady fingers pluck jars from the shelf with ease. She moves so quickly but smoothly as well, her hands confident from years of administering care. They never falter, never slip. Her eyes, too, are focused, darting back and forth. Every time I look into their brown depths, I feel something in my chest heave.

Eventually, when the jars are organized to her liking, Emma meets me at the bed. She has a beauty mark on her right cheekbone, and it almost looks like a single tear escaping down her face.

"I should refuse to help you. After what you did to Chalice and all." Emma has a soft voice, calm like winter's first snowfall.

"She deserved it," I say surely.

"You're lucky that I believe all injured beings deserve to be healed." She looks at me, puzzled, her head cocked as if she is studying a wild animal. I know what she's thinking. It's what they all think: How can I look so much like Blaine and be so different?

She takes my face in her hands and examines my chin. The open cut stings, but I focus on her touch instead, her fingers against my skin. When she is satisfied with her inspection she turns her back on me and begins to mix various ingredients in a shallow bowl. I watch her crush them, her forearm and shoulder flexing. She finishes, wipes her hands on her apron, and faces me again.

"One scoop should do," she says. She passes me the bowl,

which now holds a pasty mixture. "Rub it on the inside of your mouth, near the gash. It will numb the area, and I need to stitch up that cut."

I scoop a small handful of the mixture with my fingers and apply it as Emma instructed. Almost instantly, the pain begins to ease.

"And take this," she orders, handing me a small helping of an ingredient I don't recognize but swallow nonetheless. "I need you perfectly still, and it will help you sleep."

Emma is readying a needle when her mother enters the Clinic.

"How'd it go?" Emma asks.

"The baby didn't make it," Carter says, putting her bag down and repinning her hair on the top of her head. It is the same shade as Emma's, light brown like the hide of a young fawn, and full of stubborn waves. "Died during the labor. Just as well though, seeing as it was a boy."

Emma looks saddened by the news. "And the mother?"

"Laurel is fine." I know this girl is a good friend of Emma's. I've seen them at the market, giggling and whispering to each other as they trade for goods.

Emma breathes a sigh of relief, but I notice a single tear trickle its way down her cheek. She pushes it aside with the back of her hand and returns her attention to the needle.

"Lie back," she tells me, and I do. My head feels oddly light; and Emma, leaning over me to examine the wound, seems to shine like dew-topped grass in morning sunlight. She tells me to relax, but I'm stuck staring into her brown eyes and instead I let words bubble to my lips.

"You want to do something after this?"

"Do something?" Her face is a combination of shock and disgust.

"Yeah, like go to the pub or for a walk. I'll take anything really."

"My best friend loses her child, you're about to lose your brother, and all you want to do is take me to the pub?" When she puts it this way, it does seem somewhat despicable. "You're nothing like him, you know that?" she adds. "You two may look alike, but you're very, very different."

It hurts, those words, but they're true.

"Emma, sweetie, he's not that bad," Carter interjects from the doorway. "People cope in different ways." I'm not sure why Carter's coming to my defense. Maybe she can't stop fussing over me, even now, years after I've needed her care. Or maybe it's because she was close with my mother or the fact that I remind her of my father; she's told me countless times how much Blaine and I look like him. Either way I am grateful.

"Did they put you guys up to this? The Council?" Emma asks. "You've been slated to me, haven't you?" Her eyes cut into mine.

"No," I admit. "No, not at all. I'm not slated to anyone.

They're going light on me because of Blaine and the Heist. I haven't had to see anyone for a week, and I doubt I will for another few." My head is starting to swim now. It wants to sleep.

Emma scowls. "So I should feel honored that this is genuine? I should be happy you're trying to woo me of your own accord and not the Council's?"

Her eyebrows are furrowed and she holds her hands on her hips. I've never seen her look quite so angry.

"Forget it then, Emma, okay? I was only asking. No one's twisting your wrist."

I slump farther into the bed, exhausted. Emma leans over me, her wide eyes focused on my jaw. The needle approaches my skin, but there is no pain. It is just her, stitching me together as though I am a quilt, and then darkness, as I fall asleep.

# THREE

WHEN I COME TO, MY head is foggy. I touch my jaw and find delicate stitches sewn into my skin. The Clinic is empty except for Emma, who is tearing old clothes into bandage-sized strips by candlelight. I've slept through the entire afternoon, through dinner, through—I sit up, panicked.

"Did I miss it?"

Emma jumps. "Gray, you scared me half to death," she says, clutching her chest.

"Did I miss it?" I repeat. "Blaine's ceremony? The Heist? Is it over?"

"No, it's still under way. But you needed rest. I think you had a mild infection, and after the treatment we let you sleep. They started without you."

"Well, I'm fine now," I say, swinging my legs over the edge of the bed. I try to stand, but my vision ripples. Emma is beside me quickly, pulling my arm over her shoulders and wrapping her free hand about my waist. It takes a moment, but I feel strong with her at my side.

"I have to be there, Emma," I say, turning toward her. She's closer than I anticipate and her eyelashes nearly brush my chin. "Please? Help me get there?"

Her eyebrows rise slightly, as if she is surprised by my obvious desire to attend the ceremony. Of course I have to be there. This is the last of the lasts, the final good-bye. Emma waits for me to find my balance before leading me from the building.

It is dark outside, and late. Blaine's birthday is moments away. In the glow of the moonlight I can see the schoolhouse ahead. It's fairly large, even if it doesn't look it, broken down into three rooms. I used to spend my mornings there, scribbling on parchment with ink and reading from scrolls, all while leaning on a desk that wobbled if you applied too much pressure to its right side. It always made my script unclean. I got poor marks in writing because of the sloppiness, especially when compared to Blaine, but what did it matter? Having neat writing doesn't protect you from the Heist.

We are slow at first, the ground seeming to swim beneath me. The farther we walk, the stronger and more confident I become, but it's so nice having Emma beside me that I don't admit when I can continue alone.

In the town center, the ceremony bonfire burns brightly, illuminating the Council Bell, which is used to call meetings to order. Blaine stands beside it, receiving the individuals who line up to say their good-byes. He looks untouched by the entire affair, no fear or worry creeping into his eyes or escaping from his body in a nervous twitch. Kale lies on a mat beside him, her eyes closed in a peaceful sleep. She's still too young to understand what's going on. To her, it's merely a fun party and the excitement has worn her out.

Emma removes my arm from behind her neck. "Will you be all right?" she asks. She smiles at me painfully and I know she's referring to the fact that I'm about to lose Blaine, not my injury. I feel like I should say something, but my mouth is dry.

"Come on," she says. "Let's get in line."

The entire town is present, women, as always, far out-numbering the men. Children who do not yet understand what they are witnessing run around the bonfire, yelp-ing and playing joyfully. Everyone else exchanges forlorn looks, including the Council Heads. The Danner sisters whisper to each other, standing so close they nearly bleed into one person, while Clara and Stellamay fidget anxiously in the receiving line. The only calm Head—the only person unfazed—is Maude Chilton. She leans on her knotted cane and stares headlong into the fire. Each line that creeps its way across her weathered face and toward her chalky hairline is illuminated.

Maude has been around since the beginning, forty-seven years to be exact. I know this only because I've read the scrolls that are stored in our library. Maude was thirteen back when Claysoot was founded. There were no adults.

Now Maude leads the Council. This would be something to brag about if it weren't for all that she's lost. Every son Maude's ever known, every nephew or grandson or brother, has fallen victim to the Heist. Most of the girls she grew up with have died from disease or old age. Perhaps this is why she can stay so calm with each ceremony. Perhaps she is numb.

Emma and I join the line. We are the last two, with the exception of Maude, who always brings up the rear. As I wait for my turn, I watch the villagers greet Blaine. Some clasp his hands, give him a firm pat on the shoulder. Others cry. Sasha, while she hasn't been slated to Blaine in years, brushes aside tears after breaking from his arms. Finally only Emma and I remain. I let her go first.

She rushes to Blaine with surprising force, looping her arms around his neck. He returns the hug. They exchange words I can't quite make out, which is just as well, I suppose.

Emma's good-bye is not mine to hear. When they break apart, Blaine squeezes her hand reassuringly.

Before she turns to leave, Emma rises on her toes and plants a kiss on Blaine's cheek. I can't help but feel jealousy stir in the pit of my stomach. It courses through me, envious of her kiss, irritated with how clearly she will miss him. It's disgusting, hanging on these selfish thoughts when Blaine will soon be gone forever. Why can I not be decent? Why can I not say good-bye?

It's my turn.

Blaine speaks first.

"Hey, Gray." He is still wearing the new jacket.

"Hey." It's all I can muster.

"You missed the feast."

"That's okay. There will be others." And it's true. For every Heist there is a ceremony, and for every ceremony there is a feast, to take our minds off the gravity of the situation.

"You seem well," I add, looking up at him, my mirror image with blue eyes. I doubt I will be so calm this time next year. I don't have the composure he does. I'll likely be one of the boys who melts down as the Heist approaches, becomes a fidgeting mess during the ceremony, and collapses in panic.

"There's nothing I can do to stop it," Blaine says. "It's coming either way, so I might as well try and enjoy these final moments with everyone."

Final moments. Last moments.

"I'm going to miss you, Blaine." I can't bring myself to look at him.

"I'm going to miss you, too, but I'll be seeing you soon. Whatever comes next, death or otherwise, I think we'll meet again."

He winks at me. It catches me off guard, such a playful gesture on such a grave night, but then I realize he is consoling me. I should be comforting him, especially with what he faces, and yet here is, telling *me* that everything will be fine. He plays big brother so well.

I grasp him tightly, locking my arms around his back, and he returns the hug. It is not long or drawn-out, and neither of us cries; but when I finally let go and walk away, I feel as though an integral piece of me has been ripped from my chest.

Maude approaches Blaine and I want her to go slowly. I don't want it to end, because when she finishes, it will be time. It has to be almost midnight; and with midnight a new day will break: a day that is Blaine's birthday and also his end. Maude hugs Blaine delicately and she whispers her good-bye into his ear. She steps away. We wait.

And then it happens, the same way it always does. The ground begins to shake. It is soft at first, tiny pieces of dirt and rubble bouncing about our feet, and then, suddenly, more violent. Some people drop to their knees, unable to stay balanced. The wind howls. The world spins. And then, light. It breaks from the sky like a spear shooting through parchment, effortless and fluid. It expands, stretches, becomes so bright that it hurts my eyes.

I'm usually on the ground at this point, shielding myself from the light and trying not to throw up. I feel sick even now—the Heist always seems to have that effect—but I force myself to stay upright. I focus on Blaine. I keep him in my sight. His eyes are open wide despite the blinding glare, but he does not look afraid. The light encircles him, as if drawn to his body. He is a gleaming spectacle, a burning flame. And then there is one final jolt of the ground, an explosion of brilliance, and he's gone.

As quickly as it began, the disturbance is over. People stumble to their feet, brushing dust from their bodies and rubbing their eyes in relief. We moan and cough, our senses steadying, and then Maude calls out through the crowd.

"Let us have a moment of silence," she croaks in her dry, brittle voice, "for Blaine Weathersby, who on the morn of his eighteenth birthday, was lost to the Heist."

# FOUR

**BLAINE BEING GONE IS KIND** of like when Ma died, only this time I'm alone for good. I spend the first few days forgetting his absence is permanent. I catch myself looking up from dinner, expecting to find him walking through the door. I feel him moving through the house behind me, but when I twist around, the room is desolate and cold.

About two weeks in, when it begins to feel real and I know he's not returning, I break down for the first and only time. I spend an entire evening in bed, muffling cries into my pillow. I don't let anyone see it, but I'm terrified. I feel empty, as if half of me is gone, and I have no family left; Ma had a brother, who had a son, and both are long gone. I have Kale, I suppose, but I can't be the father she needs. I'm not good with her the way Blaine was. I think the most sickening thought is that I only have a year left myself. I have one year until I'm eighteen and no one to even share it with.

In Claysoot I am a spectacle. People give me sympathetic looks and halfhearted smiles, as if they mean to say, "Oh, Gray, it's all right." I find peace in the woods. Amid the tree limbs and pinecones, I am free; no eyes follow me, no thoughts flood my mind. There, I feel like myself.

On the bright side, at least I was able to say good-bye to Blaine. I read a scroll in the library when I was younger that documented the phenomenon of the Heist. The people of Claysoot didn't always know what it was. In fact, when the very first Heist took place, no one even realized until the following morning. It was Maude's older brother, Bo Chilton, who mysteriously went missing. After a thorough search of the town and woods, he was declared dead even though a body was never found. It was odd, Bo disappearing like that, completely out of character. He was the eldest of the original children, their main leader. Calm. Smart. Responsible.

The day the originals opened their eyes to find their town in ruins, they panicked. They suspected a strong storm had been the culprit, knocking them unconscious in the process, but they couldn't remember the bad weather rolling in. They couldn't remember anything from before the disaster, and with the exception of siblings, they couldn't even remember each other. In the blink of an eye, neighbors had become strangers.

Before the group could fall into chaos, it was Bo who rounded up tools and started rebuilding the community. He shook sense into the others, assigning each person a specific task. In a matter of months, the town was well on its way to recovering. The crops were nursed back to life. The fences around the livestock fields were refortified and the animals, which had wandered off into the woods, were corralled and brought back to town. Bo set up the Council, comprised of five heads elected by the community, and since no one could recall the name of their home, he even rechristened the place, slapping two words together that all too accurately described the makeup of most of the town's earth. Clay-rusted roads, and a film of soot-like dirt so persistent it could only be avoided by escaping into the woods.

When the Wall was discovered, Bo volunteered to go over first and scout things out, but he was unable to see what lay on the other side. The view from a large oak tree in the northern portion of the woods yielded nothing but pitch blackness beyond the Wall, and he deemed it unsafe. He tried to talk others out of climbing, claiming the Wall was likely built to keep something at bay, but a few tried. Their bodies came back a charcoaled mess, burned and lifeless, and Bo's assumptions were proven right.

Bo was the reason that the original children, wild and panic-stricken, were transformed into a united team capable of rebuilding their community. But there was still no explanation for his disappearance. A few months later, another boy went missing, and a week after that another. Eventually Maude noticed that the disappearances seemed to be happening to boys of a certain age. It was always the oldest one, and then, finally, she realized it was always the boy turning eighteen.

They ran the first experiment on Ryder Phoenix. He sat in the center of town on the eve of his eighteenth birthday, everyone else around him, and they waited. That was the first night they all witnessed it, felt the ground shake and saw the sky light up. That was the night they had proof.

Maude convinced the group to repeat the experiment. For the next several birthdays, the same thing happened. Boys disappeared, swiped from the town in a matter of seconds, and always on the morn of their eighteenth year. Each one was taken, stolen, lost to a consistent and time-specific Heist.

Once they understood this, some boys began to panic. A few tried to escape before their eighteenth birthday. They climbed the tree in the northern portion of the woods that grew close enough to the Wall to aid in their crossing, but they always reappeared. Dead. Most of the boys came to accept that the Heist was unavoidable. Maude took over for her brother as Head of the Council, and arranged the first-ever ceremony. While the Heist was inescapable, a preparation for it was not. With a ceremony everyone could at least say good-bye, something Maude was never able to do with her brother. With a ceremony, people could make peace.

I haven't quite made peace with Blaine's Heist, though. I'm not sure I ever will. I know it's just the way life is, that part of living is dealing with the consequences of the Heist, but Blaine's loss has made it personal. He's gone and he's never coming back. It feels wrong in a way I can't quite pinpoint. Above all, it's simply unfair.

There is a knock on my door and I'm pulled from my thoughts. It's bright out, late morning. I should be hunting already, but I had dreams littered with Heists and my internal clock has been off since Blaine disappeared. I climb from bed, pull on a pair of pants, and answer the door.

"Well, good morning, you lazy moper," Chalice greets me, her face abnormally chipper. She looks whole again, any damage I inflicted long gone.

"What do you want?"

"Maude wants to see you."

"Is that all?"

"Yes."

"Great." I slam the door in her face and a picture hanging

on the wall crashes to the floor. I probably shouldn't be so rude, but I've never liked Chalice. Unlike Blaine, I refuse to make excuses for her.

I stoop to collect the fallen frame, which houses a charcoal drawing of the Council building done by Blaine as a child. The frame has broken on impact, and as I collect the pieces, I notice something behind Blaine's childhood sketch: a second piece of parchment that is coarse, but not as faded as the original artwork. I lift it from the debris and unfold it carefully.

It is a letter, written in script I would recognize anywhere. *To my eldest son*, it begins. This is Ma's handwriting, careful and clean. I take a deep breath and keep reading.

*It is imperative that you read this, know this, and then hide it immediately. Gray cannot know. I have thought many times of how to share this with you—both of you—but have come to terms with this secret being one that you alone must bear after my passing. Know that I write this to you in my final hours, that I wish so much to be able to explain it in person, but I am a prisoner of my bed.*

*This world is a mysterious one, with its Heists and Wall, so unnatural that I have never been able to accept it outright. And I believe, come your eighteenth birthday, you will understand why I've shared this secret with you. The truth, or the pursuit of the truth, must not die with me. Above all, you must not tell your brother. I know this will be hard for you, but if Gray knows, he will look for answers. He will risk everything, and in turn jeopardize your discovering the truth. And you must. You must discover the truth for me because death will take me before I am able to witness it myself.*

*And so I share this with you now, my son: You and your brother are not as I've raised you to believe. Gray is, in fact—*

I flip the letter over, but there are no more words. I search the debris on the floor, but whatever sheet once accompanied the first is no longer hidden within the frame. I reread the letter once, twice, several times over.

*Gray is, in fact—* I am, in fact, what? I race into the bedroom and throw open the chest that still holds Blaine's things. I rifle through clothing and gear until my hands find a small journal, bound with stubborn twine. I flick through it noting the dates, and stop when I find the one where our mother passed. Blaine's entry is short.

*Carter had no magic left to spin and Ma died today. She left me a peculiar letter. It made me angry at*

*first, and confused, but I realize now that I am*
*incredibly fortunate—to have my brother with me*
*still. Gray, who I value more with each passing day.*

I hurl the journal back into the chest and return to the
kitchen, where I clench the original letter from Ma in my fist.
How dare they keep a secret that so clearly affects me. And
now what? They are both gone and I am left alone in the dark
without any answers. Whatever truth Ma had hoped would
be revealed at Blaine's Heist remains a mystery. Especially
to me.

I read Ma's note again, and again, and when I am boiling
with feelings of resentment and betrayal, I storm from the
house. I have to get away from the letter, as far away from it
as possible, but then I remember Chalice's original words,
the ones that sparked its discovery, and I don't get very far.

I stand before Maude's house and take deep breaths. I let rage
settle to anger and dwindle into irritation before I knock on
her door. She opens it immediately and invites me in.

Maude's place is one of the nicest in town. She has floor-
boards instead of dirt and her water basin has an attached
handle that can actually be pumped to supply water. A kettle
whistles over her fire as I enter, and the scent of fresh bread
lingers in the air.

"Tea?" she asks as I take a seat at the kitchen table. I
decline, probably not as politely as I should, and wait as she

pours herself a cup of hot water and brews her herbs. She joins me at the table eventually, cautiously sipping the piping drink.

"You wanted to see me?" I ask.

"Yes, yes. I've got a name for you." I know what this means and I don't want to hear it. It's the last thing I want to think about at the moment.

"I thought you said I didn't have to deal with that for a little while."

"It's been nearly three weeks, Gray." The steam from her tea rises, twisting delicately before her nose and blending in with her white hair before it continues toward the ceiling.

"Has it really?"

"Mhmm," she hums in agreement.

"So who is it this time?" Here comes another month of awkward formality. Me, hanging out with some girl openly enough that Maude thinks I'm sleeping with her, and then trying to turn that same girl down when the opportunity actually arises. The latter part is harder than I expect sometimes, even with the potential of fatherhood at stake.

"If there's someone you'd prefer to see, Gray, that's fine," she says. "But we have to make plans when we don't see anything materializing naturally."

If the slatings weren't so pressured and formal, then maybe things would happen naturally. But for me, it's just like when

I was a little boy. Ma told Blaine and me not to play with fire, and because of that we did. On the other hand, if she had forced us to play with fire, we'd likely have entertained ourselves with rocks instead. And so it is with this. I'm uninterested in the fire they force on me. I don't like being told what to do.

"Lately I only feel like myself when I'm in the woods," I admit. "Nothing is going to materialize on its own."

"Very well," she says, placing her cup on the wooden table between us. "You've been slated to Emma Link for the next month. You know Emma, right? Carter's girl? Works in the Clinic?"

A knot forms in my chest. "Yeah, I know her."

"Good. Well that is all, Gray. You may go."

I leave without thanking her. For the first time since shattering the frame, my mind shifts away from Ma's secret. I should like this matchup, but I don't. Emma isn't just another girl. I don't want to be with her because I've been told to. I want to be with her on my own terms and with her reciprocating that feeling, or not at all.

Perhaps it won't even matter; Emma will likely reject me. It's been rumored that she hasn't accepted a single one of her slatings, that she turns them all away. Blaine's friend Septum Tate, who was lost to the Heist a few months back, claimed Emma had actually lodged her knee into his groin when he refused to believe she truly meant no thank you. No one believed him. Mostly because Emma is so sweet, so gentle.

I look up to find my feet have subconsciously carried me to the Clinic. I suppose now is no worse a time than any to face her. I push open the doors and step inside.

Carter is attending to someone in the front of the room. I can make out their silhouettes through one of the thin curtains. Emma sits at a desk in the rear, scrawling something onto a piece of parchment. She is wearing a long white dress and her hair is gathered haphazardly atop her head. A few stray pieces fall into her eyes as she writes. I run a hand through my bangs anxiously and then march back to her desk, plopping myself in the seat opposite her without an invitation.

"Hey."

"Hi," she says, barely looking up. "Do you need help with something?"

"No." I'm still trying to work out what to say. Maybe coming to the Clinic was a bad idea. Maybe I should avoid Emma for the month.

"Then what are you doing here?" She puts her quill down and folds her arms across her chest. She looks pretty when she's cross.

"I've been slated to you," I say. There, it's out.

"Oh, is that all? Good. I'm not interested." She picks the quill up again and returns to writing.

"Yeah, I know. I was just hoping I could get the truth out of the way so that we can actually enjoy spending the next month together."

She looks at me, confusion on her face. "I'm not sure you heard me, Gray. I'm not interested. We won't be spending any time together."

"See that's the thing, Emma; I don't want to be a father. Not in a million years. I don't want to end up like Blaine, leaving a kid behind. And you're not interested. You've made that clear. But the Council still wants me slated to you, and if we hang out for a few weeks, they'll think we're doing what they want us to, and then they'll be off our backs. Heck, I could probably even convince them to keep me slated to you for several months, and then you won't have to deal with match-ups at all."

She's quiet for a moment, her dark eyes searching mine. I'm not sure what she's looking for or what she's thinking. She's too good at being blank.

"Okay," she says finally. "It's a deal. What do you want to do?"

"What, right now?"

"Yes, right now." She smiles, ever so slightly. It causes that pain in my chest, that heave I get when she looks at me, to pulse.

"We can do anything. What do you want to do?"

"Let's go to the pond," she says, putting her things away.

"What pond?"

"The pond. The only one. The one near that field of purple bellflowers."

"That's more of a lake."

"Oh, it's a pond in my mind. Come on, let's get out of here." And then she's grabbing my hand and pulling me from the Clinic. I guess I won't be hunting today.

# FIVE

**WE HEAD SOUTH THROUGH TOWN,** passing the school and black-
smith shop and the numerous houses, including my own,
that create the border of the village. Where the dirt fades
away, tall grass begins, sprouting up in patches, until finally
we are entering the woods. I don't usually hunt along the
southern portion of the forest. It's marshier, and the larger
game sticks to the drier areas. The ground grows soft beneath
our feet as we continue, but there's been little rain lately and
we avoid sinking into the doughy earth. When we reach the
coarse thicket that I know to be concealing the lake from
view, Emma grabs my arm and pulls me to a standstill.

"This way," she says, motioning to our right.

"But it's straight ahead. On the other side of this brush."

"I know, but the view's better if you climb the hill."

"View? There's no view."

"Trust, Gray. Have trust." And then without waiting to see if I follow, she starts cutting through the trees and brush, no path to guide her. She holds her dress up about her knees, and I stare at her legs as she steps over fallen logs and rocks in our path. We move slowly and up a steady incline. Maybe there will be a view after all.

When we break loose from the trees, I'm nearly speechless. We are standing on a hill that overlooks the water. From this angle it appears rather small and narrow, its thinness stretching out of view beyond another crest in the land. Surrounding us are the bellflowers, tall, thick stems that grow higher than my waist. Delicate purple petals hang from each, grouped together and dancing in the soft breeze. The southernmost portion of the Wall is barely visible in the distance.

Emma leads us into the field and toward a lone rock that sits on the hillside. The purple flowers nearly reach her shoulders, but she climbs out of their grasp.

"I used to come here with my uncle," she tells me as we get comfortable on the stone. "Almost daily. At least until . . . you know. I was nine when he was lost. I haven't been back in years."

"It's beautiful from up here," I say. "And, to be fair, it seems much smaller from this angle. I can almost understand why you called it a pond."

"See?"

"Yeah, well, it's still a lake. I'm just trying to be nice."

She sighs. "Ah, yes. That must be difficult for you."

"You know, despite what you might think, I'm not a mean person."

"What you did to Chalice wasn't mean?"

"That's different."

"It was still mean."

"Okay, fine. I'm not inherently a mean person."

"I'll give you that for now." She plucks a clump of grass and sprinkles it into the breeze.

"So why'd you do it?" she asks, looking at me. "Why were you honest about the matchup?"

I'm not quite sure how to answer the question. There are explanations on many levels. I don't want to be a father. I hate the formality of slatings. I want her, but not if it's forced.

"You were being honest, right?" she asks. "You're not going to try to attack me later or something are you? I'm stronger than I look. Everyone always thinks I'm this kind, caring thing, because of my healing hands, but I can be forceful if I need to."

"So I've heard." I chuckle. "And, yes, I was being honest."

She gives me that look again, the same one from the Clinic. I still can't read it.

"I hate the slatings," she says.

"Me, too."

"How many have you gone through with?"

"You don't want to know." I can count them on two hands and even though it's been a long time since I've slept with anyone, the number is still more than I want to admit to her. "You?"

"Just one." So the rumors are wrong. "You remember Craw Phoenix?" she asks.

I nod. He was lost to the Heist about a year and a half ago.

"I liked him," she continues. "And I mean *really* liked him. It was so nice for that month, and for some reason I thought it would last and we'd have something. I don't know what. It was stupid, really. I wanted to continue slatings with him, but I guess the feeling wasn't mutual. Two weeks later he was seeing Sasha Quarters, and then he was gone completely."

"We're all gone eventually," I say. "That's half the reason I hate it, too. I don't see the point of the scheduling and the moving around. I only have 'til I'm eighteen. I'd rather find something good, something comfortable, and stay in it."

She gives me a half smile. "You mean be with one person? Like, beyond the duration of the slating?"

"Forget the slating. Pretend there's no slating and there's no rules and there's no Claysoot and then, yes, one person. Forever. Is that weird?"

It's quiet for a moment. I know it's an odd question, completely hypothetical and outlandish, and for a second I think she's going to laugh at me.

"You know, some hawks mate for life." She bites her lip and looks back out over the water. It's a ripple of icy silver in the earth, the valley bleeding blue into its depths.

"Really?"

"Yeah, the red-tailed ones. My uncle and I used to see them here each year. Always returning, always the same pairs together. If the birds pick one mate for life, why can't we?"

I feel foolish for a moment. I spend hours in the woods every day and I've never noticed this in the hawks. Then again, I was never looking for it.

"Maybe some animals mate for life and others don't," I say. "Maybe we're not supposed to be like the birds."

"Maybe we are."

She looks so pretty, sitting there, twisting grass between her tan fingers. I wonder if we are the only people who wish this, who long to ignore the matchups and procedures and settle into something that feels right. There I go again, thinking with the feelings in my chest instead of using my head. If we were like the birds, we'd die out in a matter of decades, once all the men were gone. I still wish it were possible though, wish I were a bird and Emma were a bird and we could fly away without looking back.

"You really are nothing like him," Emma says. It pulls me from my thoughts and I find her staring at me, again with the same inquisitive look I can't read. "Like Blaine," she clarifies.

"I know, I know. He's kind and responsible, and I'm reckless. He thinks things through. I react."

"Yeah, I know, but I don't think that's necessarily a bad thing. Maybe it's good to just react, to not overthink everything. If we were wild and free, like the birds, you'd survive. Blaine probably wouldn't. He'd be too worried with pleasing everyone and making everything fair."

"Sounds like I'm pretty selfish."

"No, that's not what I meant." She wrings her fingers anxiously. "I'm trying to say that I think doing what you *feel* can't always be easy, but at least you're being true to yourself."

"It's okay, Emma, you don't have to try to make me seem like a better person. You don't have to justify why it's all right to spend time with me."

"No, I'm not . . . ," she says, frustration on her face. "Dammit, Gray, I'm trying to say I admire you for what you said about the slating, that I agree with you, that it's not crazy to want to be like the birds, but above all, I'm trying to apologize for how I've judged you all these years. You're different from Blaine but maybe not in a bad way. Maybe in a very good way, and I'm only seeing it for the first time."

She's staring right into me with those eyes of hers, dark orbs as large as walnuts. Something in my chest surges. Suddenly it is very warm.

"You want to go for a swim?" I ask, jumping from the rock. As much as I want to be near her, I need distance. It's those words. What do they mean? Earlier today she despised me, thought me wicked for hitting Chalice, and now she admires me? All because I follow those feelings in my chest?

"Swim?" she asks. "Right now? It's not even that hot out."

"Suit yourself," I say, tearing away from her and running down the flower-filled hillside. When I reach the edge of the lake, I turn back and can see Emma gazing down at me, perplexed. She's probably still trying to figure out why her kind words sent me running.

"You coming?" I yell back up the hill. She shrugs her shoulders and then hops from the rock.

I pull off my boots and strip down to my drawers and am in the water before Emma is even halfway to the lake. The cold hits me savagely, biting at my lungs. It's refreshing, though, and I feel like I can breathe again, Emma's words falling aside as I kick into open water. I'm floating on my back, staring up at an impressive mass of clouds forming overhead, when something splashes beside me. I twist over and see Emma along the shore, tossing pebbles in my direction. She has waded in up to her shins, the hem of her white dress gathered in her arms.

"Are you coming in or not?"

She shakes her head. "It's too cold."

"Wimp."

"Oh, please."

"Well, you are." I swim in until I'm close enough to the

shore to splash her with a well-placed kick. Water catches the front of her dress and her face goes wide with shock. It probably feels like ice to her.

"Oh, you're going to get it," she shouts.

"How? I'm already in." I swim back toward the lake's center.

She's fuming. She tugs her dress up over her shoulders and throws it aside before running and diving headlong into the water. She's the better swimmer and catches up quickly. With a strong kick her hands are on my shoulders and pushing me beneath the surface. I'm too busy admiring how her undershirt clings to her body to prepare myself for the dunk. I resurface, sputtering and coughing.

"Who's the wimp now?" she asks. Her hair is wet and stringy, pieces of it clinging to her neck. It looks dark in the water, nearly as black as mine. I lunge at her, but she's too quick. She darts away, slipping underwater and resurfacing behind me, where, to my embarrassment, she dunks me again. We continue like this for a while, me always trying to catch her and she easily avoiding my attacks. When I finally surrender, she's dunked me four times and eluded me seven.

"Fine, you win," I admit as we climb out of the lake. "But I would slaughter you in an archery match." I pull on my pants and use my shirt to dry my hair.

"You hunt daily, Gray. That's hardly fair." She's turned away from me, pulling her dress on. She shakes out her wet hair and braids it back.

"It doesn't have to be fair to be true."

"Fine. Teach me," she retorts.

"Really?"

"Yes, teach me how to shoot and then we'll have a match."

She spins to face me. There are wet patches where her dress meets the curved parts of her body.

"Okay," I agree. "Start tomorrow?"

"Tomorrow."

We walk home in silence. I try to figure out what it all means, Emma being so nice, so playful. The last time the two of us got along so well was when I was six.

"Today was actually a lot of fun," I tell her as we approach the outskirts of town.

"Yeah," she agrees, "like being a kid again."

We cut down a side street and head for the Clinic. Up ahead I can see Maude and Clara sitting outside the Danner sisters' house.

"Emma, take my hand."

"What? Why?"

"Just take it." I reach out and grab hers before she can argue. Her skin is soft and delicate, unlike my callused hunting hands. I spread my fingers between hers and squeeze them lightly as we carry on. My chest heaves ever so slightly. As we near Maude, I watch how her eyes linger on our entwined hands and I flash her a devious smile as we walk by.

# SIX

**THE NEXT WEEK FLIES BY.** I spend mornings hunting and afternoons with Emma, passing my knowledge of archery to her in the empty fields behind the livestock pens. We start with the basics: understanding the curve of the bow, the form of the arrow. I teach her how to hold them, when to release, the posture to possess. She squirms impatiently for two days because I refuse to let her shoot until she can nock an arrow with her eyes closed. When she finally takes her first shot, she is terrible, but only because she's forgotten everything I managed to teach her. Excitement pushed it from her mind and anxiousness took hold of her muscles. She improves over the following days, her arrow flying straighter, her aim more precise.

As happy as I am to spend so much time with Emma, the words of my mother's letter continue to haunt me. I turn the house upside down, searching for the slightest of clues. I read Blaine's diary from front to back, but nothing further is revealed. I try to forget I even discovered the letter, and yet I can't. I want to know what secret Ma shared with Blaine. I want the truth the way I crave to breathe. It is subconscious and it plagues me.

On a hot afternoon, when the weather is muggy and heavy and the air presses in on my lungs with vicious intent, I decide it is time for Emma to shoot at her first real target. Sending arrows into open fields is one thing. Hitting a mark is another.

We make our way to the eastern portion of town, past the crop and livestock fields, to our normal shooting grounds. I set up a basic target and hand Emma some arrows and my childhood bow—I have since outgrown it and it better suits her frame. As I'm slinging my quiver across my back, I hear the thump of an arrow hitting grass. I look over to see Emma's discouraged face.

"You're rushing," I tell her. The arrow is burrowed in the soft earth in front of the target.

She frowns. "It seemed so easy when we were just shooting and there was no mark to hit."

"Everything's simpler without constraints. Keep your arm parallel to the ground as you pull it back. Remember your stance, too." I draw my bowstring back in illustration. She attempts to mimic me and fails impressively. I suppress a laugh.

"Here, I'll show you." I move behind her, hold her bow hand in mine and wrap my other arm around her so that I, too, am grasping the string.

"Now focus," I say. "Nothing exists in the world except for the target." I drop my arms and step away from her. She lets the arrow fly, and this time it strikes true. It barely manages to hang on to the outermost ring, but nonetheless, it is there.

She jumps in excitement, turning to face me. "Did you see that?"

"Course I did. I'm standing right here."

She nocks another arrow and reaims. I watch her muscles clench as she focuses, admire how her eyes narrow. I wonder how she hasn't caught me staring at her like this, not even once since we started hanging out. Perhaps archery has been a worthy distraction.

Emma releases her bowstring. This time she does much better, missing the bull's-eye by only a single ring.

With a triumphant yelp she throws her arms around my neck and hugs me. It takes me by surprise. She feels small in my arms, even though she never seems small in person.

When she breaks away, I can see how truly proud she is.

"I think you're a natural," I tell her.

"I think you're a good teacher."

"No, seriously. Teaching and correcting form can only do so much. The rest is either in a person or it's not."

She walks up to the target, twists the arrows free, and returns them to her quiver. "Let's have a match," she says.

"You really think you can beat me after hitting a target twice?" I ask skeptically.

"Oh, come on. Let's play. Besides, I'm not the one that challenged you to a match that day back at the lake."

I smirk. "Fine, have it your way. Just don't say I didn't warn you."

And with that, we play, shooting three arrows from twenty paces, then three more from forty, and then a final set at sixty. Emma does extremely well at twenty paces, but her arrows start to stray at forty. From the farthest distance she misses entirely, all three arrows landing in the soft ground around the target. I shoot a perfect game without even trying. We retrieve our arrows and then sit down in the grass, our foreheads lined with sweat.

"Okay, you're right," Emma admits. "When it comes to shooting, you can absolutely crush me."

"Told you." I take a swig from my waterskin and then pass it to her. I watch as a bead of sweat trickles down her neck and across her collarbone, disappearing beyond the neckline of her shirt.

"If I tell you something, do you promise to not repeat it?" she asks, handing the water back to me.

"Sure."

"Have you ever read the scrolls from the library that document the beginnings of this place?"

"The history of Claysoot? Yeah, I've read them."

"Don't you find them odd?"

"How so?"

"For starters, their memories were so shoddy after the storm destroyed Claysoot. They remembered certain skills—like how to tend crops and work a loom and rebuild collapsed buildings—but they forgot the names of their neighbors. And their own town. And *anything* they might have been doing before the weather hit. How does something like that happen? And where were their parents? The scrolls don't mention having to bury the deceased, and if the adults weren't lost to the storm, it means they weren't here when it rolled in."

"So you think their parents were somewhere else?" I ask, taken aback by the idea.

"Maybe? I don't know. The children must have been born in Claysoot, to mothers that were living here also, because nothing can cross the Wall and live to tell the tale. But at the same time, it seems very unlikely that every single mother died in a storm that small children survived."

I've never thought of it this way, but she has a point.

"It's unlikely," I say, echoing her. "But possible."

She wrinkles her forehead. "It still feels off."

"We'll never really know, I guess. The scrolls could be incomplete or poorly written. They could have left out burying the adults because it was too difficult to write."

"Yeah, maybe," she says, but I can sense the doubt in her voice. Emma's questions remind me of Ma's letter and her mention of how mysterious life is. Like my mother, Emma is obsessed with inexplicable details.

I take another swig of the water. It's warm now, but it's still nice to wet my lips.

"So why can't I repeat any of this?" I ask.

"You know how the Council freaks out every time someone suggests there's something else beyond the Wall. But there *has* to be. I just don't see where all those children could have come from otherwise. Every living thing inside this Wall was born to a mother. And if those kids didn't have mothers *here*, they had mothers someplace else."

Again, a valid point.

"You're quiet," Emma says. "You think I'm crazy."

I laugh. "I don't think you're crazy. Not one bit."

"And you won't repeat this?"

"Your secret's safe with me."

"Thanks, Gray." She smiles—it's a crooked one, only one corner of her mouth pulling up—and then flops into the grass with a heavy sigh. The sky is cloudless today, a giant stretch of blue filled with nothing but a glaring sun. Emma wriggles about to get comfortable, and ends up closer to me than when she first lay back. I can feel her hip pressed against my side. Every muscle in my body yells at me to roll over, to grab her face in my hands and kiss her, but I lie there motionless. What we have is almost perfect, so comfortable I'm afraid to ruin it. I want it to be more, but this is manageable. For now.

"All right. My turn to ask something *you* promise not to repeat."

"Okay," she says, still staring at the sky.

"What would you do if you discovered that someone was keeping a secret from you?"

"Confront them, probably."

"What if you can't? What if they're gone?"

"Then I guess I'd confront whoever else made sense. Or start digging for answers."

"And what if you found no answers?"

"Then you're not looking hard enough."

I snort, thinking of the still upturned state of my bedroom. If answers exist, they are certainly not in my home. But maybe there are other places to look. Maybe, as Emma suggests, I'm simply not searching hard enough.

"Does the Clinic keep patient records?"

"What kind of records?"

"I don't know. Anything, really. Births? Deaths? Stuff a patient said during a visit?"

"Sure," she says, rolling onto her side to face me. "But that information is not exactly available to the public."

"Look, Emma, I need to peek at one record. It will only take a few minutes."

"Whose record?"

"My mother's."

"Is she the one that kept something from you?"

"Yes. Her and Blaine." I know I can trust Emma, and so I pull the letter that has been haunting me for days from my pocket and pass it to her. She reads it carefully, her eyes widening, and then her hands flip it over, searching for more words as she comes to its end.

"Where's the rest?" she asks.

"I don't know."

"Well, it won't be listed in her scroll, I can tell you that much."

"But some answers might be." I take the scroll, fold it, and return it to my pocket. I can feel a headache starting between my eyes and I pinch the bridge of my nose.

"I really don't think you'll find anything," Emma says.

"I still have to try. I need to know what she's talking about, or I'm going to go crazy."

"Okay. Tomorrow morning my mother has a house visit. We can check then, but quickly."

"Thank you, Emma."

She stands and offers me an arm. "We should head back. Mohassit's ceremony is tonight and the feast is probably starting soon."

Another boy turning eighteen. Another life to be lost. I'm not close to Mohassit, but I know him well enough from the market. He works in the livestock fields, tending sheep and cattle. He's thin and frail and manages to get sick more often than anyone I know in Claysoot. The odds seem always stacked against him, and yet somehow, he refused to give in to them. Unfortunately, I know he will not beat the odds tonight.

We gather up the gear and head back to town. By the time we've dropped everything off at my place, the sun is starting to set. As we approach the Council Bell, it becomes obvious that something is wrong. People are gathered as usual, but the group is quiet. No one is huddled around the bonfire or feasting on the food. Instead, everyone is standing rigid and staring up the road toward the hunting trailhead. Emma and I follow their gaze and when we see it, we freeze.

Two boys are carrying a stretcher from the woods. On it is a body, black and crisp, the features scorched beyond rec- ognition. But there is no mistaking that frail, thin frame, no second-guessing who would have risked the Wall today. He was likely late to arrive at his ceremonial dinner. And then the search party went out. And found him somewhere along the base of the Wall, where all the climbers reappear. Dead.

There will be no Heist tonight but a funeral instead.

# SEVEN

IT DOESN'T TAKE LONG FOR the funeral to commence. Maude keeps the bonfire lit, and the boys carrying the stretcher—one of whom I recognize to be Mohassit's younger brother—add the body to the flames.

Emma stands very close to me, her arm hooked around my left elbow. Sasha must be nearby, because Kale finds us in the crowd and tugs on my other arm. I lift her and she buries her face in my neck. People hang their heads; friends and family cry. When Maude stands up, everyone grows still.

"Let us have a moment of silence," she calls out solemnly, "for Mohassit Gilcress, who, on the eve of his eighteenth birthday, was lost to the Wall."

I drop my chin into my chest, but the moment of silence

never begins. A voice breaks across the crowd.

"To the Heist!" it shouts frantically. "He wasn't lost to the Wall. He was lost to the Heist!" A figure emerges near the bell. It's Mohassit's mother. She is smaller than even Mohassit was, and frailer still. The brown tunic she is wearing nearly drowns her.

"The Wall may have killed him," she continues, "but he was lost to the Heist. They all are. Whether they disappear or run straight to their own deaths, that damn Heist is the reason we lose them. I curse it, and I curse this place for stealing our boys from us. I hate this place. I hate it!"

She's a mess now, hiccups rising to her throat. She crumples to the ground and shudders like a lost child, until her remaining son pulls her into his arms, much as if he were the mother, and consoles her. Emma presses her face against my shoulder. My sleeve grows damp and I know she's started crying. Many are.

"As much as death is a part of living, the Heist is a part of life," Maude explains. "We may not understand it. We may not find it fair. But we cannot be at peace with our ways, or those lost to us, if we curse the very place we call home. Let us remember Mohassit and the joy he brought into our lives."

Mohassit's mother nods feverishly, her son still holding her in his arms. "A moment of silence," she prompts, and this time, the crowd bows their heads in remembrance.

Several people then step forward to say a word or two about Mohassit: memories, thanks, things they will miss. Kale has fallen asleep by now, and so has my arm. I have to shift her to my other side, and in turn, am forced to shake Emma off. She doesn't seem to mind, though, brushing her tears away and then smiling at me as she strokes Kale's blond curls. It's funny standing there, the three of us. Almost nice. Almost like a family. I wonder if in a different life, in a place without a Heist, if such a thing even exists, I might actually want to be a father one day.

When the funeral ends and the bonfire is put out, the sun has long since set. People begin to filter back home. Sasha finds us and lifts Kale from my arms but not before extending an invitation for drinks. With our spirits low and no Heist to fill the evening, we agree.

Sasha puts Kale to bed and then pulls out a jug of ale, pouring three tall drinks. After several rounds of Little Lie, a game where you tell four truths and one lie and those unable to spot the farce drink in defeat, we have forgotten the lull of the funeral and are light-headed and giggling.

"You lit your own hair on fire trying to light candles on a matchup. That's the lie," Emma says to Sasha.

"No way that's it," I say. "I'm going with that story about how you ate so many strawberries as a child that you got sick for a week. I know for a fact you hate berries and wouldn't have touched them to begin with."

Sasha chuckles. "You're both wrong. I do hate berries, but it's because of that childhood trauma, and I completely singed off half my hair during one of my first slatings."

Emma and I groan in disappointment. "So which one was the lie?" Emma asks.

"The I-can't-climb-a-tree statement. I know I don't come across as very adventurous, but I can actually shinny up a tree trunk without much trouble."

Emma and I exchange doubtful looks.

"Oh, shut it, you two. I'll show you sometime when it's not pitch-dark out . . . and when we haven't had quite so much ale. Now drink up." We do, emptying our mugs entirely. Somehow, Emma and I are terrible at this game, and Sasha, who still has half a mug left, is quite the trickster.

We play a few more rounds, in which I learn that Emma is terrified of midwifing, that she can deal with blood and guts, but the idea of delivering a child scares her senseless, and that Sasha, despite selling herbs at the market, is a self-proclaimed failure as a cook. By the time Emma and I leave Sasha's, our heads are spinning and the trip home seems far more difficult than it ought to.

I walk Emma to her place, the two of us swerving about the dirt path like dry leaves on a windy day. Emma is humming to herself, spinning in graceful circles, her arms outstretched. While tipping her head back to look at the stars, she stumbles and bangs her knee against the rocks making up her front stoop.

"Look, I'm bleeding!" she announces almost gleefully. It's not funny that she's hurt, but I'm smiling anyway.

"You okay?" I ask, eyeing the smear on her knee.

She nods. "Uh-huh. Doesn't even hurt." It's amazing how ale will do that to you, wipe all the pain away and replace it with a mesmerizing dizziness.

"Here," I say, offering her a hand. She's lighter than I expect, and I pull her straight into my chest without meaning to. She stands there, her hands resting over my heart, and stares up at me. Everything outside of her seems to be twisting, drifting in and out of view. Is it the ale, causing my world to spin or her? I take her hands in mine. I think of doing something, anything, but we just stand there, our fingers clutched together and our eyes locked.

A door slams somewhere in town, and, startled, we break apart.

"Well," Emma says, tucking her hair behind her ears. "I'll see you tomorrow? Meet at the Clinic?"

"Sure. If we feel well enough."

"Okay." She grins at me, another smile I am unable to completely read. She looks confused and happy at the same time. And then she slips into the house, latching the door before I can even attempt to say good night.

# EIGHT

**I AWAKE THE NEXT MORNING** feeling groggy and weak. There's a subtle pain pulsing behind my temples and my mouth is dry. I groan as I pull myself out of bed. I eat some bread, which nearly comes back up, and eventually give up on food and splash water on my face instead. I sit at the table, my head pressed against the grain, and close my eyes.

Will she pretend nothing happened? Will she even remember that moment, that second when something clearly danced between us? I remember, but maybe all that magic was in my head, a trick of the alcohol. Maybe I felt something because I'm always looking for feelings. Without them, I don't know how to act. Either way, had it not been for that slammed door, perhaps there would have been more to last night.

Then again, maybe it's better that there wasn't. The details would be a blur now anyway, the lines between real and imagined lost in the shadowy corners of my hangover. I like remembering the times I spend with Emma. I like to know they are real and honest. Ale has a way of turning both such things into dazzling illusions.

After another unsuccessful attempt to eat some bread, I change into clean clothes and head out. Except for Emma, the Clinic is empty when I arrive. She's sitting at the back of the room, searching through tall shelves that house hundreds of scrolls.

"Morning," she exclaims, bright and chipper. Clearly the ale did not punish her as it did me.

"Morning." I slump into a chair and rub my temples. Emma hands me a revolting wad that looks like nothing more than weeds.

"It will clear the headache. Promise. Mine's gone." So she did feel ill this morning after all.

The concoction tastes even worse than it looks, but I force it down and within several minutes, the pain in my skull is indeed subsiding. I must look better, because Emma flops into the seat opposite me and tosses me a scroll.

"That's her record," she says. It seems rather small, and when I look at her apprehensively, she adds, "It's all we have."

I roll it open and slide some clay jars over the edges to

keep the parchment from curling in on itself. Emma and I bend over and begin reading. The entire thing is a list, dates followed by brief descriptions written by Carter and various Clinic workers from earlier years. At the very top is my mother's name, *Sara Burke*.

Year 11, January 3: born to Sylvia Cane, healthy

Year 14, February 10: treated for bad cough

Year 14, February 13: treated again for cough, seems to be recovering

Year 21, August 14: broken bones set in wrist from fall

Year 29, June 23: gives birth to boy (Blaine Weathersby), healthy

Year 30, June 23: gives birth to boy (Gray Weathersby), sickly, will need additional care

Year 44, November 8: treated for high fever and cough

Year 44, December 1: diagnosed with pneumonia

Year 44, December 21: health failing, receiving treatment via house visits

Year 44, December 27: patient lost

The entries stop here. No item is elaborated on, no comments scrawled in the margins. I push the weights off the scroll in frustration, and it springs back together.

"I told you I didn't think you'd find anything," Emma says

heavily. "We don't keep very detailed records, only the bare minimum, in case we need to check something against a patient's family tree."

"Oh, good idea. Can I compare these dates to the ones in my scroll? And Blaine's?"

"I don't see the point."

"Please. This can't be all there is."

Emma sighs, but then returns to the shelf and pulls down two more scrolls. Blaine's has but two dates: his birth, as noted in our mother's scroll, and his Heist. Mine also has my birth date, one year to the day later than Blaine's, but dozens of other entries. The first thirteen alone document house visits from when I was an infant, sick and feeble. I read through the later notations, recounting my more recent trips to the Clinic for treatments of hunting injuries and accidents. I'm remarking at what a healthy child Blaine was in comparison to me, when Emma interrupts my thoughts.

"Gray?" I look up and find her sitting at Carter's desk. "I think you should see this."

"What is it?"

"Well you mentioned comparing records and I thought maybe, just maybe, I should check some of my mother's personal ones."

"She keeps personal records?"

"It's her notebook from house visits." She holds up a

leather book with *Year 29* written on its cover. "She brings them with her, records any necessary information, and then copies them into the scrolls later. That way, if she makes multiple stops before returning to the Clinic, nothing gets forgotten or left out."

"Okay, well let me see," I say.

Emma hesitates, her lips pinched as though she has something to say but can't find the nerve to spit it out. She looks over the page again and finally pushes the notebook into my outstretched hands. "Read here."

I take the book cautiously, and as my eyes fall on the words, I suddenly understand Emma's uncertainty. Scribbled between two other house visits, is a note of a visit to my mother. Even I cannot understand the words before me:

Year 29, June 23: gives birth to twin boys
(Blaine and Gray Weathersby), both healthy

I pause. Shake my head. This must be a mistake. I reread the line again and then sit with the book in my lap. I'm not sure if I'm furious or pleasantly surprised. If anything, at least for the moment, I am blank. Shocked.

I suppose this explains a lot of things. Why we looked so identical. Why I felt half of me had been ripped from my chest when he was Heisted. Why we could read each other so well, know what the other would say before the words even escaped our lips. It explains a lot of things and I can almost accept it. Almost. Except for one small, tiny detail.

"Gray, if this is true, you shouldn't be here," Emma says. "If you're really Blaine's twin, if you're actually eighteen, you would have been Heisted weeks ago. With him."

"I know." It's the piece that doesn't make sense, the element I cannot fathom.

"Maybe the journal's wrong," she says.

"Why would it be wrong? Would your mother write down something that didn't really happen?"

"No," she agrees. "But why would she record one thing in her notebook only to return to the Clinic and record something completely different in Sara's scroll?"

"I have no idea."

"Do you think this is what your mother was about to tell Blaine in the letter? That you are twins?"

I think of the last few words of the letter, which, from reading over and over, I have practically memorized. *And so I share this with you now, my son: You and your brother are not as I've raised you to believe. Gray is, in fact—*

Gray is, in fact, your twin. This must be it. It fits so perfectly. This is the answer I have been looking for, the secret that's been kept from me. I accept it as if it were fact. The idea takes hold of me, drills itself deep beneath my skin and penetrates marrow. I am a twin, still here—the only boy over eighteen to ever beat the Heist. But why? Because it was kept secret?

"We have to ask your mother," I say finally. "She wrote that note in the journal, and I want to know why she changed it when she copied things into the scrolls."

Emma shakes her head frantically. "No, we can't do that. She'll know we were snooping around in her personal records."

"Emma, this is so much bigger than that. I might actually be eighteen, and if I am, I think everyone here deserves to know that I wasn't Heisted." I can feel my pulse gaining velocity in my chest.

"But that's just it, Gray," Emma says sadly. "If you are really eighteen, you *would* have been Heisted. The journal is wrong."

"If we ask your mother, we'll know for sure."

"Ask me what?" Carter is standing in the doorway of the Clinic, her gear bag in hand.

"Nothing," Emma says quickly. "Gray and I were just stopping by to get out of the sun." And then she grabs my arm and pulls me toward the exit, dropping the book on Carter's desk while her back is turned.

# NINE

**I SPEND THE MAJORITY OF** the next two days in the woods, alone with my thoughts. I hike to the northernmost points simply to stare at the Wall. I imagine the answers sitting on the other side, waiting. They tug at something in my core, urging me to climb, telling me that everything I want to know lies just beyond that towering structure. The idea of the truth, the fact that there could be more to this place than any of us know, begins to drive me mad. What if the Heist really isn't as straightforward as we believe, as consistent and unavoidable as death from old age? Aren't I proof that there is something greater at work?

When not in the woods, I pore over parchment. I reread my mother's letter time and time again. I visit the library and study every historical scroll in the place. I replay my conversation with Emma that day in the fields and I keep thinking of Blaine, how he had winked at me when we'd said our goodbyes. Was he trying to tell me something?

The longer I sit with my thoughts, the more I am convinced that something is not right. It's Claysoot. Everything about it now feels wrong: the Wall, the Heist, the original children. How did people living in an enclosed space have no memory of how they got there? How did they arrive when the thing enclosing them cannot be crossed? And why does the Heist, which steals every boy at eighteen, steal every boy but me? I spend hours wondering why no one else is questioning these things, and then realize I only just started questioning them myself.

On a still, windless morning, without Emma's knowledge, I visit Carter in search of answers. I sit at her desk in the Clinic and ask her, outright, if I am Blaine's twin. She looks at me with calm eyes and simply asks, "Where on earth would you get an idea like that?"

"I don't know," I say. "I miss him so much. And we looked so much alike. Maybe I'm just going crazy with loneliness."

"Well, if you ever need to talk, our doors are always open," she says reassuringly. She then explains that I am a year to the day younger than Blaine but certainly not his twin. It is infuriating, because I'm positive she knows otherwise. She's aware of the truth, had scrawled it in that small journal. Why is she not racing through town and proclaiming that a boy over eighteen has beaten the Heist? Why has she chosen to keep such a miracle secret? Fearful that the reason lies upon the second page of the letter I will likely never find, I leave the Clinic not with answers but more questions.

That afternoon, as Emma and I sit at my place playing checkers in the dreary lighting of a summer storm, I reach a breaking point.

"I have to do something, Emma," I say. "I can't sit around here anymore, hoping the answers will fall into my lap."

"What's there to do?"

"I don't know. Find Blaine. Discover the truth."

"What do you mean, find Blaine?"

"The last couple of times I've been in the woods, I've been *this* close to climbing over the Wall and searching for him." I hold my hands up an inch apart.

"Searching for him? What's to search? It's not like he took off to enjoy a stroll beyond the Wall. He was Heisted."

"But that's just it, Emma. When you climb over the Wall, something kills you, so there must be more on the other side. There has to be more than just Claysoot."

"You'll die, Gray, like they all do," she says.

"Maybe not. I survived the Heist. Maybe I can survive the Wall, too."

"Gray, promise me you won't. Please. I understand what you mean, that feeling that there has to be more, some explanation. I get it every time I think about those original children. But it's crazy, what you're talking about. It's suicide."

"But what if there really is more, Emma? What if we just have to climb over that Wall to see it, and instead, we spend our whole lives in here because we are too afraid to try?"

She stands up and walks around the table. Before I realize what she's doing, she's wiggled her way onto my lap so that her back is to the game board and her face right before mine. She looks me over, brushing my hair away from my eyes. She doesn't say anything, but I'm too focused on her hands to care. She is tracing the contours of my face, dragging her fingertips along my chin. And then she leans in ever so slowly and she kisses me. She knows exactly what to do to win me over, to bend me to her will. I lean into her and every inch of me livens.

Her lips are soft but dry, and her hair smells like soap from the market. I return her kiss, my hands finding the curve of her back. I'm about to pick her up and carry her into the bedroom when her palms push against my chest. I open my eyes to find her, inquisitive, before me.

"Promise me," she demands. "Promise me you won't do anything stupid."

"Emma, you know I can't make a promise like that. I do

stupid things all the time. Blaine's the one that thinks things through."

"I'm not interested in Blaine. I'm interested in you."

"Fine, I can promise you this much: If I am about to do anything stupid, you'll be the first to know, before I actually do it."

"Assuming you can even identify it as stupidity."

"Yes, that."

I kiss her again. My hands go to her back for a second time, but as I begin to lift her, she giggles and climbs from my lap. She puts the kettle on and looks back to me, smiling. I don't know how she can be so calm. My chest is still heaving, my body electrified.

"You know, maybe you're overdoing the whole thing," she says. "Maybe your ma really did have twins back then, but the younger one died or something. And then a year later you came along and she named you in his memory. You could really be a year younger than Blaine."

"But then a lost child would have been stated in my mother's scroll. And I would have been listed as the third."

"Or maybe the scrolls are incomplete," she counters. "After all, that's the excuse you gave me when we originally talked about Claysoot's founding."

I raise an eyebrow at her. "That's different."

"How so?"

"I don't know. It just is."

"Maybe you should go talk to Maude, Gray. If there are any more answers to be found, she has them."

"And, what? Admit that we snooped around the Clinic and read private records and now I don't understand why, at eighteen, I haven't been Heisted?"

"At this point it seems a far safer option than climbing over the Wall."

I catch myself staring at her wavy hair, the way it has grown wild in the damp evening, and decide she is the most beautiful being I have ever seen.

"You are so smart, Emma, you know that?"

She blushes and pours the tea.

Much later, after tossing in bed for hours, I give up on sleep entirely. I sit at the table and think about Emma's suggestion. Maybe I can get information from Maude without admitting I snooped around at the Clinic. Maybe I can say I discovered I was a twin through Ma's letter by pretending I have both pages. Before I can decide if this is a good idea or rather foolish, I am pulling on a hooded shirt and stepping into the rain.

I knock on Maude's door several times, but she doesn't answer. She's probably asleep, but I pound again. This time, the door swings inward ever so slightly from the force. I nudge it cautiously with my foot. The kitchen is empty, but a faint, flickering light seeps from the bedroom, casting an eerie blue glow about the room.

"Hello?" I step inside, mostly to get out of the rain. "Maude?"

Still no answer.

I move cautiously through the kitchen, and that's when I hear it, murmured voices, coming from the bedroom.

"Any other happenings to report?" It's the voice of a male, so soft I can barely hear it.

"Nothing out of the ordinary," Maude says.

I peer around the doorway and find Maude's back to me, the rest of her facing an oddly illuminated section of her bedroom wall. I lean forward to better hear who she is talking to, but my foot steps on a squeaky floorboard that cries out under my weight.

Maude spins around and her eyes narrow as she sees me. She stands up quickly, far quicker than I've ever seen her move before and slams closed the cabinet housing the light. I step away from the room, ready to bolt for the door, but she marches right at me and I know it's no use.

"What are you doing here?" she wheezes, leaning on her cane as she moves into the kitchen. She does not look angry but terrified.

"I came to talk to you. I had a question." My eyes search the room behind her. "Who were you talking to?"

"No one," she says. "I was preparing my notes for a meeting with the Council Heads tomorrow and sometimes I like to review them out loud."

"But I heard a man's voice." Again I crane my head around her, searching the bedroom.

"You heard nothing of the sort," she says bluntly.

But I did. I know what I saw, what I heard. Suddenly, I no longer trust her. Maude, who always seemed to guide our people, show us the way. She has become another element that feels unnatural, and so quickly.

"I'm leaving," I tell her.

"Good. It does not do to enter others' homes by force."

"No, not just your house," I explain. "Claysoot. I'm leaving."

"Don't be rash. You know there is nothing beyond the Wall."

"I'm not being rash. I don't trust you. I don't trust this place. So much about it is wrong and if I can't find answers to my questions here, I'll find them elsewhere." I back away from her, feeling my way toward the door, but she grabs my arm. Her grasp is surprisingly strong for such frail hands.

"Don't be stupid, Gray," she says slowly. "You won't find any answers beyond the Wall because you'll be dead."

"But I'm eighteen! It might be different."

Maude's fingers tighten around my wrist. "Eighteen? What are you talking about? Have you lost your mind?"

"We were twins . . . *are* twins," I say, twisting my arm free. "I can't stay here anymore. I just can't."

I find the doorway and stumble into the rain.

"Wait!" she cries, but I don't. As I tear through the water-logged streets, she calls after me. I can't quite make it out, but it sounds like "stay." And "please."

I run straight to Emma's house and pound on the door. I promised to let her know if I came up with any stupid ideas, and while this doesn't exactly feel stupid, I know it is risky. But I have no other options. My only hope for truth now lies beyond Claysoot.

"Gray," Emma remarks when she opens the door. "It's the middle of the night. Are you okay?"

"I need to talk to you."

"Okay," she says, yawning. "Come in."

"No, I need to *talk* to you." I draw the words out, but she looks at me blankly. "Come here," I grunt, grabbing Emma's arm and pulling her outside so that our conversation will not wake Carter.

"Ow, Gray. What's the matter with you?" she says, rubbing her wrist.

"I have to leave."

She looks at me, bewildered. "Leave? Why do you have to leave? Where are you going?"

I tell her about Maude, the voice, the blue light coming

from her room. I tell her how Maude has become another mystery, like the Heist and Wall, that is too unnatural to trust.

"Please go home and sleep on it. We can talk in the morning," Emma says. "You're not thinking clearly."

"I'll feel the same way tomorrow. I can't stay here any longer, Emma. It's all wrong and I need answers. If they come in the form of death beyond the Wall, at least I'll know for sure that nothing exists outside this place."

"I don't understand why you're doing this." She's close to tears now.

I analyze every aspect of her. The way those large eyes pinch together in the corners, the exact angle of her eyebrows, the placement of that mark on her cheek. I want to remember these things. It's the last time I'll see them. More lasts.

"You don't have to understand," I say. "I'm doing it for me, because that's what I do. We talked about this on our very first trip to the lake. I think about myself, my needs, and I act on them. I need the truth, all of it, and I'm going to get it. I can't spend my entire life not knowing."

"Gray, please. Please don't be that selfish." She grabs my hand in desperation.

"I have to do this," I say. I'm not sure if this is really true. It feels it, though. Every ounce of my body screams that this is the only way, and that's all I need. Those feelings have always been enough to justify action.

"Gray?" she whispers.

"If I survived the Heist, what's to say I can't survive the Wall? I'll come back. After I get some answers. I promise." And then I grab her face and kiss her before she can argue. She kisses me back, her hands gripping the base of my neck. This figures, that when I finally manage to connect with Emma, I am running in the other direction. Before her lips can change my mind, I break away. She stands alone, her nightgown blowing about her shins as I sprint home.

I pack my bag with food and water. Gather my bow and arrows. It is mindless work, like my body's been preparing for this moment my entire life. I am calm, free of nerves. I feel nothing—nothing but the warm rain that pings against my skin as I leave my house, a torch in hand.

The trailhead lies quiet and somber before me. As I stand in its mouth, lightning snakes through the sky, illuminating the town I leave behind. I admire it for the last time, holding the torch overhead. It sizzles in the lightly falling rain. And then, without looking back, I shoulder my pack and head north.

PART TWO

# OF WALLS

# TEN

I'VE NEVER BEEN ANXIOUS IN the woods before, but tonight nerves find me. It's not because of the dark or the constantly rumbling thunder or even the reality that I am trekking toward what for all before me has been death. It's the answers, calling to me from beyond the Wall. Blaine would say I've lost my mind, and maybe I have. Maybe it takes going crazy to face the truth.

When I reach the Wall, it is more ominous than I remember. I press a hand against it. The stone is cold, and the surface smooth, like rocks in a riverbed. I look up, past the rain that drips from my eyelashes, to the top of the towering structure. A flash of lightning brightens the sky; for a split second, I can make out the figure of a lone crow. He is perched on the

Wall, his feathers slick and glistening in the rain.

Something moves behind me, bolting through the brush. I squint through the rain, but my torch reveals only flickering raindrops. I turn my attention to the tree, a massive oak whose limbs grow close enough to the Wall to serve as bridges, and begin the climb.

It's slow going with the torch, but I need it. I climb higher than I ever have before, past the point I'd clambered to as a child in hopes of glimpsing what lay beyond the Wall. I reach a branch that stretches out toward the top of the stone shelf, and shinny across it, my legs doing most of the work. Soon I am crouched atop the Wall, staring into the black void that fills the space on the other side.

There is nothing to make out beyond the structure, not even with the torch. It is a thick black fog, a nothing so dense and heavy that if you awoke within that murky space you might think yourself dead. I sit there for a few moments, breathing heavily. My heart pounds stubbornly against my ribs. I try to calm it but can't.

For a moment, I consider climbing down the tree and returning to town. I must be crazy, thinking I can do this. No one survives the Wall. No one. But then again, just days ago I believed no boy survived the Heist. And the answers are waiting, on the other side. All I have to do is climb over.

The crow beside me ruffles his feathers, annoyed by my

panting and indecision. He cocks his head, caws at me with a shrill screech, and then, as if to show me how simple it is, soars effortlessly into the dark void. His black feathers blend seamlessly with the empty air. I stare for quite some time at the space into which he vanished.

I follow the crow's example in the end. I wedge the torch in my bag so that my hands are free and shift my body over the edge of the Wall. The opposing side is as smooth as ours. There are no crannies or footholds to aid in my descent. I hang from my arms, lowering myself as far as possible, before dropping to the ground.

My knees buckle when I land, pain jolting through my ankles and back. I retrieve the torch and straighten up.

I can smell smoke in the distance. I hold the torch before me, hoping to see something, anything. Slowly, the darkness begins to fade. It's melting away, changing, as if setting foot on this side of the Wall has made the space visible. It is still nighttime, but I can finally see, the flames from my torch lighting the world around me when just on the other side of the Wall this space was forever dark. There is indeed grass beneath my feet. Pebbles and brush. It's another forest, much like the one I've just left, but there are no trees growing near the Wall; they have all been cut down. I shudder at the sight of their stumps, which are cut almost as smoothly as the surface of the Wall itself. No ax could chop that flush.

Things are still coming into view, morphing and trans-forming in the air, when another waft of smoke reaches me on a gust of wind.

I hear a shuffle to my right. It grows closer.

I drop the torch and ready my bow, aiming into the unknown. This is it, coming. This is what killed all the others.

A figure emerges from the shadows, and my heart plum-mets to my feet. Nothing could be worse than this, more terrifying. Emma has followed me over the Wall.

# ELEVEN

I STOOP TO RETRIEVE THE torch before it goes out in the wet grass, and then I stand there, my mouth hanging open. Emma takes advantage of my silence and races toward me. She's wearing pants and a well-made jacket. There's a bag strung about her shoulders. She's thought this through, deliberately followed me.

Her arms link behind my neck. I hug her and kiss her hair, which is wet with rain. She's saying something, but the words are muffled, her face pressed into my chest. And then the initial shock of her arrival wears off. It sinks in, the severity of her actions. I grab her shoulders and push her away from me.

"What is this?" I demand.

"Gray," she starts, reaching for me, but I slap her arm away.

"No, seriously, Emma. What were you thinking? Why did you follow me here?" I'm almost certain now that the movement through the brush earlier was her tailing me.

"I . . . I wanted . . . Well, fine, Gray! It's nice to see you, too."

"That's exactly it, Emma," I spit back. "It's not nice to see you at all. How could this possibly be nice? I have a chance here, but you, you'll be like all the others. Am I supposed to like that?"

"I'm not dead yet," she retorts.

"Well, it hasn't found us yet. It's going to happen, whatever it is, and there's nothing I'm going to be able to do to save you." I want to tell her to leave, to climb back to where it is safe, but the Wall is too smooth to scale and the lack of nearby trees has her trapped.

"Maybe I don't want to be saved," Emma continues. "Maybe I'm here because I want the truth, too, no matter the cost. What you're feeling right now, that drive for answers, I've had it my entire life. Why is your seeking the truth any more justifiable than my wanting to?"

"It's justifiable because I actually have a chance."

"That's really two-faced," she snaps.

"I don't care!" I shout. "I escaped the Heist. I don't know how or why, but maybe that same magic will spare me here. You don't have that chance."

Emma bites her lip and looks down at the grass. It's quiet

for far longer than is comfortable and when she finally speaks again, her voice is soft. "There's nothing for me back there anymore, Gray. The two things I want, answers and you, are now on *this* side of the Wall."

I hear Emma say this, and know that I want her, too, but in a more dangerous way, in a way I've always been afraid to admit, maybe even to myself.

I love her, and *love* is a word too heavy for couples to exchange in Claysoot. It is rarely spoken, and when it is, it is passed solely between parent and child. Feeling so strongly about someone your own age is nothing but foolish; the Heist shatters all relationships, regardless of their strength. It won't ruin us, though, not when I've beaten it. But this world beyond the Wall, what happens to all the climbers . . . that could.

"Gray?" Emma is still waiting for my answer. She looks so pretty, even with her hair growing wild in the humidity. I can't stay mad at her. Not here, not when there's no guarantee we'll both make it. I want to tell her the truth, to speak that word, but it feels clumsy on my tongue.

"I'm sorry," I say, "for yelling."

She nods. And then I'm kissing her, because it's easier than forming words. Her lips taste like rain, and I want her closer, even though I want her far away, safe behind the Wall. When we finally break apart, the storm is faltering.

"I need you to promise me you'll listen from here on in. Any order I give, even if it sounds weird at the time, just trust me, okay?"

Again, she nods. "I promise."

We drink some water and then I lead the way, moving through the dense woods and away from the smoky scent that continues to ride the air. I have an uneasy feeling that should we meet its source, Emma will meet her doom.

We left Claysoot so late in the evening that it isn't long before dawn penetrates the overhead canopy. We squint in the light, continuing until the trees open onto an empty field. It's much larger than the clearing in Claysoot's woods, and free of stones and dirt trails. It's almost inviting, and because of this, I grow suspicious.

A breeze whips through the meadow and the smoke again reaches us. It smells thicker, more pungent. I thought we'd been moving away from it, but now I'm not so sure.

"What's that?" Emma whispers, pointing ahead through the meadow.

At the far end, where another line of trees begins, is the faintest hint of a structure, a building perhaps. The hairs on my forearm rise.

Answers.

We make our way into the field carefully. I lead, pausing whenever I hear a foreign sound or get a bad feeling. Slowly, the shape reveals itself to us.

It is indeed a building, a narrow, skinny thing that has long since been deserted. Parts of the roof are failing, and the front door swings aimlessly on the breeze. There's something odd about the place, though. Even in its state of decay, it is too perfect. You can tell its frame was once meticulously aligned, its windows uniform, its roof even. I think of our homes in Claysoot that, while built with care, are flawed and imperfect. Whatever hands made this building were extremely skilled.

Or not human.

"Maybe there's people," Emma says. "Come on. Let's go see."

I grab her wrist and pull her to my side. I can tell the place is abandoned, and has been, for sometime. "I think we should wait a minute." There's an odd feeling creeping over me. I suddenly feel as if we're being watched.

"I always knew there had to be more, out here, beyond that Wall," Emma says. "Gray, you know what this means, don't you? Someone has been here. People! Just beyond Claysoot. Maybe this is where they came from, the originals. Or maybe the adults were here when the storm hit, and the children got stuck inside!"

I don't know what I expected to find on this side of the Wall—a gaping black hole through which I'd drift forever, perhaps—but this place changes everything. There is life beyond Claysoot, life and earth just like there is inside the Wall.

"Come on, let's get a better look," Emma urges again.

I want to, so badly. I can feel the answers pulsing in the air before us. They reach for me, soaking over my skin like the warmth of a strong fire, but they cannot outshine the doubt that fills my mind. I can still feel invisible eyes on us and I look around the field, almost hoping to find an intruder to shoot.

We are alone.

When I can no longer fight the desire to know, I agree to Emma's request and we head for the building. Once inside, I twist a rusty bolt to secure the door and we take to exploring.

The place has a finished floor, like Maude's house in Claysoot, only it is not wood but some smooth material I have never seen before. Even under a layer of dust and grime, you can tell it once shone brightly, reflecting light and movement. We also find a sink that spits rusty water from a pipe at the turn of a handle, and there are odd branches hanging from the ceiling that flicker light about the room when Emma presses something on the wall. The place is magical. I'm now certain it was built by something other than human hands.

"Can you believe it?" Emma asks as she spins about the

empty foyer. "I wish we could tell them about this. Imagine if we all climbed over the Wall together! We would have running water and magic candles and—"

There's a deafening crash as the bolted door is kicked in.

Emma sinks into my side. Two figures stand in the entryway, dust settling about them. In their arms they hold metal instruments, long, slender, and narrow, and somehow I know that even if I fired my arrows, I would be no match against these intruders.

"Thank God it didn't find you yet," one of them says. He has a scar that stretches from below his left eye down into a thick beard that covers his mouth, and his head is completely free of hair. The man at his side looks younger and is clean shaven. Both men are older than me though, and since I've never seen a man over eighteen, they look ancient. They wear matching garb: black pants with black jackets, a red triangle emblazoned with a cursive white *f* upon their chests.

"Are you alone?" the bearded man asks.

Emma and I nod at the same time.

"Something patrols this area. Something dangerous. You're lucky we found you first."

"Something?" It's all I can manage, and my voice is unsteady as I say it.

"It's not safe here," he says. "Come with us."

He walks up to us, grabs Emma at the elbow, and tugs.

"Get your hands off her," I snap.

He twists around, his face right before mine. The eye above his scar is disconcertingly foggy. "If you know what's good for you and your girlfriend, you will shut up and follow us to safety. But if you want to burn, by all means, stay here."

Burn. Are we the first climbers to encounter these black-suited saviors, the first to avoid the death every other met?

The bearded man straightens up. "Well, Romeo?" It takes me a moment to realize he's addressing me. "What will it be?"

I look at Emma. Her face is nothing but fear and I'm certain mine is the same. She gives a curt nod, takes my palm in hers, and squeezes.

"We'll come," I tell the man.

"Good. Let's move. We don't have much time."

Outside, waiting atop the hill before us, are two oddly shaped contraptions on wheels. They are identical in size and color, both large enough to hold several people but not grand enough to be a home, like their windows and doors suggest. The bearded man pulls a small, rectangular box from his jacket pocket. It is not much larger than his palm, but he speaks to it as though it's a person.

"We're good," he says.

A split second later, the device talks back. "We'll see you back at Union Central then, Marco." A figure waves from one of the wheeled cages on the hillside and I get the feeling it was his voice I just heard responding to the bearded man.

The cage growls and then springs to life, hurtling toward the woods Emma and I hiked through earlier. It is faster than anything I have ever witnessed. Unnaturally fast. I blink, and it's gone.

We follow Marco up the hill. "In the car," he orders, pulling open a rear door.

The idea of being trapped in the thing he called a *car* makes me anxious, and I'm no longer sure I want to follow them. What if it's all a trick? What if they claim to be helping, but really they plan on delivering us straight to our deaths?

Marco's partner pushes at my back, but I resist. "Why are you helping us?"

Marco shifts his weight, the door still held open. "I'm not at liberty to discuss that with you right now. Nor do we have the time. But if you get in the car, I can take you to the man who has answers."

Wind, followed by the scent of smoke.

"Come on, Marco," the other man says. "We have to get out of here. I'm not risking my own life just because these two are too stupid to save their own."

The men climb into the car. Marco lowers the window and stares at me with his one good eye. "Last chance, Romeo."

Why does he keep calling me that? I want to correct him,

but Emma touches my arm. "I think we should get in," she says.

"I don't trust them. We don't know who they are or how they found us. If they can save us, why didn't they save all the other climbers?"

Emma tucks a strand of hair behind her ear. "I'm not sure, but you know what will happen if we stay. I can smell the smoke. We've both seen the bodies. And they say they can take us to the man that has answers. What other choice do we have?"

The car growls and Marco urges us again. "I'm not waiting a moment longer. It's now or never."

I beat the Heist, and maybe, just maybe, I can beat that smoky scent as well. But Emma can't. This is her only shot and I know it.

"Let's go," I say. I slide into the car and she follows my lead. Marco says something to his partner, but a clear panel divides the front seats from the rear and his words are muffled and flat. I can hear the car, though, rumbling beneath us. Emma leans into my shoulder, and suddenly we are flying.

# TWELVE

**WE RATTLE AHEAD, THE CAR** lurching over uneven ground. I put an arm around Emma and let my thoughts drift back to the odd light in Maude's bedroom. I can't help but think she knows there's more beyond the Wall. I try to tell myself that it is not possible. If she knows, if she's known all along . . . I don't want to think about what that means.

The car slows and we stop before a stretch of wall. Not our Wall but a second one. Emma and I were trapped all along, both in Claysoot and even when we were beyond it. In the front seat, Marco takes the communication device and again talks into it.

What happens next doesn't seem possible. A small section of the wall twitches, and then it's moving, parting like a cloud splitting in two. Not a moment later, a vacant expanse lies before us, a clear passageway right in the center of the structure.

Emma sits upright. "Did you see that?"

I nod, dumbfounded.

"Do you think we could do that? Back in Claysoot? Do you think there's a section of our Wall that opens and we just never found it?"

But I don't get a chance to answer her because we are hurtling forward again, the speed so great I grow nauseous.

We emerge onto a frozen black river, so straight and precise that I wonder if it is a river at all. It cuts through the earth. The sky hangs gray. The grass grows dry. There is a whole lot of nothing out here, just land that goes on and on. I wonder how much of it exists, how small Claysoot is in comparison.

At one point, we pass several rickety homes and faltering structures. A town, like Claysoot. The people are holding a funeral, obvious from the downturned eyes and a mound of fresh earth. Farther outside the community I see two young boys carrying buckets of water, their forearms strained. I imagine they will have blisters by the time they get home. That, or they make the trip so often their palms already boast proud calluses.

We drive for a long while without seeing anyone else.

Finally, a forest of tiny tree trunks appears on the horizon, stretching toward the clouds. Above them is a glint of light, shaped like an arched rainbow or overturned bowl. It catches the sunbeams and shoots them into the car. As we get closer, I realize that the shapes within are not trees but buildings—hundreds of buildings of varying heights, all stretching up toward the brilliant arch.

Marco drives the car toward the gleaming barrier at a stunning speed. Again he says something into the handheld device, and again, an entrance reveals itself.

*Welcome to Taem*, a sign above us reads, *the first domed city.*

Taem is like nothing I have ever seen. I keep thinking that I must be dreaming, that I will wake up in my Claysoot bed to discover that everything from when I first entered Maude's house to now has been nothing more than the workings of my slumbering imagination. I blink rapidly. I pinch the flesh on my forearm.

I don't wake up.

The sheer size of Taem makes it hard to breathe. Buildings tower at heights so precarious I am certain they will topple in on us. I realize that the frozen river we travel on is actually a road, dark and solid, so opposite our dirt variety. As we travel through the city, the road splits and forks and multiplies, twisting in intricate patterns as cars fly past. There is a long series of silver buckets that hang from cables and whoosh by overhead, their sides scrawled with letters that read *trolley*. I repeat the odd term in my head, wondering how it's pronounced. Emma and I don't exchange a single word; we are too busy gawking.

Things here are made of materials I have never seen. Lights illuminate the city, their brightness trumping every candle and torch in Claysoot combined. Some cast their brilliance along the road we travel. Others fill the sides of buildings, flashing words and symbols in a frantic manner. And the people: There are people everywhere. Walking. Talking. Coming in and out of buildings. They wear odd clothing and some of the women walk in awkward shoes that appear to be raised beneath their heels. Many carry bags that seem impractical, too large or too small. I can't stop staring.

Beyond all the things I don't understand—the new shapes, sounds, materials—there is one thing I do: the men. They are abundant. There are as many as the women. Some are young—my age or children—but there are old men, too, middle-aged to ancient. They have creases on their faces and gray hair on their heads. They have skin as dry as parchment and eyes that droop, tired. It makes my stomach uneasy but in an exhilarating way.

We pass more buildings, pausing near an open center where men, dressed in the same black uniform that Marco and his partner wear, stand on a raised platform. There is a golden statue at their backs, shaped like the emblem atop

their chests, and an incredibly lengthy line of civilians filling the square before them. Several of the black-suited men
hold the same slender objects Marco and his partner carried,
only these men point theirs at the crowd. I know the form.
They are aiming. At people. The objects they hold are weapons. Behind the statue, a smooth section of an aged building
is illuminated with words: *Water distribution today. Segments
13 & 14 only. Must present ration card.*

With a lurch, we are moving again and the square slips
from view. The next street seems to be the city's main artery.
I have never seen so many people in my life. I think of the
struggling community we'd passed earlier and wonder why
they couldn't live here as well, in these immaculate buildings, under this glowing dome. Maybe the city has no more
room. Or no more water. The thought is terrifying; Claysoot
always seemed to have enough rain, and our lake and rivers never ran dry. Then again, we were only a few hundred
people.

The road squeezes between two towering buildings, both of
which are plastered with a repeating piece of paper, climbing
up, up, up toward the city's domed ceiling. A man's face fills
each sheet, staring at us. Resting on his ears and the bridge
of his nose is some sort of protective eye gear, its frames
thick and black. He wears an odd ribbon about his neck
that dangles down the front of his shirt. The visuals cut off

at midchest, but the man's shoulders slouch forward within the frame. He looks delicate and brittle, as though his entire body might crumple from even the slightest breeze.

"How do you think someone drew those?" Emma asks, pointing at the man. "They are identical. And they look so real."

"Maybe it's not a drawing."

We both look back at the maybe-drawings. The words *Harvey Maldoon* appear beneath each picture. There are several smaller words beneath those, but I can only make them out when Marco brings the car to a standstill and lets people cross the street. "Wanted alive for crimes against AmEast, including sedition, espionage, and high treason; crimes against humanity, including torture, murder, and unethical practices of a scientific nature."

Most of the words are foreign to me, but I know enough to be disturbed. We had little crime in Claysoot, thanks to laws set up and enforced by the Council, and our scrolls documented only one attempted murder, a failed one at that.

I look over Harvey again, trying to fathom one person doing all these terrible things and more. At first I thought he looked weak. Now, after reading the description, something in his eyes appears sick and twisted. I don't like the way they follow me as the car moves down the street. Emma shudders, and I do the same.

When we break free of the crowded corridor, we travel a few more minutes before arriving at a building more grand than the rest. It sits atop a manicured plot of grass, each blade cut with precision so that their tips seem to match up seamlessly in height. The entire place is surrounded by an intricate fence, made of metal and sculpted with such care and embellishment that I know it would have taken Blaine a lifetime to forge in Claysoot. The building itself is immaculate. It bends and sweeps in odd areas, giving way to arched windows and whimsical coves. The roofline varies in height, creating stepping-stones into the sky. The shapes are all wrong and yet mesmerizing. I can make out the words "Union Central" above a massive front doorway.

A man in black nods at Marco as we head through the front gates. Marco takes the car around the side of the building and then we sink underground, moving into a space filled with idle cars. When ours ceases to rumble, Marco climbs out, opens the back door, and squats beside us.

"I'm Marco. This is Pete." He jerks his head backward to where his partner now stands. "I apologize for not introducing ourselves sooner, but it wasn't safe."

"It doesn't really seem safe here either," I think aloud, images of a wanted man and rationed water and men pointing weapons at their own people still clear in my mind.

Marco snorts. "Sure, don't bother thanking us. We only

just saved your lives."

"Thank you," Emma says. She reaches across me and shakes Marco's hand. "I'm Emma, and this is Gray. He seems to have forgotten his manners."

Marco smiles at that, but I don't like the way his lips look devious or the way his eyes are working over Emma.

"Maybe I'd be more polite if we could get some answers," I say. "I still don't know who you are. Or why we were the first climbers to ever be saved."

"Like I said, I can't discuss that," Marco says, standing. "But after you clean up, we'll take you to Frank. Come on."

Emma and I climb out of the car. "Who's Frank?"

"Just the only thing holding this crumbling country together."

I don't understand the differences between towns and cities and countries, but given what I've seen today, if a city is a large town, I'd guess a country is a large city. Or something even bigger. "And he has answers?"

"Yes," Marco responds. He shifts his weapon in his hands and adds, "This is where we split. Emma, you go with Pete. Gray, this way."

"Emma stays with me," I say.

"That's sweet of you, Romeo, but she can't." Again with that name. I want to correct him, but he keeps talking. "Boys have one washroom, girls another. That's just the way it is."

We never divided outhouses in Claysoot. The idea is ridiculous, not to mention inefficient. So much more construction and upkeep and maintenance.

"It's okay," Emma says to me. "I'll be fine."

I nod in agreement even though I'd feel better if she never left my sight. Everything about this place makes my skin crawl, and since climbing the Wall we've met not answers but more questions. If Emma is not with me, I am incapable of ensuring her safety. I stare over my shoulder as she disappears with Pete. Marco and I head in the opposite direction.

"You regret climbing yet?" Marco asks, his voice condescending. He's walking ahead of me, but I would bet a week's worth of hunting game that he's smirking.

I scowl. "Not at all. Besides, I didn't get Heisted like I was supposed to. It was worth risking the Wall."

He freezes. "Wait. Say that again. The part about the Heist."

"I didn't get Heisted like I was supposed to."

He turns to face me, slowly. He looks as dumbfounded as I felt taking in Taem moments earlier. "What do you mean by that?"

"I mean I was the only boy who stayed *in* Claysoot when he turned eighteen."

"Impossible." His mouth hangs open.

Why would he think that impossible? Why does he even recognize the term *Heist*? I shiver, cold, and against my better judgment I add, "It's not impossible. My twin brother—he disappeared and I stayed."

"Twin?" Marco gasps. He runs a hand over his head, looks off down the hallway, and then back at me. "Change of plans," he says. "This way."

And then he practically sprints down the corridor, backtracking. My feet work feverishly to keep up. We step into a box. It lurches downward, metal walls surrounding us. Doors open and Marco leads me through a hallway, down stairs, around corners. I lose my sense of direction. One thing is certain, though: the area of Union Central through which we are now walking is not nearly as glorious as its outer shell. The walls are a gray stone. Dust gathers in the crannies, moss clinging furiously to damp corners. Hallways are lit overhead with odd panels of light that flicker and cast an unnatural bluish glow about the space.

We head down a final set of steps and the moisture in the air seems to triple. A man in black sits on a lonely stool within the hallway we've entered. It is narrow, lined with doors to the left and right that are too short to walk through without ducking.

"We're all full," he calls out.

"Well, double him up," Marco says. "Throw him in with our pal Bozo the clown. He'll be good company." Marco pushes me at the man with impressive force, and then darts off the way we arrived, looking more frantic than ever.

"Where's he going?"

The man says nothing but shuffles me toward a door at the far end of the hallway, where he presses his thumb to a metal plate before it slides open.

"Sorry, kid," he says to me. "This guy's a bit of a loon." And then he shoves me through the doorway. It's dark inside and smells of mold and urine. The door slams behind me and it takes the click of metal echoing in my ears before I realize I'm in a prison.

# THIRTEEN

**AT FIRST I PANIC.** I tug on the door frantically, and when it doesn't give, I sink to the floor and bury my face in my hands. I shouldn't have trusted these people. Maybe this was Marco's plan all along. Maybe he never had any intention of helping us. My stomach twists at the thought of Emma also in a cell, trapped somewhere in this massive building, and me, powerless to help her. I lash out in frustration, punching the door behind me.

"That won't do any good, you know," a voice croaks from the corner, "losing your temper." I'd forgotten I had a cell mate. I can't see his face and I don't really care.

"You're new," he remarks, his fingers tapping against stone in the dark. They create a funny little rhythm, an awkward beat that is always just a hair off, as if a finger has darted out against his will and struck rock prematurely. "Which group did you come from?"

"I'm sorry?" I don't feel like talking, especially not to some man so gone he's been given a nickname that induces ridicule. *Clown* means nothing to me, but I heard the way Marco pronounced it, saw the way his lips curled around the word.

"Group," the man says again. "What group are you from? A? B?"

"Look," I snap, unsure what he's talking about, "I'm not from any *group*. And I'm not from Taem, either."

He shuffles out of the corner, crouching beneath the low ceiling, and into the little light that filters through the window of our cell door. The man is gawky, thin. There are creases and wrinkles on his face, and he has a gray beard that grows in haphazard patches. His eyes appear as if he has not slept in weeks, and his dark clothes are tattered and worn.

"An outsider, eh?" He flashes me a crazed grin. "You like it there? Outside the city?" His fingers dance over the stonework again, tapping frantically as he speaks.

"It was better than here," I admit.

The man breaks into a terrible cackle at this comment, throwing his head back like a wild dog and howling deeply. "I like you," he says. "Quite a sense of humor." I don't tell him I wasn't trying to be funny. He laughs until he's worn himself out, and then his fingers are back to tapping.

From behind us, somewhere down the hall, there is the sound of footsteps approaching and then guards talking. I try to make out what's being said, but Bozo's tapping grows louder, as if he is deliberately trying to block out the conversation. He rocks back and forth on his heels, and mumbles—no, sings—to himself.

"Five red berries in a row, sown with love so that they'll grow. Five red berries in a row, sown with love so that they'll grow."

He repeats it, over and over, his voice raspy. It almost sounds like a lullaby. Almost. The words are echoing in our tiny cell, and soon I can't tell which are his and which are just bouncing back to me off the walls.

"Will you shut up?" I snap. He freezes, looks at me, tugs at the hair on his head. "I'm trying to hear what they're saying. At the end of the hall."

He doesn't seem to care. The tapping continues, as does the singing, the same two lines and nothing more. His hands are moving across the stones so quickly that they become a massive blur of flesh. I notice the faded imprint of a triangle on his dark, fraying top. Was this madman once like the uniformed men in Taem? Like Marco and Pete?

"Five red berries in a row, sown with love so that they'll grow. Five red berries in a row, sown with love—"

"So that they'll grow! I get it. Enough already."

He stops tapping and sits bolt upright, nearly banging his head on the low ceiling. And then he's scuttling across the floor like a spider, until he's right before me, his face so close I can smell his sour breath.

"Do you know that song?" he asks, his nose practically touching mine.

I push him away. "I've got the first two lines memorized, thanks to you."

He deflates. "And the rest?"

I shake my head. He starts tapping and singing, but doesn't move back to his corner. I lean away from him, put my ear to the door, and listen for the guards. I hear nothing but footsteps. They are growing louder and louder, until they come to a standstill just outside our cell. Someone is wrestling with the door. Bozo clutches his knees and rocks. "Five red berries in a row, sown with love so that they'll grow."

There's the click of the plate and then light floods the cell.

Bozo chants louder. "Five red berries in a row, five red berries in a row."

"You there, kid," a voice calls to me from the hallway. "They want you upstairs."

The guard steps into the cell and grabs my wrist. Bozo starts screaming, mostly to himself, "Five red berries in a row, five red berries, five red berries, berriesberriesberries!"

"Hey!" the guard yells, kicking at the old man. His boot connects with the faded triangle on Bozo's chest and sends him tumbling into the corner.

The guard slams the door shut and tugs at my arm. "Shall we?" It's quiet for a moment, and then the frantic tapping picks up again, followed by Bozo's eerie melody. We turn a corner. I can no longer hear Bozo, but I know he is still singing—about berries and love, two things that will never, ever save him from that damp prison cell.

Frank's office is an oblong room that has so much decoration I am unable to tell what is functional and what is for show. The guard tells me to sit in one of the chairs that face a massive desk, its wood a deep red, and wait. I lean back to admire the ceiling as I do.

I never knew ceilings could be so intricate. Square panels impressed with patterns fill the space above my head. In the center of the room is a massive, hanging object. It has perfectly spaced arms that each hold a candle, only the candles don't flicker or melt. Instead, they transmit an even and unfading glow about the room.

Everything is carefully positioned; a coatrack beside an immense window, a plant near rich purple curtains. Even the papers that are spread about the desk match up, their edges aligning beneath a stone weight. Artwork hangs on the walls, framed in materials that glisten under the light. One piece shows a family, two parents and two young boys, standing with their backs against a shiny black car. It's not like the other art, which is clearly the result of a paintbrush on canvas. This image looks like the maybe-drawing of Harvey in Taem, stunningly authentic. The mother has an arm slung over the younger boy's shoulder, while the second child eyes something of interest beyond the frame. It looks sunny where they stand, and windy, too, given the way the mother's hair whips into her smile. I'm wondering if the father depicted is Frank when the doors behind me swing open.

The man who enters is too old to be the parent in the maybe-drawing. His skin is softly leathered, as if he spent one day too many in the sun. Cheeks droop delicately into the corners of his mouth and his lips are chapped. The little hair he has is a brilliant white, wispy and thin about the tops of his ears. He is built lean but not very tall. Nothing about him indicates that he would be a man in charge. A man with answers.

"Gray, right?" he says, smiling as he extends an arm toward me. Dozens of fine lines bloom around his lips. His voice is soft like cotton, smooth like butter. It instantly makes me confident that I might finally find the truth here. This man, with his unassuming face and organized papers, might have answers.

But even still, I hesitate to shake his hand.

"Ah, yes. Why trust me? We swiped you from the Outer Ring, explained nothing, threw you in a cell." He puts a finger to his lips and sits. "I cannot apologize enough for how you were treated when you arrived here, Gray. You and your friend . . ."

"Emma."

"Yes, Emma. You are the first we've been able to save, so our procedures are not quite ironed out. Marco reacted rashly to some very interesting information that you shared with him. I want you to know that if I could do it all over again, a jail cell would have absolutely no place in your entrance to Taem. None whatsoever."

He pours two cups of water from a clear pitcher and hands one to me. Not having had anything to drink since dawn, and not knowing how much water exists in Taem, even for someone like Frank, I take it and drink eagerly. Frank sips his with equal parts grace and formality. He doesn't smile, but his eyes do.

I put the water down. "So you're Frank," I say.

"Dimitri Octavius Frank." He extends his hand once more, and this time, I shake it. His fingers are long and slender, but his grip, firm.

"Gray Weathersby."

"Ah, I see." Again, a finger to the lip.

"See what?"

He puts his elbows on the desk, aligns his hands so that pinky is to pinky, ring finger to ring finger, and so on. They move in a steady wave as he thinks. He looks not at me but through me, deep in thought. My patience runs out quickly.

"Look, forget the cell and Marco and all that. Apology accepted. But I can't just sit here while you tap your fingers. I need to find Emma. And then I need to go back to Claysoot. I need to tell them there's more and I need to get them out. You can wait with those car things while they all climb and then we can—"

"We've tried, Gray," he says softly. His eyes stay focused on something behind me, some item of interest that must lie square between my eyes on the far side of the room. "We've . . . how do I put this?"

I feel like throwing my cup into the wall and watching it shatter. "Just say it. I can handle it. Just tell me already."

"There is no easy way to explain." He stumbles, pauses, stares at the top of his desk. "God, you'd think it would get easier, but each time is as hard as the first."

He looks at me now, not through me. His face appears as broken as my mother's did the day she closed her eyes for the final time. Frank's eyes have gone dark, too, just like hers.

"You saw some posters on your way in. Wanted posters."

It's a statement, but he waits for me to nod in confirmation.

"Harvey Maldoon is a scientist, and one of the best that this country has seen since the Second Civil War. Many years ago, Harvey started something—an experiment, if you will. He wanted to study human nature and the building of societies and I'm not certain what else. We only know so much. I'm sure once upon a time he had good intentions, but his work was unethical. When we discovered what he was doing, we tried to arrest him. He ran. But the experiment, the things he started, it's as if they are on autopilot. Pieces of it continue to function even though it has been a long time since he set foot in Taem."

A knot has formed in my throat, so coarse and stubborn I can barely swallow. "What are you saying?"

"I'm saying that Claysoot . . ."

I think I know. But it can't be true.

"It's not what you think it is."

No.

"Everything you know—your world, your people . . ."

This can't be happening.

"It's Harvey's experiment. Claysoot was, and is, an experiment."

No. No. "No." The last one escapes me. "So it's all . . . Someone made it like that? Someone built the Wall? And put us in there?" My hands are shaking.

Frank grimaces, his eyes downturned. He takes a piece

of paper from his desk and writes six letters on it. *LAICOS*. "Claysoot is nothing but an experiment, Gray. Harvey called it the Laicos Project in the little documentation we've managed to confiscate. We don't know much else. I'm so sorry."

My hands are in fists, my knuckles whitening. "I'll kill him," I say, without realizing the thought had even entered my mind.

If Frank is surprised by my reaction, he doesn't show it. "I can't say I wouldn't do the same, son. Taem has suffered much at Harvey's hands. When we tried to arrest him, he killed our men rather than come quietly. After he ran, he stole resources from his own people and slit throats for good measure. Things are bad enough here, far from perfect. We don't need Harvey making them worse. Perhaps it will help you to understand a bit of our history, here, and how Harvey fits into it."

He takes another sip of water and then continues. "Before the earthquakes and the flooding and the Second Civil War, this country was a large, sprawling, united thing. We are now two rifts, two pieces: AmEast and AmWest. Here in AmEast, and especially in Taem, I've tried to restore order, and I've done a decent job. It's taken me most of my life to bring Taem to its current state. This country lost so many lives in the war that the precious resource we once fought over, freshwater, is now plentiful enough if carefully rationed. I give my people water. I give them safety by way of the Franconian Order." He places a palm against the red triangle on his uniform.

"We keep the traitors of AmWest at bay, Gray. They started the war years ago. They attacked us first; and even with the worst of the fighting behind us, they still attack us today. And Harvey, as if the injustices he's done are not great enough, helps them. He sells them trade secrets and weapons and information in exchange for safety. He thinks I will forget his crimes if he can scare me enough. He uses fear as a weapon, but I will not bend. He will be punished for all he's done, to our people as well as Claysoot's."

Frank pinches the bridge of his nose and I realize that my mouth has gone dry. Too much is happening too quickly and I can't comprehend it all. I try to picture the divided country that Frank mentioned. Taem seemed large in comparison to Claysoot, and the thought that something even larger exists—land that is exponentially greater than them both—is impossible to fathom. The massive war he speaks of is foreign, too, a concept so different from the carefree game I played as a child: Blaine and me against Septum and Craw, shooting imaginary arrows until someone scolded us to stop. Frank's story is not a game.

And then there's Claysoot, an experiment. The original children that Emma and I had debated over were never stranded in the ruins of a town. They didn't lose their mothers to a terrible storm. It was just Harvey, picking up people as though they were playing pieces in a game and placing them where he wished. Suddenly, anything I've ever done, anyone I've ever known, everything I've ever said seems like a lie.

"So the Wall? The burned bodies? The Heist?" I blurt out. "That was *all* Harvey? It's all just part of this Laicos Project?" The name feels dirty on my tongue.

Frank nods.

"And even though he's in hiding, you can't stop it? You can't just climb over the Wall and free Claysoot?"

"We've tried. But we've lost so many men to the thing that patrols the Outer Ring." I want to ask him what that *thing* is, but Frank continues before I have the chance. "We have no means of fighting what Harvey set in motion beyond your Wall, so we focus instead on saving the climbers. We spot them from observation towers, but we've never reached them in time. You and Emma are the first." He leans back in his chair and smiles kindly. "But there may be hope, Gray. Marco was an idiot, putting you in a cell, but he did so because you said something very, very interesting. Something he thought too valuable to treat lightly."

I'm almost afraid to repeat the statement since it landed me in a cell the first time, but Frank's voice is so reassuring. He almost reminds me of my mother, calm and concerned.

"I'm a twin," I say. "I'm eighteen and I wasn't Heisted."

Frank leans forward and points at me. "Exactly."

"What does it mean?"

"You tell me," he says. "I find it incredibly fascinating. Not lock-you-in-the-prison fascinating, but this means something. If we can figure out how or why you escaped the Heist, we may have the slightest chance of saving the rest of your people."

I could easily tell him what I read in Carter's notebook, but I'm caught wondering how Marco and Frank already know so much about the Heist.

"And if you don't know what it means, that's fine, too," Frank says in my silence. "We can figure it out together. I'm extremely busy, but I promise you that Claysoot remains one of my top priorities. You are important, Gray—to unraveling this mystery. I can feel it. You can stay in Taem, right here in Union Central, even. You and Emma. It's really the very least I can do if you are going to help me crack this. What do you say?"

What *can* I say? There is nowhere else for Emma and me to go. I picture Carter behind the Wall, longing to be reunited with her daughter. This is a chance to make that possible. Maybe I am the key to figuring everything out and ending Harvey's project. I'd be both selfish and dense to not see this through.

"We'll stay," I say. "And thank you."

Frank smiles, lines again racing over his cheeks. "The unHeisted boy, staying right here in Union Central. I feel honored to be in the presence of such mystery and hope."

When he mentions the Heist, I get that feeling again, the sense that he knows more than I ever shared.

"About the Heist . . . If Emma and I are the first climbers to be saved, how do you know so much about the Heist?"

"I told you much of the Laicos Project still continues, running as though on autopilot. We know boys are Heisted at eighteen because they end up on our training field in the dead of night, claiming as much. *Poof*, and there they are, as though they've sprouted from the grass like dandelions."

My face must look shocked because Frank chuckles.

"I don't understand it, either," he says. "It's as much a mystery to you as it is to us. Maybe your unique situation will shed some light on things."

I nod, baffled, and then freeze. The thought hits me like a punch in the stomach.

"Wait? Here? The Heisted boys appear *here*?"

"Weathersby you said, right?" Frank flips through some papers he's pulled from his desk. He finds what he is looking for and winks at me. "Blaine. He'll be in the cafeteria this time of day. Breakfast."

I almost forget to breathe. Frank motions for me to stand and places a hand on my shoulder. His palm is warm, reassuring. He is shorter than me and raises his eyes to meet mine before saying, "Come. Let's go find your brother."

# FOURTEEN

**FRANK LEADS. WE PASS THROUGH** a series of corridors and he has to unlock several of the doors as we progress, but does so by swiping his wrist before a plain, silver box. The hallways are impressive, adorned with radiant lights and a plush floor comprised of the Franconian Order's triangular emblem. It repeats itself in several shades of red, edges lining up to form an intricate pattern.

When we arrive at a towering set of double doors that I suspect to be concealing the dining hall from view, there is a subtle beep and Frank puts one hand to his ear. His fingers pinch a small device that rests wrapped about his earlobe. He raises one finger toward me, motioning for me to wait, and paces the hall. He *hmmms* and *ahhhs* a few times, nodding curtly. I realize he must be talking to someone, and through that tiny object. He speaks just once, at the tail end of the conversation.

"Get a team together immediately. If this is true, we may get fantastically lucky. I want them sent out first thing tomorrow, at the latest. And, Evan, round up the necessities for a meeting. I'll join shortly."

The device beeps a second time and Frank lowers his hand. "My apologies," he says.

I point at his ear. "What is it?"

"Just a way for us to talk—the Order—even when we are far apart. You'll see all sorts of new technologies in your time here. Harvey didn't exactly have you living in the modern era."

I'm not fully following, but I nod. Frank rests a hand on my shoulder. "I'm very sorry to do this, but I have to attend to some pressing business. Find your brother, get some food in your system. I'll make sure someone retrieves you in a bit to show you to your room."

I nod. As soon as Frank removes his hand from my shoulder, I wish he'd put it back. He makes me feel anchored in this strange world.

"My scouts think they spotted Harvey outside Taem," Frank says, walking backward down the hallway so that he still faces me as he speaks. "We just might be able to intersect his travels if we act quickly enough. But, *shhh,* you didn't hear that from me."

He winks, rounds a corner, and is gone.

I put a palm to the double doors, and push my way inside.

The dining hall is extremely large and filled with numerous tables and even more chairs. Each item is identical, crafted with such precision I long to meet its maker. The place is packed with Order members. Some chatter while they eat. Others stand in line, gathering their meals from a long table at the rear of the room. It almost reminds me of the feast during our Heist ceremonies.

My stomach growls at the smell of hot food, but not even hunger is enough to distract me. Blaine is here. I stand near the entrance and scan the crowd. It is a sea of black suits, each Order member blending into the next. And then, I spot him. His hair is gone, shaved close to his head, but it is him. Like everyone else, he wears the dark uniform of the Franconian Order. He's laughing at something, and I feel whole. I dart across the room. I'm still several tables away when he sees me.

"Gray!" he exclaims. And then he is jumping from the table, spilling water on his lap. The people around him duck as his tray is knocked askew. The next thing I know Blaine is clasping his arms around me, and I'm almost crying because I thought we'd never see each other again.

"What are you doing here?" he asks, shaking me.

"It's a long story."

"I can't believe—I mean, I'm glad to see you—but how did . . . This isn't happening."

My cheeks hurt from grinning, but I can't stop. To see him so utterly confused is beyond amusing.

"Did you . . . Did you *climb*?" he asks quietly.

I nod, still smiling. Although I would have thought it impossible, his face grows even more startled. I have a million questions for him—about what's happened since he's been here, about the letter he kept from me—but in this moment, all I can do is enjoy his reaction.

"Hey, Blaine," a voice calls out behind him. "Where are your manners? Aren't you going to introduce us to your kid brother?"

Kid brother. No one else knows we're twins.

Blaine snaps back to reality. "Septum, it's not like you actually need to be introduced."

I crane my neck around Blaine, and there's Septum Tate, exactly how he looked a few months ago when he was Heisted, with the exception of his now short hair.

"Hey, Gray." Septum grins at me through a mouthful of bread. Behind him, Craw Phoenix motions his fork at me in a friendly gesture. My mouth falls open.

"You guys are here, too?" I gasp. Frank had told me as much, but it's still hard to believe.

"Everyone's here," Craw says. Dimples appear in his cheeks as he smiles. "Except the ones that have died in service." Behind him, I see a few other faces I recognize, and beyond those, a dozen more.

"Service?"

"Frank's got a lot on his plate," Blaine says. "We've been helping the Order with smaller tasks as he fights the larger ones."

"Such as?"

Septum takes a huge bite of his bread and then talks, mouth full and words garbled. "Like water distribution or scouting missions."

"And people die from that?"

"Not water distribution," Blaine clarifies. "But the scouting missions have gotten a little risky lately. There's talk that Harvey's gaining followers. Rebels. Here, in AmEast."

So they know. They know everything.

"Vermin," Craw mutters, and spits on his empty plate. "That man is no good."

"You mean varmint," Septum says. "Wild and sly and sneaky."

"No, I mean vermin. Like the pest, the worm, the rodent."

Septum screws up his face. "Wait, maybe those words mean the same thing."

"Of course they don't mean the same thing," Craw says,

rolling his eyes. "Being sly is actually a little bit of a compliment. I'm talking about pure filth. Harvey. Vermin."

As they continue to argue, Blaine grabs my arm and says, "Come on. We need to talk."

He ushers me from the table and we leave the dining hall through a side door that opens into a small, circular courtyard surrounded by the tall walls of Union Central. The morning air is still cool and damp and the place is deserted. I'm finally starting to feel the side effects of fatigue. It was late when I left Claysoot—nearly dawn—and I still have not slept.

"That was really stupid, Gray."

I'm surprised to hear anger in his voice. "Stupid?"

"Climbing." He folds his hands across his chest and gives me a disappointed big brother look. "Do you know how lucky you are that the Order managed to find you? Save you? Why'd you do it?"

All the anger and betrayal and hurt I'd felt when I first discovered Ma's note comes surging back.

"I climbed because of you, Blaine," I snap. "I did it because *you* lied to me and *you* kept the truth from me. Maybe if you and Ma trusted me enough to be honest, I wouldn't have gone searching for answers myself."

"What are you talking about?"

"The fact that we're twins, Blaine. You and me. Born on the same, exact day." I pull Ma's note from my pants pocket and throw it at him. "Next time you don't want me discovering something, you should burn your evidence."

He smooths out the letter and his eyes grow heavy as he recognizes it. When he speaks again, he sounds embarrassed. "And you pieced it together? This page doesn't even admit anything."

"Well, Ma was right about one thing—I did go looking for answers. Carter's records, her private ones, had an interesting note claiming that you and I are twins, born the very same day back in year twenty-nine."

"You weren't supposed to know," he says quietly.

"What was on the second page, Blaine?"

"I'm sorry, Gray. I didn't think it would matter. Ma . . . I thought she was crazy. She gave me that letter and I didn't want to disgrace her memory by betraying her trust. But I swear I thought you'd be Heisted with me. I always thought it would be the two of us."

The memory flashes before my eyes. How Blaine had winked at me, said we'd see each other again soon. Inside I am burning, angry and hurt, and yet I cannot raise my voice. I slowly repeat myself. "Blaine, what was on the second page?"

He reaches into his pocket and pulls out a piece of parchment. I take it from him and unfold it with unsteady hands. I remember where the previous page left off—*Gray is, in fact*—and begin reading.

your twin. You are not a year apart but several minutes. I did not know I was carrying two, and when Gray arrived just moments later, I saw my chance to test things. I had Carter keep Gray's birth secret. A full year later, after a faked pregnancy, Carter returned to "deliver" Gray. She deemed him "sickly" and forbade him visitors. Gray saw his first day of sunlight at age two and a half. By then, no one questioned a thing. You were nearly identical, but brothers, believed to be a year apart.

If the Heist really is just a part of life, none of this will matter. I had wanted to see this myself, so that I could finally accept the mysteries of Claysoot, but I will not, and so the rest is on your shoulders. Should you and Gray disappear together, you can accept the Heist for me. But in case the Heist is something more, well, this is why Gray must not know. His knowing will foster questions, and I fear with questions he will not stay put. And if he is spared, he must. He will be proof that some of our boys have a chance.

Carter and I have devised a plan if this is

*the case, but the closer death creeps, the more*
*likely it seems that the Heist is just an unfair*
*portion of life I never managed to accept. I*
*hope you do not hate me for this, for turning*
*your lives into an experiment. I love you*
*both very, very much. Not a day goes by that*
*I don't see your father in the two of you. You*
*are his mirror images, but only Gray has his*
*stubborn nature, so remember that even in*
*keeping this secret, as painful as it may be,*
*Gray is your brother, your twin, and will*
*forgive you in time.*

There is no signature, only a splotch of ink at the bottom of the parchment.

This is the information that Frank wants, right here in this letter. This could be what he needs, proof that a concealed birthday made all the difference in my escaping the Heist.

"Can I keep this?" I ask, not looking up.

"Sure."

I fold the parchment in on itself, matching premade creases. Blaine passes the first page back to me, and I return the complete letter to my pocket. It's odd finally having Ma's letter in its entirety. For so long, I thought that reading the message would make sense of things, but even now, I'm still perplexed. And plagued by questions.

"What was Carter's plan? What did I mess up by leaving?"

"After Ma died, Carter filled me in," Blaine says. "She said if we were not Heisted together, her plan was to simply wait. After your Heist, if it came on your nineteenth birthday, she'd have proof that the Heist was somehow based on public records and not actual birth dates. She was going to talk to Maude then, start devising a way to hide other boys' birth dates on a more grand scale, buy them more time. Test out the theory. After that, I don't know."

I snort. I don't think telling Maude would have been much help, not after what I saw the night I climbed. I start to tell Blaine this, but he speaks over me.

"I thought she was crazy, too. I thought they'd both lost their minds and I only stayed quiet because I'd made a promise to Ma." Blaine looks at the ground and then back to me. "She said you'd forgive me. For keeping secrets."

Ma was right about me being his brother, about the fact that I'll forgive him. I'm just not ready. Not yet. You can't read that your whole life is a lie, that you were a test, and then carry on like everything's normal. Nothing about me is normal. Nothing about where I am now is normal. I am completely and utterly lost.

"Gray." It's another *I'm sorry* without saying the actual words.

"It's done, Blaine." There's an awkward pause. I try to

remember if one existed between us before, and come up with nothing. "So you know everything?" I continue, desperate to break the silence. "About Claysoot? And Harvey?"

He nods. "You?"

"Yeah, Frank told me."

"You met him? In person?"

"How else would he have told me?"

"I watched it all on a video." He must read the confusion on my face, because he continues. "They have these things called cameras here. It's like a set of eyes that can watch things at all times. It can even save some of what it sees and trap it permanently, so you can watch it later, anytime you want. I think they did that with Frank—had him talk about Claysoot, saved his speech, and then showed it to me when I was Heisted. Septum and Craw saw the same thing. Frank's so busy, he doesn't have time to meet each boy after every single Heist. I'm amazed he had time to meet you." He pauses for a second and then adds, "What's he like?"

"He's really nice."

Blaine sticks his hands in his pockets. "I hope he figures things out soon. I think about Kale every day. I need to get her out of there."

The mention of Kale makes me think of everyone else still trapped behind the Wall. Of Carter and Sasha and Maude. "Do you think they'll all climb now?" I ask, panicked. "If

Emma and I were the first the Order picked up, that means there won't be bodies. If there aren't bodies, everyone might—"

"They won't," Blaine says.

"You don't know that."

"The video . . . it mentioned that if the Order saves a climber, they will use someone from the prisons as a replacement. Leaving a criminal of similar build in the Outer Ring ensures that a body goes back to Claysoot."

I think of the second car waiting on the hill when Emma and I were found by Marco. It had driven off, but not in the direction we did. Its driver had more business to attend to. "I guess it makes sense," I say. "If Emma and I are the first they've ever saved, and it's hard for them to save climbers in general, it's better for Claysoot to stay put until Frank solves things."

"Or until he gets his hands on Harvey."

"Exactly."

I smile and Blaine smiles, too, but for some reason it doesn't feel right. If we are not encircled by a Wall and standing on clay streets, are we the same brothers? The thought is exhausting.

"I'm really tired," I say. "I think I need to sleep."

"Sure. I'll find you later. We can catch up." As I walk away, he adds, "I'm sorry, Gray. About the twin thing. Really."

I could accept it. But I don't. "I know," I say, and then I keep walking.

As I wind back through the dining hall, I am engulfed by a wave of doubt. The likelihood of Frank solving things or capturing Harvey seems so remote, so improbable. I want to go home. I never thought I'd say that, but I just want to go back to Claysoot, where everything was simple. Where things with Blaine were uncomplicated, where I had a future with Emma. Not knowing made everything easier.

I leave the way I came in, brushing through a group of people entering for breakfast. I keep my head down, buried in my thoughts, but someone grabs my arm.

"Gray?"

Emma is standing before me, her hair brushed out so thoroughly it is pin straight. It makes her look oddly formal. I am overcome by every emotion I have ever felt for her. Love, joy, pain, want, all mingled with relief.

"I missed you," she says. She's wearing all white: a pair of pants that look uncomfortably tight and a top that flutters when she moves, almost as fluidly as water. Something is different about her. Her eyebrows have suddenly become too thin, and her skin too shiny. There's something odd about her face, too, as though all of her features have been exaggerated with a fine-tipped quill.

"What did they do to you?" I ask. Her lips are dark, painted with a color too even and bold. Even her eyes, which I thought I could never forget, seem to be surrounded by dark shadows.

She groans. "I don't even know. I feel like I have three layers of grime on my face, while every other inch of my body feels like it's missing three layers of skin. At least they didn't make me wear the *heels*. I kept falling in them anyway." She points to a pair of flat, white shoes on her feet and then steps into my arms.

"We have to get out of here, Gray," she whispers into my ear. "This place isn't right. They're keeping something from us. I don't trust them." Her hair smells burned beneath my chin.

"They didn't tell you about Harvey?" She pulls her head from my shoulder and frowns. I guess that's a no. "I met with Frank. He had some answers." My stomach growls audibly and I realize I haven't eaten in hours. Sleep can wait. "I'll fill you in over breakfast."

"Hey, Romeo!" Marco comes strolling up the hallway and Emma and I break apart. "I need to borrow you." I notice for the first time how truly ridiculous his massive beard looks in comparison to his shaved head. His eyes fall on Emma.

"Well hello, girly. Don't you clean up nicely." I watch his eyes linger on the low neckline of Emma's top and have to stifle a strong desire to punch him in the face. Marco grabs me by the upper arm, carting me down the hall before Emma and I can say good-bye.

"Where are we going?" I ask as he takes a turn and guides me down a flight of stairs.

"The infirmary. You need to be Cleansed. Standard procedure for all Order members."

"Cleansed?"

"Shots and pills and medicine. And we've got to shave that head of yours. Don't tell me you haven't noticed how we all sport the same clean look? We just want you to be part of the family." He smiles at me viciously.

My free hand instinctively feels for the wild strands against my neck. It's only hair, nothing really, but I want to keep it. I want to look different from the Order, from Marco. I want to keep Claysoot with me.

"No thanks," I say. "I'm fine as is."

Marco slaps the back of my head. "Did I say you had a choice? This is not negotiable." I rub my head, startled. "Hair is cut short to prevent lice. Pills and shots are given to ward off illness. It's for your own good, and for the good of everyone in Taem. Now let's move."

I'm dragged roughly in his wake. Marco was far nicer when he was trying to convince Emma and me to get into his car earlier. Now, inside Union Central, it's as if something has changed, as if he hates me. I wonder if Frank reamed him out for putting me in that cell with Bozo.

We pass a door marked Authorized Personnel Only and stop at a second one marked Cleansing Infirmary. Marco waves his wrist at the box beside the door and guides me down the now accessible hallway, his fingers pinching my elbow. When we finally enter a room, he pushes me into a cold, metal chair.

The last thing I remember are two red pills being shoved down my throat, and the razor, waiting to strip me bald.

# FIFTEEN

**WHEN I COME TO, I'M** no longer in the infirmary. I wake in a bed in a private room, still wearing my muddy pants and hooded shirt from Claysoot. It's dark outside. I'm not sure how much time has passed—a few hours, days. I roll over on my side. My head feels abrasive atop the pillow, as if it is clinging to the fabric. I reach up, and a brittle, coarse landscape greets my hands. It feels wrong. I've never had such little hair before, never in all the years I can remember.

I sit up and swing my legs over the edge of the bed. Every muscle in my body aches. My arms feel like cumbersome weights, and a dull throb radiates from the base of my neck. Someone has left bread and fruit on a table beside my pillow, and I scarf it down before stumbling into a small side room beyond the bed. There, I find an outhouse—*inside*.

There is no tub, but when I twist a series of handles behind a panel of glass, water rains from a pipe mounted on the wall. It reminds me of the miraculous feature Emma and I had discovered back in the deserted building beyond Claysoot. I peel off my dirty clothes and step in. It's much easier than bathing back home. I stand under the hot stream of water, scrubbing the dirt from my skin and watching the suds drip their way down the drain. The pain in my neck is finally beginning to subside when the water abruptly turns off. I jiggle the handle. Nothing. A small panel illuminates on the wall, flashing a message: *Two-minute daily shower allotment used*. I grab a towel and dry off, wiping away excess soap. Next time, I will have to be faster.

A pile of clean clothes sits on the bathroom counter: an Order uniform. The material is heavy, extremely durable. I wonder how they've stitched it. The pants aren't half bad, but the top fits oddly. The collar is too tight, softly choking me, and the sleeves and body are narrow, causing the material to cling to my skin. I feel absurdly rigid, as though my movements are restricted and my neck limited to look only ahead.

In a mirror above the sink, I see my new haircut for the first time. My forehead now appears too large, and I look dull, my gray eyes no longer able to hide behind long bangs. My neck still hurts and the uniform isn't helping. I tug the top off and leave it on the floor. Then I crawl back in bed and sleep easily, pressed into the bedsheets as if they could massage away the pain.

The next time I wake, the sun is just rising. I sit up in bed, my limbs still tight and sore, and pull on my boots before retrieving the other half of my uniform from the bathroom floor. I should find Emma. I still need to tell her what Frank told me about Harvey and his project. We could get breakfast together, talk over our meals, and attempt to block out all of Union Central around us. If we try hard enough, maybe it will be like we are back in Claysoot, where things were easy. Maybe.

As I approach my door, I hear voices on the other side: Marco and Frank.

"He's still out?" Frank asks. I feel a surge of gratitude, knowing he's checking in on me.

"It's been roughly twenty-four hours, but that's pretty standard," Marco says. "He should be up soon."

"I want to know the moment he is. In the meantime, get me answers. I'm too busy with Harvey to deal with this right now, and, so help me, I do not want all this hard work crumbling because of one missed Heist."

"I understand, sir."

"Good," Frank says. His footsteps click down the hallway,

but then they pause. "Are you coming?"

"I haven't slept in a while. First the boy, then that meeting you called yesterday. I thought maybe I could take a break."

"You don't deserve one," Frank says. His voice is still as buttery and smooth as ever, but it makes the obvious authority in his words that much more powerful. "We're receiving an update from Evan's team before they head out to the forest. I want you there."

Marco sighs. "Yes, sir."

I listen to their footsteps trail off, and then open my door a crack. The hallway is empty. I try to comprehend what this means.

Yesterday Frank told me I was a miracle, a mystery, the potential key to saving our town, but while talking to Marco just now, he hadn't seemed nearly as pleased with this possibility. If I'm honest with myself, he sounded terrified by the idea.

I realize my hands are shaking. Frank is upset because he hasn't been able to free the people of Claysoot or make sense of my escaping the Heist yet. That's all. That must be it. I'm being irrational and suspicious because everything is so new here and I'm still trying to adjust.

I repeat this to myself as I leave my room in search of Emma.

~∽~

The door at the end of my hallway is locked. I halfheartedly wave my wrist in front of the silver box as I saw Frank do when he led me to the dining hall, and to my surprise, the door slides open.

I walk through, staring at my hand. There is the faintest purple bruise on the inside of my wrist. I must have been granted access to these doors during my Cleansing. How, I'm not sure, but it's the only thing that makes sense.

I wander the hallways until I come across a stairwell. I take it to the main level, again using my wrist to gain access, and walk to the dining hall by memory. I grab some food and find Emma eating oatmeal and sipping a hot cup of tea. After she reacts to my haircut, running her hand over my scalp and teasing me endlessly, I fill her in. I tell her about Harvey and the Laicos Project, Frank and his goals, the curious conversation I just overheard. Her fists ball up the way mine had when I tell her about Harvey's experiment.

"I'm being paranoid, right?" I ask when I recount Frank's tone outside my bedroom, how he sounded upset that the Heist failed to take me on my eighteenth birthday.

"I don't know," Emma says. "If he's trying to solve the Heist and free Claysoot, he should be happy you weren't Heisted, not worried."

"Exactly what I thought." I touch Ma's letter in my pocket. The answer Frank seeks is written on that parchment, but I suddenly feel that sharing the note would be a terrible idea.

Emma looks down at her tray. "They think we're dead, don't they?" Her voice is dull and flat.

"Who?"

"My mother. Maude. All of them. Blaine told you they planted replacements. If he's right, bodies went back, like they always do, and they think we're dead."

I picture Carter, collapsed and sobbing on a bed in the Clinic. She'd had a baby girl. She wasn't supposed to lose her child. I don't answer Emma's question, but we both know the answer is yes.

"Let's go for a walk," I say. "We could use some fresh air. And maybe we can dig up some details on this place in the process."

"What exactly are you looking for?"

"Why Harvey even started the Laicos Project. What kills climbers in the Outer Ring. Why the Heisted boys appear here in Union Central."

She smirks at me. "And you think you'll find those answers on a walk?"

"Who knows. Walls talk sometimes. Think of how much we learned from Harvey's wanted poster the day we arrived in Taem."

The dining hall begins to empty out, Order members returning to their duties.

"Will you always be obsessed with the truth?" Emma looks at me, her brows raised.

I shrug. "Until I see it with my own eyes, I guess. And you said you wanted answers just as badly, back when you followed me over the Wall."

"I did. But now look where we are. I want it to be like it was before we left. If I could do it over, I'd stop searching and just be with you, Gray. You weren't Heisted and so maybe we could have been together in Claysoot. Forever. Like the birds."

"I would have been Heisted when I turned nineteen," I point out. "And we're not birds."

"I know. But I wish we were. We could fly away. Right now."

She stares at her tray again, and for a second, I'm afraid she might start crying. I reach out and take her hand in mine. "We can't do that. Not yet. But some more answers, the truth, and then I promise we can fly anywhere you want."

Her customary half smile comes first, the one I can never fully read. And then she leans across the table and kisses me, a quick, tempting thing that leaves me hungry for more. As we leave the dining hall, my heart races, and not because of answers waiting to be discovered.

It's Emma. It's always been Emma.

# SIXTEEN

OUR WALK FROM UNION CENTRAL, through the corridor littered with Harvey's wanted posters, and to the public square
downtown is much longer than we anticipate. Emma and I
find a small piece of shade blanketing a bench and sit. I face
the golden statue, but Emma leans her back against my arm,
swings her feet up onto the seat, and gazes off in the opposite
direction. Her hair no longer smells like Claysoot soap—that
scent is long gone, replaced with something foreign—but I
kiss her head anyway. We sit there, in a comfortable silence,
for quite a while.

"You know, I haven't found any answers yet," she jokes.
"It's very disappointing. I'm starting to think you just wanted
an excuse to spend time with me."

I smile as she twists around to sit properly. "Maybe I did."

The square has steadily filled with civilians since our arrival. Now, their numbers border on crowded. They shuffle in, forming a line leading up to the platform and pushing each other aggressively as they jockey for position. A wall illuminates with a familiar message: *Water distribution today. Segments 1 & 2 only. Must present ration card.*

The Order members come next, filing from between various buildings, cars bringing up the rear. Those on foot take their place on the raised platform, weapons ready. The instruments are the same as the ones I saw during our initial drive into Taem, and again, the Order points them at the growing crowd. Taem's citizens are a steady pulse, filtering by our bench and surging toward the stage. They all hold red slips in their hands, papers that must be their ration cards. A middle-aged man, looking desperately nervous, races by us, crushing my feet as he does.

"Watch it," I say.

He looks back at me, eyes livid, and mumbles something. Then he runs off, disregarding the line and pushing his way through people. The bag slung across his back swings wildly, hitting anyone standing too close. Up ahead, the distribution begins, a single jug of water handed to each civilian in turn.

Emma and I decide to leave—it's getting far too crowded— but our progress is slow. We are fish going upstream, an unyielding current of bodies pressing against us. Just when we have reached the outer perimeter of the square, I hear the shouts.

"Stop him! Stop that man."

Behind us, things remain relatively calm, the crowd still moving toward the stage. And then a ripple, a small steady thing in the center, which grows larger and larger, people parting in its wake. The voices keep yelling. "Stop him! Thief!"

And then I can see him, the same man that trampled over my feet. He is sprinting from the crowd, pushing over anyone in his path. He clings to not one jug of water but two.

The Order members on the stage are frantic, fighting their way into the crowd and after the thief. I look back to Emma and see the man barreling toward her. She is blocking the alley he approaches.

She attempts to jump out of his way but is too slow. The thief throws his shoulder into her and she crumples. As the thief rushes by me, I stick my leg out and trip him. Water jugs tumble from his arms, contents spill from his bag. He stumbles to his feet and takes off down the alley, but I am quicker. I lunge at him, seize the back of his shirt, throw him against the wall.

"You should really watch where you're going," I snarl.

"Please," he says. "You don't understand. My wife. My kids. They're sick."

His eyes no longer look livid. They look broken. They look moments away from hopeless. I peer down the alley to where Emma is climbing to her feet. Her white pants are torn, blood dripping from her knees. I shove the man into the wall again. The Order is coming. I can hear their shouts.

"Please," the thief begs. "We need the water."

"It seems like everyone needs it."

"What would you know?" he says, eyeing my uniform. "Living in that place, following the orders of a corrupt man."

The first Order member rounds the corner, and the man wriggles in my grasp.

"Please. My son, he's just five. There's still time. Just let go. Tell them I stabbed you. Or kicked you. Or spit in your eye."

I almost do it. I almost let his shirt slip from my fingers— his words sound so sincere—but Emma falling is replaying in my mind, her body being thrown to the side by the thief's frame. I hold his shirt just a second longer, and then an Order member arrives. He presses the thief into the wall. I watch his cheek scrape the brick while his hands are bound with not rope but an odd chain of metal links, two of which are snapped closed around his wrists.

"Turn around," the Order member says. When the thief doesn't, he is shoved. Hard. He hits his head on the wall and with fresh blood trickling into his eyebrows, he continues to beg.

"Please. We need it. You don't understand."

"Turn around."

"I'll do anything. Just let me bring the water to my family first."

"Now!"

The thief puts his back to the wall. He is crying, blood mixing with tears. The Order member steps back and repositions his weapon.

And then there is an explosion, a noise so loud it rattles the space between my ears, echoing for an eternity. I blink, and when I open my eyes, the thief is on the ground, dead. There is no arrow, no spear, no knife. Nothing. Just a gaping hole. I stare at his bleeding skull until I turn to dry heave against the wall.

Emma shakes the entire way back. She doesn't cry, but at least her reaction is better than mine. She's showing fear or remorse or nerves or *something*. I do nothing but look blankly ahead, wondering what on earth happened, wondering if I'm somehow responsible. Everyone wanted water. Everyone was waiting in line. He stole something. He was a thief. But did he deserve to die over a jug of water?

I keep the thoughts to myself because I fear that if I speak them aloud, Emma might collapse right beside me. We walk to Union Central, my arm wrapped around her and the blood drying on her pants. I take her to her room, which happens to be on the same floor as mine, just in a different wing, and then march straight to Frank's office. I pound on the door until someone comes and tells me Frank doesn't have time to talk to me. I demand to see him. They tell me to leave. I demand some more.

I end up sitting on the floor outside his office, arms folded across my chest. I doze off momentarily and wake to a foot prodding my side.

"Gray." Frank stands above me, a pile of documents in hand.

I scramble to my feet. "I need to talk to you."

"I've heard. I only have a moment, but, please, come in."

We sit at his desk, and when he puts the papers on them, everything suddenly looks out of place, that one disorganized pile throwing the entirely methodical room out of orbit. Frank leans back in his chair, places his fingertips together in a calming wave, and says, "So, Gray. What can I help you with?"

"There was a man today, in town. He was—"

"Shot," Frank finishes.

"But there was no arrow."

"This is true. You carry a bow in Claysoot, correct? You shoot arrows?"

I nod.

"In the Order, we carry guns. We shoot bullets." He lifts

his shirt, and removes something from a belt at his waist. It is much smaller than the weapons the other men had carried in the public square. Frank points it away from us and slides a slender box from its base before pulling back on the weapon's top. He fishes something from the gun, gold and glinting, and hands it to me.

It is small in my palm. So small I wonder how it killed the thief. But it had also traveled unbelievably fast, erupting from the gun and hitting its mark so swiftly I couldn't even see it happen. Small and powerful. Quick and deadly. It makes my bow and arrows look laughable.

I let the bullet roll from my palm and onto the desk. "He didn't deserve to die," I say.

Frank smiles, a kind one, the way my mother used to when Blaine or I was acting up and she had to scold us but didn't really want to. "Sometimes we have to do things that are not completely agreeable."

"No," I say firmly. "It didn't have to be that way. His family was sick. He just needed a little extra water."

"They all want more water, Gray. Each and every one of them. And what I wouldn't give to provide it. But we only have so much. He took what was not his, and, sick or not, he is not privileged to receive any more water than his neighbor. Surely you understand."

"But he never even got to defend himself."

"He was guilty," Frank says.

"But what if he wasn't? What if it isn't that black-and-white?"

"It is. He was fleeing with the water. He knew what he did was wrong." Frank leans forward on the desk and lowers his face to meet mine. "You did the right thing by stopping him, Gray. Taem is a more just place today because of your actions."

I nod, but the thief's final words echo in my mind. His begging, pleading. I feel like I'm missing a critical piece of the puzzle, like I'm staring at the situation from an incorrect angle and if I could only get a better view, it would all make sense. The only thing I know for certain is that I don't agree with Frank. No matter how obvious something may seem, there are two sides to every story, and the thief never had a chance to tell his.

I want to tell Frank this, and yet he's been so good to me. He's clothed me and fed me and he's trying to free the rest of Claysoot, all while juggling his own country's problems. Maybe he's justified in having the Order act so swiftly. What do I know? Claysoot is so small, and things here are far more complex.

"What you saw is not typical, Gray," Frank assures me. "We reserve such treatment for thieves and criminals only. The corrupt."

I nod, but something has sprouted in my gut, a tiny seed of doubt, a seed that feeds off an idea the thief had planted. *What would you know . . . following the orders of a corrupt man?*

I excuse myself and head for the door. Before I step into the hallway, Frank calls after me. "And, Gray? I don't know how it happened, but we must have mixed up your access codes during your Cleansing. The front doors should not have opened for you. Taem is often in an unsettled state, the world beyond the dome even more so. I can only ensure your safety if you stay here, in Union Central. I'm sure you'll understand when I ask you not to wander until further notice."

Just yesterday I might have thought his words endearing. Today they sound like an order, a demand.

"Absolutely," I say.

But when the office doors click shut behind me, I head straight for Emma. There is a seed in my gut and only she will know if I should stamp it out before it has a chance to secure its roots.

# SEVENTEEN

BY THE TIME I GET to Emma's room, I've made up my mind.
The doubts I have are too real. The thief must know things I
do not, to think Frank corrupt. And then there was the conversation I overheard earlier, Frank's sounding upset at my
beating the Heist, when the idea should make him hopeful.
Something doesn't add up.

Emma pulls her door open within seconds of my knocking. Her room has windows on the far side, and they
illuminate her from behind. Her hair, damp from a shower,
hangs on her shoulders. She's stopped shaking.

"Remember when I said walls could talk?"

She nods.

"There's a hallway marked Authorized Personnel Only

down by the infirmary. I saw it when Marco took me to get Cleansed. I figure those types of walls know more than others."

She looks at me cautiously. "Those walls sound like the type that you shouldn't mess with unless you are Authorized Personnel. Maybe you should talk to Frank. He seems to like you."

"I already did. And he does. But he likes me because I escaped the Heist and nothing more."

"All right," Emma says, stepping into the hallway. "What exactly are we looking for this time?"

"A library."

She pauses. "Why?"

I look over my shoulder. We are alone, but I lower my voice anyway. "Because no matter how many questions I ask, we're not getting all the details. But libraries are full of details. This place is mountains larger than Claysoot, and even we had a building housing historical notes and facts. There have to be scrolls or books *somewhere* in Taem."

Emma says nothing but offers me her hand. I take it, and the search begins.

When we get to the hallway Emma has started shaking again. I keep stealing glances over my shoulder, but no one has followed us. I don't even bother trying my wrist at the door's silver box. I know I won't have access. Instead, I eye a unit on the wall that says, In Case of Fire, Pull. Whatever happens after will probably create some sort of distraction. I hesitate for a moment, wondering if there is another option. But Emma nods reassuringly and I figure the only way I've ever gotten answers is by following my gut, by taking risks and hunting down the truth myself. Before I can change my mind, I reach out and pull the small handle. A series of alarms ring through the corridor and water erupts from the ceilings.

We are definitely going to get caught.

A group of Order members bursts through the locked door, but miraculously, they don't even look at us. They run for drier corridors, papers held over their heads for protection. Before the door slides shut behind them, Emma and I slip through unnoticed.

Inside, the hall is poorly lit, long and narrow. The floor is a deep blue and with the water raining from the ceiling, it takes on an eerie, underwater feel. The alarm echoes endlessly. Emma, shivering, searches for my hand and lets her fingers fill the spaces between mine.

We pass a series of offices and meeting rooms. Their doors are locked, but we can see chairs and tables through a window in each. There is a lone door at the end of the hallway, its windows frosted in a way that distorts everything behind them. We can make out one thing though, a figure moving on the other side. The shadow grows larger. It's approaching us, about to burst into our hallway.

I tug Emma's hand and we skirt to the side, frantically trying offices. Just as the door at the end of the hall begins to open, I find a handle that twists, and Emma and I spill into a room. We press our backs against the wall, panting. I peer out the window of our door. A figure is racing up the hallway.

I take a deep breath. "I think we're okay."

Emma breathes a sigh of relief, and as the raining water shuts off in the hallway, we turn to explore the office. We are in a plain meeting room. There is one long table, surrounded by chairs and covered with odd-looking books. The page contents are not stitched into a spine, but merely resting within their pale covers. Emma grabs the top one, marked Operation Ferret, and flips it open. Inside is the same maybe-drawing that is plastered all over Taem. This version holds additional information.

"Target: Harvey Maldoon," it reads. "Age 55, Caucasian, height five foot eleven. Brown hair, brown eyes. Wears glasses; nearsighted." Those must be the things surrounding his eyes and resting on his nose. I wonder if they improve his vision rather than serve as protection, like I originally thought. "Wanted alive."

We look at each other, and then pull up chairs hurriedly.

Emma flips to the next page in the unbound book. It is a

map. We had one in Claysoot, a bird's-eye view of the town center and surrounding woodlands, drawn by Bo Chilton before he was Heisted. This map shows Taem, as well as an expansive batch of trees marked the Great Forest north of the city. Far within the forest, nearly at its most northern point, is a vast range of mountains, one of which is labeled Mount Martyr. Someone has circled it and scrawled "possible Rebel headquarters" in red. Several areas of the forest leading up to the mountains are marked with arrows.

There are other pages as well, full of scouting reports and landmarks and areas where Harvey has allegedly been spotted. We don't read them all; there are far too many.

"I hope they capture him," Emma says when she closes the record.

"Me, too."

The rest of the records are thinner. Each houses several sheets of paper, urgent words pressed upon them, crisp and uniform, too precise to be handwriting.

Emma holds out one of the pages for me to see. On it is an image of a boy, roughly my age. His head hangs forward a little, but his eyes are narrowed defiantly. "Elijah Brewster" it reads beneath his maybe-drawing. "Rebel." Emma runs her finger over the word.

"I heard Harvey is gathering followers—Rebels—outside the city," I tell her. "He's working with them to leak information to AmWest."

"Why would people want to help Harvey?" Emma asks, her lips curling in disgust.

"Here. Look." I point to a paragraph within Elijah's records.

**Brewster suspected to be one of the first to start the Rebellion. Subject took to the woods after the burning of his father's business. Sister was taken for questioning, but deemed useless. Exact whereabouts of Brewster unknown. Believed to be manning Rebel troops from hideouts within the Great Forest. Brewster is to be shot on sight.**

"That's odd," I say, thinking aloud. "Frank made it sound like Harvey started the Rebellion. But here . . . it sounds like Elijah did."

Below the paragraph, Elijah's family is listed, his mother as *deceased*, his father and sister as *executed*. I shift uncomfortably in my chair.

"Executed?" Emma repeats. "Does this mean Frank . . . the Order . . ."

I look back at the words. *Deceased* would mean the mother simply died, but *executed* . . . "I think they killed them, his father and sister. I think Elijah did something bad and so they killed his family."

"Like the thief today?"

"Maybe."

We look through the remaining papers. They show similar stories. Some of the people are marked as Rebels and Traitors. Others are marked as executed. But all have something in common: They are targets. Frank wants them all dead.

Sometimes it is justified to execute someone, I suppose. In all the years of Claysoot, it happened only once. I read about it in the scrolls. A boy by the name of Jeq Warrows went mad with jealousy. He was just sixteen and infuriated that the girl he admired could not return his affection. She had eyes for someone else, continually arranged her slatings with that someone. Jeq snuck into that boy's home one evening and attempted to slit his throat. He failed. Jeq was called to Council for attempted murder and was sentenced to climb the Wall. His body came back a day later; and in this sense, the people of Claysoot executed him.

But this seems different from the stories filling the pages before me, where people are targeted for things not comparable to murder: for reading a certain book, for speaking in a public square, for teaching subjects deemed inappropriate. Elijah seems innocent. As do most of the people. Especially the ones marked executed. I felt conflicted about the thief's fate earlier, but these records are indisputable. These people had done nothing wrong.

"Gray, what do you think this means? These records?" Emma's face has grown pale.

I glance at the door and then back at the table. Frank knows about these executions. His signature is at the bottom of each page. Frank, who put his hand on my shoulder and talked to me like a father and wanted me to help him. And maybe I still need to help him. Harvey is the true enemy, but Frank feels less and less like an ally with each record we read.

"I wonder if the Rebels are just victims," I offer, trying to make sense of what I've read, "banding together, rebelling against Taem." I drop my voice to a whisper. "And against Frank."

"But to join sides with Harvey? That's disgusting."

"Maybe they think he's the lesser of two evils. Frank is killing—no, executing—their friends and family. Harvey ran one experiment, on people they don't even know. If they don't have all the details, I can see why the Rebels chose to join Harvey. Or Elijah, I guess, based on these files."

Emma twists her fingers anxiously. "Gray? What if Frank's not the good guy?"

I think about that for a moment. I can't say the thought hadn't crossed my mind since reading the documents. "But then why did Frank even bother helping us? Why waste efforts saving us from the Outer Ring?"

Emma keeps kneading her fingers, thumbs over knuckles. "Because he wants us to think he's on our side. Maybe it's all part of an act."

If I had any hesitations, Emma is watering that seed of

doubt. The details in these records don't match up with what I've been told. And even if Frank does manage to free Claysoot, is his world the kind I want to live in? One where a seemingly harmless act can get you killed?

"We need to find Blaine," I say. "We need to tell him about these records and we need to get out of here. We can find Harvey ourselves, break Claysoot free; and when we do, we have to take everyone as far from this place as possible."

"What a valiant plan." Marco is standing in the doorway, his smile malicious. "And to think Frank was actually enjoying your company, Gray. He's going to be so disappointed when he hears you've both turned against him." Marco looks thrilled with himself, and it's all crashing down on me—what this means, how much trouble I've gotten not just myself into but Emma as well. Why had I thought this was a good idea? Why did I have to pull her down with me?

Marco grabs Emma first. I'm shouting and shoving him, but he's stronger, and then there's another Order member in the room, seizing Emma so that Marco can bind my hands. He snaps two metal links around my wrists, tethering my hands like the water thief's, and then grabs my jaw. He leans in so close I can see my reflection in his good eye.

"Seems I was right from day one, putting you in a cell. How ironic." He straightens up. "Now let's go see what Frank wants done about this."

# EIGHTEEN

EMMA IS DRAGGED TOWARD THE prison and I'm brought to
Frank's office even though Frank is not there. The windows
are open, giant panes of glass pushed outward, and the curtains flanking them flutter in a late summer breeze.

Marco drops a set of keys on Frank's desk and then shoves
me into the seat before it. Two guards stand at either side,
guns in hand. I struggle against my restraints, and the metal
digs into my skin more deeply. I quit struggling and take to
staring out the window instead. The truth wasn't worth this.
My mouth suddenly tastes sour, like spoiled milk.

Marco flops arrogantly into Frank's seat and eyes me with
disdain. "The unHeisted boy. Such a mystery you are, and
what a shame that it comes to this—you turning on Frank." He
clucks his tongue. "I hope Frank is creative with his choice of

punishment. There are so many exciting options."

He pauses, as if he expects me to offer up a suggestion for my own sentence, and then continues. "We could throw your girlfriend back in the Outer Ring and wait for her to burn, for example." A sly smile. "But maybe that would be too quick, too painless. I think we should leave her in a cell, let her rot and wither into old age. That would bother you more, too. Wouldn't it?"

My fists clench and Marco smiles. "Oh, Romeo," he coos, "you should thank me. She'll live a long life this way."

An image of Bozo fills my mind: his tapping fingers, his crazed stare, his endless singing. Emma can't sit in a cell for her entire life. It will break her. I tug against my bindings, and again, the metal drives into my skin.

The doors burst open, but Frank does not enter. Instead it is an older Order member who walks in briskly and motions for Marco to join him. They meet beneath the maybe-drawing of a family on Frank's wall and talk quietly. I can't make out a single word.

Marco eventually loses his patience. "All right, all right. What's the verdict? What did Frank say?" he snaps.

The Order member jerks his head toward me and says, "Execute him."

Straight ahead, out the open window, a black crow soars past. I think of the crow in the Claysoot meadow, how I couldn't shoot him from the sky. I think of the crow atop the

Wall, urging me to climb over. And I see this one now, flying along the roofline, guiding me again. I don't think about it. I don't contemplate if it's the right choice. I react.

I bolt from the chair, scrambling over Frank's desk and grabbing Marco's keys in the process. I've darted between the two guards and am halfway to the window before Marco starts screaming.

"Shoot him! Shoot him now!"

My feet are almost there, then a boot on the ledge. I push off, throw my body from the windowsill. Gunfire erupts, loud and deafening. The fall seems to take forever, my feet kicking as though I am underwater and searching for the surface.

It is not a long drop to the roof below, but my knees buckle from the impact. I topple forward, my bound arms unable to break my momentum. Tiles scrape the side of my face. I feel the blood almost instantly, warm as it trickles past my ear.

The gunfire continues and I run. Bullets speckle the roof around me. I don't know where I'm going, but I don't stop. The crow is ahead, fleeing, and I race after his black form, running until I can duck behind the safety of a broad chimney.

I pant for a moment, attempt to catch my breath. My ears still ring and a stitch has formed in my side. I brush the blood from the side of my face with my shoulder and spend an awkward moment grappling with the keys. I find the one that fits my metal links, and swing each jaw open, freeing my hands.

I wait a moment longer, and then I run. The crow has disappeared and I am on my own. I sprint toward the sun, clambering down the varying levels of roof as I do. When I come to the lowest level, I am still rather far from the ground. The drop is not impossible, but I could break something. As I sit there, breathless and weighing my options, a dark shape appears on the horizon, beyond Taem's dome.

At first, I think it is a bird, another crow maybe. But it is flying too quickly, and it is incredibly loud, an angry roar growing as it approaches the city. And there is not one but four. They soar in a precise line, wings never flapping. Soon they are directly overhead and the noise is unbearable. I cup my hands over my ears.

The first of the strange birds drops something, an abnormal egg tearing toward Taem's dome. It hits with a monstrous clamor. The sound echoes through my ears, the world seems to shake. The sky is momentarily brilliant. The other birds drop their eggs as well, one right after the other. Taem's dome holds.

The birds speed overhead, circling around. I catch an odd marking on their sides; a red triangle, like the Franconian emblem, only this one has a blue circle in its center, and a white star in place of the Order's cursive $f$.

A series of alarms erupt behind me, ringing through Union

Central. They are almost immediately echoed in downtown Taem. The noise is an endless shrieking, a sound of panic, of fear. I don't need to be told that these flying contraptions are the enemy Frank spoke of or that his words regarding AmWest were honest and true.

As the birds flip on their sides and navigate their turn, several cars emerge from below me. They are large green things, much bulkier than the one Emma and I traveled in when we were brought to Taem. These models have flat tops and hinged doors on their rear.

"Head downtown!" I hear someone shout from below the roof. "We are Code Red."

As the cars weave hastily toward Union Central's gates, the birds attack Taem's dome a second time. The roof beneath me vibrates, but again the barrier holds.

The man giving instructions, now in view, starts waving out a new stream of cars. "This batch to the Great Forest. Now!"

The map from Frank's records flashes in my mind. The Great Forest lying beyond Taem, the suspected Rebel headquarters nestled somewhere in its dense northern mountains. Rebels mean safety from Frank and the potential for answers by way of Harvey. And at the moment, I need both.

Rather than heading downtown, the second group of cars wraps around Union Central, heading for a different exit.

I'm on my feet instinctively, chasing it. Taem's dome lurches under a new attack and I nearly lose my footing from the resulting tremor.

The cars turn away from the building and onto a dirt road, and I see my only chance. I jump from the roof and onto the last vehicle. Pain shoots through my right ankle. There's nothing to grab hold of, and I'm sent sliding toward the rear of the car, thrown off as it hits a bump. I scramble to my feet.

The car is moving slowly because of the terrain and I manage to catch up to it. I twist open the back door and it swings wildly. I force myself to go faster, and when the timing is right, I jump into the rear of the vehicle just before the door slams shut.

I collapse on the floor. The car doesn't slow.

Gear bags are scattered about, and a series of crates marked with the Franconian emblem are stacked neatly in one corner. A row of large, slender guns is mounted to the wall of the vehicle. There are no windows, no way for the driver to see me. For now I am safe.

As we jerk over uneven ground, I think of Emma, alone in a prison cell, and me, running from her. I tell myself that I can't help her if I'm dead, that she will understand why I had to leave. This is the only way. Get safe, get a plan, *then* return for her. AmWest's attack may have been conveniently timed with my escape, but if Taem is at risk, Emma is as well. For her sake, I need Taem's dome to hold. I need the Order to fend off its enemy.

I snatch up a green gear bag and dig through it to distract my thoughts. Inside, I find an assortment of novelties. There's an odd wand contraption that shines light out one end when twisted, maps, a box labeled Matches, a heavy-duty hunting knife, a medical kit, and a pair of bulky eye extensions that when held up to my face make everything seem far closer than it should. There is a canteen of water, too, and some dried fruit. I take a swig of water and then I wait.

Several hours later, we slow to a crawl. I eye the guns along the wall, but instead fish the sheathed knife from the gear bag and stuff it into the waistband of my pants. Then I sling the pack on my back and wait for the rear doors to open.

Voices come first.

"We'll rest here for the night."

"But delivering supplies to the field is never an overnight job."

"We only left early because of the attack. Couldn't risk getting stuck in Taem when Evan is expecting supplies tomorrow."

Evan. The name sounds familiar, although I can't remember where I heard it.

The doors to the vehicle are pulled open and I let my boot

connect with the head of a surprised Order member. He falls to the ground and I start running. There is some shouting behind me, and another speckling of bullets, but I slip into the forest unscathed. There are trees again. Green trees and open air and woods that make me feel at home.

I have lots of labels now. Traitor. Rebel. Target. I am to be executed and my one hope lies deep within the forest. My arms pump, my feet fly north.

Toward uncertainties. Toward Mount Martyr. Toward Rebels.

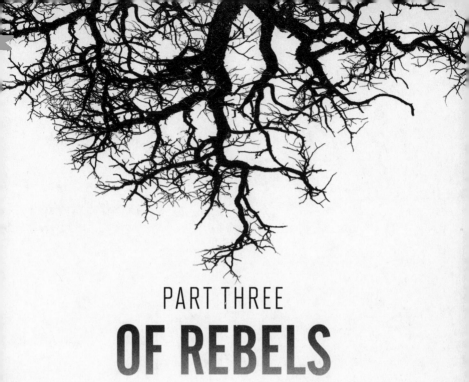

PART THREE

# OF REBELS

# NINETEEN

**I WANT TO BE AS** far from the Order as possible by nightfall, which gives me only a handful of hours to cover precious ground. I run until my lungs burn, and then slow to a brisk walk. The landscape has become rugged and rich. Trees seem uncommonly tall, and they grow so close together that I am forced to weave my way between them. It's hard to imagine that just this morning I was recovering from a trip to the infirmary.

A strong breeze whips at my back. The sky above me is barely visible through the thick leaves. It is a calm, pale blue, but the air smells like rain. A storm is coming. It's nice to feel these things again, to know and understand the world around me. It almost makes me feel like I am back in

Claysoot, hunting in the woods. Almost.

I check my map. There's a ledge ahead and some landform labeled the Hairpin, but it will be better to make camp now. The sun is already setting and the wind is too strong. I don't want to get stranded on an open ledge in bad weather.

In the very bottom of my pack is a hammock, which I tie between two trees, and a tarp, which I string overhead. Fearful of being spotted, I refrain from making a fire and instead pull the collar of my uniform up high around my neck. When the rain first begins, it is gentle. The drops fall daintily, landing in uneven beats as if the storm may pass right over, but then the sky unloads itself in one fell swoop. I dart beneath the tarp.Water comes down in sheets so thick the forest about me becomes a blur of motion.

I wonder how long it will take for Blaine to realize I'm missing. I wonder what Frank will tell him. *Emma and Gray were caught in a crossfire downtown. Emma and Gray walked beyond the dome of the city and were killed by Rebels. Emma and Gray ran away.* Lies, lies, lies. I need to return for Emma, but I need Harvey, too, otherwise Claysoot will never be free. Continuing toward the Rebels makes sense, but I have no concrete plan, no strategy. Everything has been turned upside down and it's giving me a headache.

When it starts to hail, I abandon the dried fruit I am eating for dinner, climb into the safety of my hammock, and sleep.

It rains all night.

I eat more fruit the following morning. I seriously contemplate hunting but know it will take too much time. I have just the one knife, and setting a trap would require waiting for something to wander into it. I break down camp, check the rising sun and the map, and continue north.

Maybe two hours later, I find myself walking alongside a cliff, the forest continuing beyond it, hundreds of feet below. From here, I can see for what seems like forever, an endless stretch of treetops spanning out before me. I follow a path along the ridge until suddenly it turns so sharply to the left, and downward, that it would be easy to overlook it altogether. I've reached the Hairpin.

It is slow going. The earth beneath my feet is loose from the previous night's rain and I progress with careful steps. At the base of the cliff, where the decline meets the forest plane, I notice a footprint in the moist earth. It is identical to the markings my boots create.

My heart rate quickens. The Order must be nearby.

I stick to the shadows for the rest of the day. I walk on pine needles when possible. I pause often. I hear nothing but the sounds of the forest—wind between branches and birdsong— until later that evening.

It's past nightfall, as I am setting up my hammock, when I make out the voices. I should stay put, keep a safe distance, and yet I can't help but wonder who the voices belong to and what they are discussing. I repack my gear, and with the bag on my shoulder, I steal toward the conversation.

The terrain has grown rockier this side of the Hairpin, and it offers plenty of coverage. I dart from boulder to tree to boulder, staying out of sight. Ahead, through the branches, I can make out the faint glow of a fire. As I edge closer, I realize it's a camp. An Order camp. There are perhaps two dozen of them, sitting around a central fire pit that casts warm light upon their faces. Some have their backs to me, but the man who appears in charge is fully visible. His hair is shaved so closely to his head, I wonder if any ever grew there at all.

"I want to be very, very clear about what we are doing here and how we are going to do it," he says. "Operation Ferret is perhaps one of the most critical assignments our division has ever been tasked with. It is imperative we don't screw this up."

Operation Ferret: the folder Emma and I had discovered back in Union Central. It must be the mission Frank has been planning since he heard Harvey was spotted in the forest.

The man pauses dramatically and looks over his team. I follow his gaze and recognize Septum and Craw in the firelight. They look nervous. This must be what they'd consider their first big mission.

"Mount Martyr is our final destination," the man continues. "We suspect it, or at least one of the neighboring mountain ranges, to not only be the location of Maldoon but his headquarters for the entire Rebel movement. Do not underestimate this man. He is ruthless and far more cunning than he appears. Our mission is to bring him back to Taem. *Alive*. It is crucial that he is brought back in one piece."

I picture Harvey, his frail frame and dark eyes. I can see his piercing gaze as clearly as if he stood before me. I have to tail this group. Or get to Harvey first. I need to get answers from him before Frank does.

The man folds his arms over the red triangle on his chest and continues. "Tomorrow morning, we start a trek that will take us to the base of Mount Martyr, and from there, the retrieval of Maldoon begins. Follow orders, and I am confident this operation will be a success."

The man then points to a few individuals, and asks them to join him in his tent. I adjust the pack on my back, ready to retreat and set up camp from a safe distance when a twig snaps behind me.

I spin to face nothing but dark shadows and silhouetted trees.

Another snap.

This time I see the figure: tall, dark, pointing a gun at me. It is a smaller model, like the one Frank had. "Stay right there," he orders, walking into the extended glow of firelight. It's

Blaine. He drops the weapon to his side as soon as he recognizes me.

"Gray! What are you doing here?" he whispers.

"What are *you* doing here?"

"I'm on this mission. First big one and a chance to catch Harvey, no less," he says proudly.

This is better than I could have planned it. I can fill Blaine in, tell him about Frank. I can get him to help me capture Harvey before the Order does. My chances for success have always been slim, but with Blaine, I feel more sure.

Before I am able to get out another word, a figure is approaching us.

"Blaine? Your watch is up. I came to relieve—" The man sees me and freezes. "What the devil? Where did he come from?"

"It's okay, Liam," Blaine says. "This is my brother, Gray."

Liam eyes me suspiciously. "How did he get here?"

"He . . ." Blaine pauses and looks at me, puzzled. "How *did* you get here?"

This is clearly the wrong thing to say, because Liam draws his gun and points it at us both. "Toward camp," he orders, motioning with the weapon. "Right now."

Blaine raises his hands. "Liam, this is my brother, not the enemy."

"I don't care. He shows up snooping around in the woods

and he isn't on the mission list. Move toward camp."

As we near the campfire, the other Order members stare.

"Evan?" Liam calls out. The bald leader reappears from a tent, and I remember. Evan was the man Frank talked to that day outside the dining hall, the person tasked with readying a team to retrieve Harvey. "Found this kid spying on us in the woods," Liam continues. "Blaine says his name is Gray. They're brothers."

Blaine tries to say something, mumbling in my defense, but Evan raises a hand and silences him. Someone brings Evan a handheld device that looks a lot like the one Marco had used in the Outer Ring.

"I've got a Gray Weathersby here," he says into it. "I don't know how he arrived, but he is wearing an Order uniform and has a supply pack. We found him on the outskirts of our camp. Orders?"

The unit breathes static, overriding a voice, muffled and choppy.

"Say again?" Evan shakes the device, but the vocals don't clear. He curses, tries to make contact again, and eventually gives up. "Those things never have the range we need. Bring him here."

Liam pushes me forward and doesn't let up until I am standing so close to Evan that I can see the firelight glistening off his smooth scalp.

"What are you doing out here alone?" he asks.

"Individual mission," I say hurriedly.

"That so? Funny, I wasn't aware of anything else happening this week, not with the mission my team is about to conduct. You got papers?"

"Yes." This is not going to end well.

"Let's see them." Evan snaps and points at my pack, which Liam starts rifling through. He doesn't even bother to take it off my back and I am jostled left and right as he digs.

"Sir," he says. "There are no papers. And this pack . . . it's not a standard mission pack. It's for deliveries. Enough supplies for two days, tops."

Evan pulls at my bag, takes one look at its contents, and then shoves me. "On your knees."

"Wait. What are you doing?" Blaine asks, his voice uneven.

"His bag belongs to the supply team that is supposed to be here in the morning to restock us. He's lying."

Evan draws a gun from his hip and Blaine flinches. "Put it away," he says. "If he's lying, I'm sure there's a reason."

"And whatever it is, it won't be good enough."

Liam forces me to my knees.

All that running for nothing. I should have ignored the voices and made camp back in the trees. Blaine is saying something to Evan, frantically pleading, but the man has made up his mind. I catch Craw on the other side of the flames. He grimaces.

I hear Evan move behind me, feel the weapon press against the back of my shaved head. It is cold. I'm thinking of Emma and Claysoot and unanswered questions and if it will hurt when I realize it has grown quiet; too quiet. The rustling of animals in the woods is gone. Not even the wind makes a noise.

And then I hear it, the gentle whiz of a projectile through air. It is followed by a soft thud. Evan coughs and falls onto me. I shove him off and find an arrow in his chest, red blossoming over his shirt.

"Rebels!" Liam yells. "We're being attacked!"

The arrows come in a steady stream, piercing their way through the darkness. Some are on fire and send tents ablaze when they connect with canvas. I cover my head with my hands and scramble to my feet.

Blaine grabs my arm and tugs. He's pulling me from the madness when an arrow grazes his arm. He stumbles. I turn in time to see a second arrow burrow into his leg. He falls instantly.

"Blaine!"

I bend to examine him on the ground, barely dodging another arrow that whizzes overhead. Blaine is clutching his thigh. Already there is a lot of blood and I can't see the wound.

"Is it bad?" he asks, coughing.

"You're fine," I say, even though I'm certain he's not. "Come on, we have to move." I sling Blaine's arm behind my neck. He is heavy, but in the moment, my legs don't seem to care. I run away from the fire pit, supporting Blaine's weight as best I can. Gunfire breaks out behind us, our attackers now shooting both arrows and bullets.

The camp is in absolute chaos. Order members drop sporadically while the attackers stay hidden in the evening shadows.

"Fire at will!" someone shouts. Bullets race in both directions. How the Order is not shooting their own kind, I am not sure.

"Fall back," another voice demands. "Fall back now!"

I duck behind the nearest boulder. Craw, too, is using the rock as shelter. "What happened?" he shouts over the gunfire, eyeing Blaine.

"An arrow. It hit him." My ears ring from the shooting.

"He'll be okay," Craw says, reloading his gun.

"I don't know." I watch him ready the weapon. He slams ammunition in place and then leans back over the rock, spraying bullets into the darkness. A series of arrows comes back at us, forcing us to flatten our bellies to the ground.

Craw looks at me desperately, and then Blaine. "I can't hold them off much longer," he admits. "You should go. Now."

Bullets come flying at the rock. I'm struck with the realization that this might be it, that I might not make it beyond tonight or back to Taem and I never got to tell Emma how I really felt. She seems so distant suddenly. Irretrievable.

"If you make it back to Taem, tell Emma I'll come back for her. And that I love her. Can you tell her that?"

If Craw is surprised at that word, he doesn't show it. He gives a nod, one quick jerk of his chin, and then leans back over the rock. He points his weapon into the darkness and speaks without looking at me. "Go. Now," he orders. "I'll cover you."

I shift Blaine so that my arms are better locked beneath his shoulders, and as Craw opens fire, I run.

# TWENTY

**I SPEND THE NIGHT IN** a dark cave nestled among a small rise. I build a fire and tend to Blaine as best I can. Fearful of being unable to control the bleeding, I don't pull out the arrow. Instead, I break it off low to the wound. He winces. I use most of the water left in my canteen to clear away the blood. He snarls. I wrap bandages from my pack around the remainder of the shaft and they quickly turn crimson.

"I'll be okay," he says over and over and over. I nod.

I had been running to the Rebels, and they'd shot my brother. I watch his chest rise and fall in unsteady waves. I already lost Blaine once. I can't lose him again.

In the morning, Blaine is weaker. We follow our footprints back to camp with him slumped against my shoulder. There is nothing left of the mission team but a mess of canvas and ash barely visible through a thick fog. The fire pit is run over, and most of the tents lay trampled in the dirt, smoldering. I salvage one and create a giant sling that I can rest Blaine in and drag behind me. I'm furious with the Rebels for what has happened to Blaine, but I would be foolish to not continue my trek there. I need Harvey and there is nothing but an execution waiting for me in Taem. Plus, Blaine requires medical attention. Badly.

I count seven dead bodies among the wrecked camp. I feel like I should bury them, but don't have the time. Instead, I pile the remains atop a still smoking tent and light them on fire. A team of black crows, annoyed that I have stolen their breakfast, lurk overhead as we leave the camp. They follow us for most of the morning, flying in low circles and cawing eerily as the fog dissipates.

I head north, counting fifteen dead Order members over the course of the day. More than half of Evan's mission team has been lost. The little water I have left goes to Blaine, and I have to hold his mouth open and force the liquid down his throat.

That night I catch a rabbit for dinner. I try to feed Blaine, but he can't stomach the meat. I run out of water the following morning and am forced to sip dew from cupped leaves in a futile attempt to quench my thirst.

I continue this trend daily. I drag Blaine behind me. We

eat what I can kill. I try to keep us hydrated. Blaine has been fading in and out of consciousness for the better part of a day when I begin to lose faith. The thirst is getting to me. Sometimes I'll see a Rebel ahead or Craw, and then I blink and nothing is there. I keep heading north but cover less ground with each passing hour. Night and day become one and the same. North and south blend. I could be dragging Blaine in wide circles and I wouldn't know the difference. My head hurts and my throat burns so intensely I'm afraid it may catch fire.

Maybe I will never find water. Frank said it was scarce, a rare and coveted resource. What if this forest has already been stripped dry? What if its rivers are dammed, and its lakes pumped, and I find nothing but empty reservoirs?

On the third day without water, I stumble upon a stagnant pond of filthy green slime. I drop to my knees in front of it. This? After all my searching? It's too still, completely undrinkable. I pull Blaine's body toward mine and hold his head in my lap. His lips are split and dry, his eyes struggling to stay open. I watch his chest heave, his breathing pattern erratic. I've failed the people I love. First Emma. Now Blaine.

And then I hear something: a soft, delicate flutter. My heart flips over. I strain and listen harder. It sounds like the trickle of a stream.

I follow the noise and discover that the green pond is being filled by the tiniest beads of water dripping down a rock face at its rear. There's a very small opening in the stone, but I can see light on the other side. The sound, too, is coming from behind it.

"Blaine," I say. "Get up. You have to walk."

He mumbles something incoherent.

"There's water," I explain. I want to tell him that I only need him to do this one thing and then I'll carry him again, but forming the words requires too much effort.

Blaine grunts as I pull him to his feet. Dirt and sweat cover his forehead.

"Through here," I say, pointing at the gap in the rock. He grimaces as we move forward, limping to keep weight off his bad leg. "Can you do it?"

He coughs, but nods. I let go of him. He clenches his eyes shut, blinks several times, nods again. As soon as I turn my back on him, Blaine falls. The sound of him hitting the ground is sickening: a solid, dull crack.

He's fainted, his head striking a rock in the process. I drop beside him. "Blaine?" He doesn't answer. I lift his head and my fingers grow sticky with blood. "Blaine!"

Nothing.

"You can't do this! Not now. Not when we finally found it." I shake him, curse him, yell his name, but he doesn't respond. I press my ear to his chest and when I hear his heartbeat, I release a breath I didn't realize I was holding. I fish a bandage from my bag and dress his wound, my hands shaking the entire time.

I look back at the rock face. We still need water. I'll have to go in alone, gather as much as possible. I take one last look at Blaine, and then force myself through the passageway. It is a tight squeeze and my fatigued state slows me significantly, but by the time I have scrambled through the gap, I am crying out with joy.

Steep stone encloses me from all angles. From one of the highest peaks comes water, tumbling down in a magnificent spout and filling a freshwater pool at my feet. Water from this pool drips ever so slowly through the path I have just taken, but rushes out an opposite end of the enclosed area into what must be an impressive river.

I don't stop to explore the workings of the water's natural course. Instead, I whisper my thanks that the Order has not discovered this resource and race into the shallow pool. I splash it on my face and drink anxiously. My arms feel heavy, the weight of bringing them to my mouth nearly unbearable, but the water tastes so good. The sound of the cascading falls is heavenly, the kick of the cool liquid in my stomach unreal. For the first time in days, I am hopeful.

I drink until I can take no more, and then pull the canteen from my pack and fill it for Blaine.

"Stop right there," a voice commands.

I freeze. My hands go above my head.

I take what I expect to be my last breath, but the shot never comes. With my arms still held in surrender, I look up, searching for the intruder. About twenty paces away, standing near the narrow opening through which I just climbed, is a girl. She is my age, maybe a tad younger, and holds a gun in her arms, one of the long and slender varieties. Her eyes are focused, intense. She's going to pull the trigger and I'll be dead as quickly as the thief in Taem's public square. But the girl pauses, lifts her face from her weapon. I watch as she takes aim for a second time and again hesitates to shoot.

"You," she says, barking at me. "What's your name?" She marches up to me when I remain silent and presses the gun into my chest. "I asked you what your name is." She is far shorter than me—shorter than Emma, even—with bright blond hair that is braided into a bun. "The boy outside. Is he your brother?"

"You're just going to kill us anyway," I tell her. And it's true. She thinks I'm the enemy. "You're going to murder us, the way you murdered that Order team."

"Murder?" she spits. "It's not murder when we're fighting for our lives." She looks at me carefully again, her eyes boring into mine.

"Your name," she grits through clenched teeth. I refuse to

give it and instead begin to toy with her. This is when I know I'm more dehydrated than ever, more crazy than sane.

"You were really good," I admit. "All quiet like that. How long have you been following us?" She doesn't answer. "You'd make a good hunter. Especially where I came from. I don't think we had a single girl as stealthy as you."

"Where you came from?" she repeats. "Are you with the Order or are you from somewhere else?" She pushes the gun into my chest a bit harder this time. I keep my hands over my head, but I'm pretty certain that if she hasn't shot me yet, she's not going to.

"What's it matter? You *are* going to shoot me, right?" I flash her a quick smile. Devious. Playful.

Her eyes narrow, and when she moves, she is impossibly quick. Her knee comes up and hits me in the groin. I buckle over in pain and she brings the butt of her weapon into my skull. I fall into the water and the last thing I see as I surrender to darkness is her proud face above me, smirking.

# TWENTY-ONE

**WHEN I REGAIN CONSCIOUSNESS, I** am lying on a cot, in a room that appears to be a combination of wood and rock, as though someone tried to build a space that would fuse with the land. The blond girl stands with her back to me, talking to a man twice her age and nearly four times her size. He looks worried, his arms crossed atop his bulging stomach.

"You shouldn't have brought them back here, Bree," the man says.

"Luke, just look at them. Tell me you don't see it and I'll admit I'm wrong."

Luke says nothing.

"And he said 'where I came from.'"

Still nothing.

"And they're twins."

"I don't care," Luke says, shaking his head. "They're wearing Order uniforms. They're a threat to us all."

"One of them is unconscious. Possibly in a coma due to a head injury."

"Even still."

"Owen should see them," Bree retorts. "If he wants them dead, too, then fine. But I want to be sure."

"All right, but I'm getting Clipper first. He's already dealt with the unconscious one, but I won't have that boy here a moment longer until it's out." Luke eyes me suspiciously before leaving the room.

"Who's Clipper?" I ask, sitting up. The motion makes me dizzy.

"He specializes in removing tracking devices," Bree says. "Here. Have some water." She hands me a crudely shaped cup, which I drink from anxiously.

"Tracking devices?"

"You *do* know where you are, don't you?" she asks, hands on her hips.

"Mount Martyr," I say. I have to be. Bree is with the Rebels and she has brought me back to their headquarters. "Where's my brother? I want to see him."

She sits on the edge of the bed. "What's your name?" Her eyes lock with mine as if she could stare the answer out of me.

"What's yours?"

"Bree."

"Nice to meet you."

She frowns. "I'd say likewise, but you still haven't told me who you are."

"I know. And I don't plan to." I don't trust her. She thought of shooting me, and Blaine, too, who was unconscious, as harmless as a fallen tree trunk.

"You'll tell us eventually," she says. "We have ways of making people talk."

There is a knock on the door and a small boy walks in. He is a scrawny thing, with pinched eyes and large hands. He can't be older than twelve or thirteen.

"This is Clipper," Bree says. "He's going to terminate your tracking device now." The boy smiles proudly.

"I have no clue what you're talking about," I say.

"Of course you don't," Bree sneers. "They likely said you needed some shots and pills and a haircut, called it a Cleansing. And then you woke up the next day with odd pains in your neck. They put a tracker in you."

I look at her blankly.

"As long as you are breathing and the tracker is implanted, they will get an accurate reading of your location back in Taem," she continues. "So what Clipper does is remove the device. Once he's got it out of you, it will cease to work and the Franconian Order will lose their precious reading.

In their eyes, you'll be good as dead. I explained that right, didn't I, Clipper?"

"Sure did," he announces.

This is definitely for the best. If Frank thinks I'm dead, I can start a new life. I can search out Harvey and figure out how to free Claysoot. And then, when the time is right and Frank has forgotten about me, I can return to Taem for Emma.

"Here," Bree says, passing me a wooden spoon. "You'll want to bite it. It's going to hurt like heck." She turns a cheek to me and reveals a nasty scar running from beneath her right ear toward her collarbone. She must have served in the Order at one point.

Clipper cleans an area of my neck and takes an odd contraption out of his bag. He hooks up a few wires and positions some menacing-looking tools beside me.

"Bree? Are you sure Clipper is qualified to be doing this?"

She frowns. "Clayton has been doing this for years; it's how he earned the nickname Clipper. And he did mine when he was only eleven, so he can most certainly handle yours." She smiles viciously and adds, "Chances are you won't even scar that bad."

"Ready?" the boy asks.

"Count to three," I say. "So I know it's coming."

Clipper holds something I can't see alongside my neck. "Okay," he agrees. "Here we go. One . . . two . . ."

Without warning, pain jolts through my neck. Everything burns. There is a piercing stab, like a hot iron drilling into the muscles of my neck, then a wrench and a pull and something breaks free from my body. I'm screaming so loudly, it's hurting even my own ears. I'm certain I've bitten the spoon in half.

Clipper presses something warm to my neck, but it is not relieving. Instead, I feel as though my skin is melting, burning, blistering. A moment later, he pulls the instrument away, and the pain begins to subside.

"You said you'd count to three!" I shout at him.

"Sorry." He actually sounds sincere. "It only works if the person is relaxed. If I'd counted to three, you would have braced for it, and then it would have failed."

"It's true," Bree says. She smiles as though she's happy I suffered.

"Look," Clipper says, holding out a mirror. "You barely even scarred."

There's now a pale red line on the side of my neck. He's right. It doesn't look nearly as bad as Bree's. Hers looks as if Clipper got into a knife fight with her neck.

"Can I see the tracker?" I ask.

Clipper holds out a bowl. In it rests an insignificant metal strip, no longer than my thumb. I feel dirty, knowing they had planted something in me without my knowledge.

"All right, Clipper, that's enough," Bree says. "We don't need to give him a full-blown lesson. I'm not even sure he'll be staying around."

"You're kidding!" Clipper flings the tracking device into his bag. "I just went through that entire process so that you can kill the guy later?"

"What?" I reach for the knife tucked in my waistband, but it's gone. I'm still too weak to fight even if I wanted. I think I need more water.

"We have to take precautions," Bree says, shrugging. "And in the end, it's not my call."

"Whose decision is it?" I ask.

"Owen's."

"Who's he?"

"Why don't we go find out?" She points her gun at me and nudges my shoulder.

With my hands once again held up in surrender, she guides me from the room. We head through a series of narrow rock hallways, encountering no one along the way. I think of jumping Bree and making a run for it, but I'd probably wander in circles and be captured by someone before finding an exit. That, or collapse from exhaustion. And I can't leave without Blaine.

We come to a halt and Bree wrestles a door open. "Inside," she says, motioning with the gun. "Owen will be in momentarily."

I don't bother arguing. I walk through the doorway into a dark and dingy room. Rock surrounds me. It reminds me of the prison cell I shared with Bozo back in Taem, only it doesn't smell quite as foul. A single overhead light renders the far side of the room visible. Against the wall is a lone chair and I drag my tired legs over to it. As soon as I sit, a man enters.

"Stay where you are," he says, his voice oddly familiar. I slump further into the chair. From where I sit I can make out only his shins and feet—he wears thickly woven pants and a pair of strong boots—but the rest of him is in shadows.

"Bree said I should see you before we dispose of you," he says. "Do you know why that might be?"

"She feels guilty murdering someone who had his hands up in surrender?" I suggest, my eyes still on his feet.

The man grunts. "Very clever. You Order folk have an odd sense of humor." He shifts something from his shoulder and sets it on the ground. It looks like a bow, but I can't be sure. Then he walks to the corner and grabs a tall slender pole and positions it before him. After flicking something on its trunk, brightness floods the room and he adjusts the light source until it is practically on top of me. It's blinding and I drop my head further into my chest.

"Look at me," the man demands. Again, his voice sounds familiar, but I can't place it. I keep my head in my chest. "I said look at me," he orders.

It's too bright, but I lift my head slowly. I squint, opening one eye at a time. He takes a step backward when the light hits my face.

"You . . . ," he starts, but then his voice fades out. "What's your name?"

He sounds like Bree. "I don't see the point in telling you if you're going to kill me anyway."

"Maybe we won't."

"Maybe you will."

"Boy, just tell me your name. Please?" His voice has gone from demanding to kind, as if nothing could be more important than learning my name at this particular moment. But I've kept it to myself for so long now, it seems foolish to give it away just because someone's asking nicely.

"Are you Blaine or Gray?" he offers when I remain silent. Those words make me flinch, open my eyes wider in an attempt to see him. How out of all the names did he pick these two to pair together?

"Neither," I spit, but I know my reaction has proven otherwise.

"No, you're most certainly one of them. I would bet my life on it."

"I don't know what you're talking about." Why won't he step into the light and show his face? The coward.

"Of course you don't. You never knew me, but I knew you."

204

The man is making me uncomfortable. I shrink as far as I can into the chair as he moves toward me. There is a moment when he changes from a black silhouette to a person with such recognizable features that I believe my eyes are tricking me, that the dehydration has altered my vision. Dark hair, wild as mine was before it was cut. Broad shoulders. Deep, blue eyes as bright as Blaine's.

"I'm Owen," he says when he finally stands before me. He stretches out a hand in greeting. "Owen Weathersby. You are?"

"Gray," I say, struggling to stand. "I'm Gray."

He pulls me into his chest, clutching an arm tightly around my back, and whispers, "Welcome home, Gray. Welcome home."

# TWENTY-TWO

**MY FATHER. HERE. ALIVE.**

He walks me through the cool stone passages and back to
the cot I first awoke in. I remember seeing his face above me
as I succumb to darkness.

When some subconscious drive deems me strong enough
to open my eyes again, Bree is sitting beside me, examining
her weapon. I wonder if it ever leaves her hands. She wears
an outfit oddly reminiscent of Claysoot: a lightly woven jacket
and thick, cotton pants.

"How long was I out?" I ask, sitting up quickly. I feel strong
again. Hungry, but strong.

"A full day."

It feels much longer. "Where's my father?"

"He's waiting to see you. I'm supposed to bring you in now that you're up."

"And my brother?"

"He's been brought to the hospital. At Mount Martyr."

"Aren't we already there?"

She scowls. "You think I'm that stupid? That I would have brought you both to our headquarters before confirming you were Owen's sons?"

"But you said—back when Clipper came in . . ."

"No. *You* said we were at Mount Martyr. I neither confirmed nor denied that fact."

She's right. "How come I had to stay here?"

"Because you are not in a coma like your brother. He's harmless. But you, on the other hand . . . we just don't trust you."

"Right. Don't trust the guy that practically died of dehydration looking for the so-called Rebels."

She stands aggressively and pushes a wild strand of blond hair out of her eyes. "You know nothing. Absolutely nothing. You come in wearing that horrible Order uniform, and we spare you, nurse you back to health. We take unnecessary risks for you because you're a captain's son. And instead of seeing what's happening around you, you focus on how we've treated you *unfairly*."

I roll my eyes, uninterested in arguing with her. "Maybe

you should have shot me then, Bree. Me and my brother. Maybe that would have made things easier for you."

"If you think I actually want another death on my conscience, you're even dumber than I thought." She snatches up her gun. "Do you want to see your father or not?"

"Yes."

"Then shut up and follow me. You try to run, I shoot you. You try to attack me, I shoot you. You do anything else I find to be slightly suspicious, I shoot you. Got it?"

I nod. I don't trust her, but what choice do I have? And there's my father. Waiting. Holding answers. Going forward is the only way.

"Good. Now let's move." Bree nudges me with the gun. It's not pressed straight into me, like in our earlier encounters, but it's positioned well enough, screaming that she is in control and I am still a prisoner. I'm certain I could take her now if I really wanted. I feel well enough. But that doesn't get me to my father, and it certainly won't help me earn anyone's trust.

"We don't have all day," she says, motioning more adamantly.

I raise my hands above my head playfully, as if I am truly threatened by her command. "We're back to this again, I see?"

"Always." She actually smiles a little. Not an angry smile, but a smirk, visible for a second and then gone.

It turns out I was being held in an interrogation center. We pass Luke on our way through the stone passageways. He holds bloody hands before us, an ugly, twisted tool in their grasp. From somewhere down a dark hallway behind him, I can hear a mangled cry ring out. It sends shivers down my spine that only multiply when Luke shoots me what I'm sure he intends to be a reassuring smile. I'm still attempting to shake off the chills when we step from the dark confines of rock and out into a sunny afternoon.

There is no path, but Bree leads as though there is one. After twenty minutes of a steep, uphill climb, I am out of breath. At the top of a crest, where the land levels out momentarily, I buckle over and heave for air. Bree waits patiently and then tosses me a canteen when I straighten up. Before I can thank her, we are moving again.

We hike silently until we come to what appears to be a dead end. The steep slopes of what must be Mount Martyr bear down on us. To climb over them would take days, and before us sits only a towering rockface.

"We're here," Bree announces.

I look around, thinking she's speaking to someone, but we are alone. There is nowhere to go but back.

"We just climbed the lower base of Mount Martyr. And this"—she motions back toward the monstrous wall—"is the entrance to Crevice Valley."

"Crevice Valley?" That name wasn't on Frank's Operation Ferret map.

She nods. "Headquarters."

I stare at the massive mountain. "It sure doesn't look like a valley."

"That's because you have to go through the crevice first." She moves toward the rock towering above us, and as I follow, the passageway becomes visible to my eyes. It is a dark slit, running the length of the stone, from our feet toward the sky, so narrow it's barely visible. No wonder the Order has been unsuccessful locating this place. The entrance is hard to see even when you are directly in front of it.

"You first," Bree says.

"Through here?" I point doubtfully at the cramped break in the rock. "Isn't there another entrance?"

"Yes, but that would require us to hike all the way around the mountain, and we don't have the time. Now move."

Shimmying through the crevice ends up being easier than I anticipate, not because it's spacious or well lit, but because there is only one path to take. We wiggle sideways through the tiny space, our backs pressed to rock behind us, and our noses nearly scraping the opposing side of the mountain.

Eventually, the passage begins to widen. Soon I can walk normally, the space large enough to house my shoulders. Moments after that, Bree is at my side. The light from the entrance has nearly faded out completely when a new light appears ahead.

"What if you need to escape?" I ask as we continue down the ever-widening path. "What if the Order infiltrates?"

"Then we leave through the rear."

"And what if they infiltrate both at the same time? You guys are sitting ducks in here. You've trapped yourself."

"You give us so little credit." I stare at her, confused, and she points up into the clefts in the rock walls surrounding us. High up, hidden like insects in the crannies of the crevice's tall rock face, are armed men. "Both entrances are patrolled day and night. And there's always the tear gas if needed."

Her words are foreign to me, but I shudder nonetheless. How had Evan and his team expected to be even remotely successful? This is a fortress, with no way in other than by invitation.

Eventually, the place lives up to its name. The crevice's width doubles, triples, quadruples. It grows so wide that it is immeasurable, at least to my eyes. The rock walls continue to surround us but give way to clouds and fresh air overhead. And before us lies the valley, a footpath twisting down into it. Fields and gardens are plowed out beneath the open-air ceiling. Dirt streets snake between houses and livestock pens. A market in the distance brings the scents of herbs and roasting meat to my nose. There are people, too, hundreds of them. I never would have guessed that Harvey had amassed so many followers. Or maybe it was Elijah. I think back to the records in Union Central, perplexed. I'm starting to question the accuracy of Frank's information. Something doesn't add up. Maybe Harvey's not even here.

I look down at the town. From our elevated position, the people appear as tiny dolls, dressed in drab clothes. They are young and old, women and children, men and boys. The place is oddly familiar, like Claysoot, only picked up and shoved into a hollowed-out mountain. On the outskirts of the open valley, where the steep walls begin reaching for the sky, tunnels and passageways twist into the rock's depth. If Harvey really is here, finding him will be no easy task.

"What's to keep your enemy from coming in the top?" I ask.

"We have our defenses, even if they can't be seen, but I'm not sure you can be trusted with those details yet. Better wait 'til after your vote."

We hit the base of the valley floor, and Bree cuts up the street that passes the market. People stare at the red triangle atop my chest, the $f$ stitched in its center. They have hatred in their eyes, hatred so clear I know they wish me dead.

"This vote," I say as we leave the market and turn up a side street. "What do you mean when you say it's mine?"

"Exactly that. It's *your* vote. They're deciding if you live or die."

"What? I . . . I thought that's what my father was deciding, back when he met me in the interrogation center."

"Well, yes and no. Owen was deciding if you lived to see Crevice Valley, but he doesn't make all the calls. Now the others get to weigh in."

"What others?"

We are approaching two men near one of the dark tunnels that breaks off from the valley. They are monstrous, both taller than me and nearly twice as wide.

"Bree, what others?" I ask again anxiously. She doesn't answer. Instead, the two men swipe me up effortlessly, each one grabbing me beneath an elbow. I struggle against them, but it's pointless. Why had I trusted Bree? My father? Why did I think the Rebel headquarters would be any safer than Taem itself? They are going to have me killed, just like Frank ordered.

I shout to Bree as the men drag me away, but she remains rooted in place, quiet and stoic. She has a look of pity in her eyes, if only for a moment.

The next thing I know, we are bursting into a large room housed off a torch-lit tunnel. The men throw me into a chair and bind my wrists to its armrests. Circling the table are five people: the votes for my sentence. Four are strangers, but one is my father.

# TWENTY-THREE

**THEIR EYES BEAR DOWN ON** me, inquisitive, curious. I have no clue what happens now. The only thing I know for certain is that this vote could be the end. I'll have spent the last days of my life chasing after truths that never revealed themselves, hurting the people I love in the process.

Why was I so stupid, so reckless? I need to get back to Emma. I struggle against my bindings. I *have* to get back to her. My breathing is suddenly erratic.

"Screw you. All of you." I spit at the center of the table. The liquid lands in front of a tall, thin woman. Her brows dip toward the bridge of her nose. "You especially," I shout again, eyeing my father. He looks hurt, but he betrayed me. He shook my hand knowing this vote would come; and shouting feels painfully good, like salt in a wound.

"You're going to cast my life away with a vote?" I continue. "Do you know what I've been through to get here? Do you know what you'll take away from me if you don't vote in my favor?"

An aged man with little hair smiles from the head of the table. "We've caught a fiery one, I see."

"Ryder, he's just upset," my father interjects. "And confused."

"Easy, Owen," Ryder says, running a hand across his dull scalp. "I never said fire was a bad thing." The way my father retreats at his words, slouches back into his seat, tells me who is in charge. Not Harvey, not Elijah, but this man: a face I have never seen until today.

"What's going on here?" I ask. "I want answers. I demand them."

Ryder pushes back his chair and stands, using his arms to support his weight on the table before him. His gentle nature, but unmistakable confidence, reminds me so much of Maude. Maude, who I once trusted.

The old man looks directly at me and says, "My name is Ryder Phoenix, Gray. We come from the same place, you and I, from Claysoot. I understand your frustrations because I lived them myself. Several of us here have. I give you my word, regardless of your vote's outcome, you will have the truth."

Answers. I should be relieved and yet I'm hung up on his

name. Ryder. Ryder Phoenix. Why is it so familiar? And then I remember; the early scrolls. The boy Maude had run the first experiment on. The boy that led to the discovery of the Heist. He is so much more than a boy now, aged and grown before me, but it must be him.

"The whole truth. All of it," I demand. "About the Laicos Project and why you're working for Harvey after what he did to you."

The lone woman at the table snickers. "The boy is hardly in a position to be making demands."

"It's fine, Fallyn," Ryder says. "The whole truth, Gray. I promise."

I don't thank him, even if I should.

"This is a vote in regard to the life of one Gray Weathersby, son of Owen Weathersby, captured from the Franconian Order and brought in by Brianna Nox two days ago. Votes will be one per person, nay for death and yea for mercy. Majority rules." Ryder turns to me and adds, "Do you have anything to say that has not already been spoken?"

I look around the rock-enclosed room. Eyes glare at me, my father's the only pair that look remotely kind. Blaine would tell me to reflect first, to ready my words before I spill them. I take a deep breath and begin, speaking as calmly as I can manage.

"I was supposed to be executed. I came in search of safety,

but I was planning on coming here either way. I saw records in Taem. Records that documented executions at Frank's hands. The truth is, I climbed over the Wall for answers and found only more questions. And all those questions led me here. Because I think you have answers. I know you do."

It's a fragment of the truth, and maybe that's why it comes out so easily. I *had* come for safety. But I'd also come for Harvey, for the answers *he* possesses. I keep that small detail to myself for now.

Ryder nods and sits back into his chair. "And now, we vote."

The man immediately to Ryder's right stands. He is about my father's age, maybe older. I'm not used to seeing men over eighteen and it's hard to tell. "Raid Dextern," he says, announcing himself to the room. "Yea."

That's it. No reasoning. No motive. Just yea, a vote for life, and he returns to his seat.

My father stands next. "Owen Weathersby. I'm sorry, Fallyn," he says, addressing the woman to his side. "I understand your reasoning, and I even know it possible, but if we are wrong, and he is truly my son—well, I just can't take that chance. My vote is for life."

Fallyn stands, palms pressed into the table. She has a wild look in her eyes, not unlike Bree's when I first encountered her in the forest.

"Fallyn Case," she says. "He could be a Forgery, another

trick of Taem, engineered to look like something that will tear at our heartstrings and later murder us as we sleep. And even if he's not, he's just too much of a risk. You've heard him. Irrational. Vengeful. I vote death."

This is the first vote for my death, and yet instead of fear or dread, I am hung up on her mention of *Forgeries*. What are they? Is Harvey responsible for them as well?

The next man stands, and I suddenly recognize him. It's the boy from Frank's records. He looks even younger in person than he had on paper. "Elijah Brewster," he says. "I have to agree with Fallyn. It's too risky. Nay."

It's all tied up, and down to one vote. One measly vote.

Ryder does not stand. "I do not think the Order would have engineered such a rash Forgery," he says. "Forgeries are far more reserved. They are so plain that you overlook them. But this boy is emotional. The rage in this one, the anger, the bitterness, the fire—that is real. That is what is left of a Heisted boy, a life plucked from one world and thrown without background into another. I vote mercy in this case. I vote yea."

Fallyn slams her fists on the table. "If you're wrong, Ryder, the blood is on your hands." She storms from the room. Elijah follows her, knocking his chair over as he leaves.

"You'll pardon Elijah and Fallyn," Ryder says, removing the rope that bound me to my seat. "They're only trying to protect our people."

I scoff at this and Raid whispers something to my father before skirting after the others.

"Well, that about does it," Ryder says. "I'll leave you two alone. I'm sure you have plenty of catching up to do."

"What about the truth?" I call out to him.

"Oh, we'll get to that eventually. You need to clean up first. Eat."

"But . . . you said . . ."

"I promised you answers, Gray, but I did not say they would be instantaneous, nor did I say they would come directly from me. Talk to your father. Get to know him. Visit your brother in the hospital. These things should be more important anyway." And with his carefully formulated wave of guilt working over me, Ryder, too, exits.

My father shows me to my room. I'm lost immediately, overwhelmed by the various tunnels and burrows that snake off the main valley area he refers to as the Basin. Each passageway looks the same, each turn identical, but he promises I will pick it up in time.

I want to ask him about Harvey, about the Laicos Project and why the Rebels are working alongside a monster, but the details don't add up. Word in Taem was that Harvey was gathering followers, and yet, I haven't seen him once since arriving, not even at my vote, which seemed to include influential Rebels. Maybe Frank's records are wrong and Harvey's not in charge. Maybe Harvey isn't even here at all.

Pushing the questions aside, I tell my father about my journey. I start with the letter I found and climbing the Wall. I tell him about Emma and her jail cell and my ordered execution. He is silent until we reach my room, a tiny thing set in the middle of a tunnel that looks like all the rest. There's a simple cot and a dresser and a painting on the wall that shows sunshine and blue skies in the way a windowless room within rock never could.

"Your mother, Sara. How is she?" he asks. I pause, unsure how to tell him. He's practically a stranger, and yet I know it should be personal, delivered softly and with care. I think my silence says enough.

"No," he mutters in disbelief. "When?"

"We were fifteen. Pneumonia. Carter tried everything, but she couldn't save her."

I watch as a thin sheet of water builds in his eyes. He so clearly loved her. It makes me wonder if he hated the slatings the same way I do, if he ever murmured that word to my mother despite its weight.

"Blaine's a father," I say, desperately trying to distract him from the oncoming tears. "Her name's Kale, and she's the cutest thing there is. Not even three yet."

He sits on the edge of my cot and runs a hand through his hair exactly as I do when I'm anxious. "I barely got to be a father myself," he says. "I can't imagine being a grandfather as well."

It's odd to see him lost. I guess I always figured a parent should have all the answers. When I got hurt as a child I ran to Ma. When I needed comfort or advice, she always had both. To see my father confused and conflicted is somewhat startling. He shakes whatever parental concerns he's dealing with aside and looks back up at me.

"I'm assuming you know about Sara's experiment," he says. "It's why you climbed, right?"

I nod.

"I was seventeen when she had the two of you. I came to see her that day after I finished hunting—because we'd agreed to continue slatings together—and you were both there, bundled up on her lap. She pulled me to her side and told me you didn't exist. Blaine, yes; but you, Gray, you were a ghost. With the exception of Carter and me, no one was to know that you had even been born, at least not until the following year. It was Sara's way of challenging the home she could never accept.

"You have to understand that even though I loved your mother dearly, I thought she was losing her grip on reality. She hated Claysoot and the Heist. She was always telling me about how unnatural the place was, sharing her doubts and suspicions and making me promise to not repeat her words."

I'm shocked at how little I knew about my own mother. She

never expressed any of these feelings to Blaine or me, not in all the years leading up to her death. It's like we were raised by a different person.

My father swallows heavily and continues. "She was the only one obsessing about these things. No other villager questioned the Heist, including me. And I wanted to spend my final year with *both* my sons. I wanted to be able to carry you both outside, through fresh air and sunlight. I didn't want my only time with you, Gray, to take place inside, hidden away from the world.

"Sara won, though. Above anything else, I could not bear the thought of her being unhappy during our last year together. She was so sure the experiment would prove something. I thought she was crazy." He rubs his knuckles and looks up at me. "Turns out, she was completely right. Claysoot is unnatural and the Heist is so much more than a standard part of life. It's been a giant scheme all along, and she never even got to see that."

"Yes, Claysoot is one big experiment and you go working hand in hand with the man that started it. What a great way to honor her memory." I feel bad as soon as I say it. I only want to confirm that Harvey is in Crevice Valley, but my father's in mourning and I still can't be decent for five minutes. If Blaine were here, he'd shoot me a disapproving big brother look for sure.

"Harvey is a very influential man. Powerful. Smart," my

father says. So Harvey is here after all. "We need his help."

"I think the only help you need is someone with the guts to torture answers out of him. So that we can get everyone out of Claysoot. So they can be free." Blaine would be glaring now, but I wasn't expecting this sort of loyalty for Harvey. Especially not from my father. It doesn't make any sense.

"It's not that simple," he says.

"Then tell me why you're working with him, because I don't get it."

"It's only going to make adjusting harder. Maybe you should rest, visit Blaine in the hospital, take it easy. I'm not sure turning everything upside down is a good idea."

"No, it's an excellent idea. I need to hear it."

"I'd feel better if you settled in first." I cross my arms over my chest. He looks between me and the door and adds, "What are the chances you let me leave this room without giving you any details?"

"Slim to none."

He sighs. "I should have known you'd demand answers immediately. I was the same way."

I lean against the dresser and wait. He kneads his palms together. Stares at the floor. It feels like hours before he speaks again.

"Harvey didn't start the Laicos Project. Frank did."

# TWENTY-FOUR

**MY LEGS FEEL WEAK.**

"Whatever you've heard in Taem, it's not true."

"But there are wanted posters," I say, "and a list of crimes."

"He was framed, Gray. Harvey wasn't gathering followers. He wasn't killing soldiers or selling information or plotting the downfall of AmEast. He was running from the Order because he is innocent."

I slide up onto the dresser because my feet can no longer support my weight. "How can you know that?"

"Elijah brought Harvey in a few months ago, and Harvey told us the whole story. Said he wanted to help us, too."

"What if he was lying?"

My father laughs lightly. "He's fifty-five."

"So?"

"So Claysoot has been around for nearly fifty years. If Harvey was responsible for the Laicos Project, he would have been a child during its inception. It's impossible."

Harvey's age had been listed with other Operation Ferret details; I just hadn't realized what the numbers meant. I kick myself for this. Had I noticed, maybe Emma and I would have left the room sooner, avoided Marco. Maybe she'd even be with me now, instead of in a jail cell.

"But why would Frank blame Harvey?"

"It serves him best. The more crimes Harvey has committed, the more people are on the lookout for him."

I remember Frank's words in his office that first day I arrived in Taem: *He uses fear as a weapon.* Frank wasn't talking about Harvey . . . he was talking about himself. Everything he'd told me was a twisted version of the truth, the version that he knew would earn my trust.

"I don't get it. The Heists, the entire project. What's the point?"

"It's a very long story."

"I have time."

We are in too deep to stop, and my father knows it. He barrels ahead. "Any details Frank mentioned regarding the war were probably accurate. This country suffered greatly in the wake of fighting, which happened long before the project. Even still, AmWest remains a threat. Most of its people live in ruins, like the communities do outside Taem. They have one organized force on the western shore, and right now their attacks are sporadic and uncoordinated. But put them all together—the people living in poverty and the people actively attacking—and they are many. So many. Frank knows that if they united themselves long enough to cross the borderline, claiming back land and freshwater, he couldn't stop them.

"The only way to ensure that won't happen is with greater numbers. Frank wants more soldiers, an endless supply. He wants good ones, too, physically fit and mentally strong. And what better way to get tough and stubborn and resourceful individuals than to make them grow up in the harsh conditions of a place like Claysoot?"

"That seems incredibly inefficient," I point out. "Having to wait eighteen years to Heist a single soldier."

"We are a means to an end, Gray. He is not after us, just our qualities. It's the Forgeries he cares about."

There's that word again. I know what it means in the black-smith shop where Blaine would forge new spears and axes, molding and shaping them to his liking. But in this context, I think it means something more.

"The Forgeries are the point of the Laicos Project," my father says. "When a boy was Heisted, he went into the labs, where Frank tried to replicate him. He's achieved some level of success, just not the kind he craves. Harvey told us Frank can make one Forgery off any given boy. His end goal is of course limitless copies: one Heisted boy who can be replicated one, ten, a hundred times over. If Frank had that sort of army, he could wipe AmWest out in a matter of days."

I sit there, stunned. Just a few days ago I trusted Frank, felt at home in his presence. And now . . . this. Harvey is innocent and it's all Frank. Frank, who is grooming the perfect soldier. With Claysoot as his mold. And the Outer Ring, the smoke—that's him, too. The dead climbers weren't victims of a self-functioning piece of Harvey's experiment. They fell to Frank, who burned anyone that threatened the future of his project by trying to escape it. Emma and I were the first to be saved because . . . of Maude! I told her I was Blaine's twin as I ran from her house. Maybe it was Frank she was talking to that night. Maybe she told him what I said and Frank had Emma and me saved because he wanted to know how I tricked the Heist.

"I just . . . I can't believe I bought all his lies," I stammer. "How did he get away with locking a bunch of children up? And how did no one stop him? How did *no one* question him as the Wall was raised?"

"It's stamped with Quarantine on the outside," my father says. "AmWest released a virus that killed thousands back during the war. Claysoot was passed off as a quarantined community still suffering from that illness, and people happily avoided it."

My knuckles have gone pale from squeezing the edge of the dresser. Frank put his arm on my shoulder. I trusted him. I think about my trip to the infirmary to be Cleansed, the tracker implanted in my neck. I wonder what else happened to me when I was there, if a piece of me now sits in some vial in his labs.

"We have a little documentation, if you want to see it with your own eyes," my father adds. "Ryder got his hands on some partial research records when he ran years ago."

"It's an extremely interesting read," a voice says from the open doorway. Bree is standing there, holding a clean set of clothes for me in her arms. "Full of surprising details."

I look to my father, suspicious that he's withheld information.

"I've told you the basics," he says, and I believe him. His voice is steady, and I have a feeling if he were lying, I'd be able to sense the quaver, the way I can with Blaine. "But I'm sure Bree will show you to the library if you'd like to read them yourself."

She shrugs, uninterested. "Yeah, I can do that sometime. I'm heading to the Basin now though, for dinner."

"Good idea," my father says. "Gray needs a proper meal." He eyes the state of my Order uniform and adds, "It wouldn't hurt to stop by the washroom beforehand, either."

Bree drops the clothing on my cot and turns to leave.

"You'll wait for him, Bree," my father says. "He doesn't

know his way around and I need to head to a meeting."

She eyes the door. "But I'm starving."

"You're waiting for him, and that's an order."

Something in his tone snaps Bree to attention. "Yes, sir."

Owen nods curtly and after telling me he'll see me in the morning, excuses himself. Once he's out of sight, Bree exhales dramatically and flops onto the cot. "You have five minutes."

"Or what?"

"I'll conveniently become too busy to take you to the library after dinner." She keeps her eyes on the ceiling, smirking.

I grab the clean clothes and leave in a hurry.


The shared washroom at the end of my tunnel is small and modest, but it feels good to soak my skin. I lather quickly, rubbing a bar of soap over my arms and head. To my satisfaction, I find the once brittle hair on my scalp to be softening ever so slightly.

The clothes Bree has provided are simple but comfortable. A cotton tunic and linen pants. Clean socks. I almost feel I am back in Claysoot when I slip them on. I return to my room and stuff my Order uniform into the dresser.

"You look semitolerable now," Bree says. I roll my eyes at her but she's already turned her back on me. "This way. Dinner's in the Basin."

Back in the Basin, beyond the market and crop fields and

near what appears to be a rudimentary schoolhouse, is a large building that Bree refers to as the Eatery. The layout reminds me of the dining hall in Taem, large tables and crude wooden benches filling the space. There's an open kitchen at the far end of the room, and we join the line of people waiting to get food. The angry eyes that greeted me earlier are nowhere to be found. I blend in seamlessly in my drab clothing.

The food is surprisingly tasty but carefully rationed. I'm still hungry when I finish my small meal—a cup of soup, a piece of bread, a half ear of corn—but some food is better than none. Bree and I sit at a table with several other Rebels whom she instantly joins in conversation. She avoids introducing me, so I simply listen.

"We haven't found them yet," Bree tells a stout boy sitting beside her.

"You said Luke had one, though," he interjects.

"Dammit, Hal, do you never listen?" another girl at the table argues, chucking a clump of bread at his face. "They caught one of them days ago, and Luke's been questioning him, but no new developments since then."

"Well, thanks for putting it so bluntly, Polly." Hal throws the bit of bread back at her. It hits her square between the eyes and falls into her soup, crust first. The impact splatters broth onto the front of her tunic and the brown braids that frame her face.

"If we're talking details," Bree says, clearing her throat and making it apparent that she, and only she, has all the facts, "the man we caught isn't giving up anything. Won't tell us any of the operation's details or a possible location of Evan's troops. My guess is they're long gone."

"Gone where?" Hal asks.

"Back to Taem," she says. "I think our chances of catching them are few and far between, and the man in the interrogation center will likely die under Luke's blade before revealing anything."

"Bummer." Polly sighs. She drags her bread across the base of her cup and sops up the remaining broth.

"Yeah," Bree agrees, "but at least we've got Gray now. Maybe he can shed some light on the mission."

"You were with the Order?" Polly nearly shrieks, acknowledging me for the first time.

"No . . . not really," I say. "I was about to be executed, so I was trying to come here. But then I ran into the Order's camp, and my brother was there, and I tried to—"

"So your brother's with the Order," Hal interrupts. "Trash. I don't know why we show mercy to your lot. I think we should only take the ones that show up at the Crevice with their hands over their heads and walk in, begging to join. The ones that risk their lives attempting to get here are the only trustworthy ones."

"That's what I was trying to do," I argue.

Hal snorts. "Sure. Or maybe that's just your story. Besides, running to us because you were going to be executed proves nothing other than the fact that you only care about your own hide."

"He's Owen's son," Bree says. "If he's anything like his father, we just might end up happy we have him. And his brother, too, if he ever wakes up."

"Maybe," Hal says. "Or maybe he's a Forgery. It's a crap-shoot with these flaky acquisitions."

"Excuse me folks, but I think I'll determine if he's a Forgery." There's a middle-aged man standing behind Hal and Polly and staring at me. He's wearing an odd sweater that lacks arms and struggles to hold an otherwise bland shirt in place. I know who he is. Those eyes, those dark, dark eyes.

"Sorry to interrupt your dinner," he continues, "but I need to borrow Gray here. Turns out, Fallyn convinced Ryder it would do good to run a few tests to be sure."

"To be sure of what?" I ask.

"That you're who you say you are. That you're not a Forgery." He smiles, and it fills out the otherwise hollow coves of his cheeks. His eyes even brighten a little. He is so plain in person, so feeble. I wonder why Frank wants him back so badly—and alive, no less—if he isn't actually responsible for the Laicos Project.

"Oh, go on already," Bree grumbles, elbowing me in the side. "Harvey couldn't hurt a fly."

Harvey chuckles lightly and lifts a hand from his pocket. "How foolish of me, not introducing myself. I'm Harvey Maldoon. I head up all technological operations here in Crevice Valley."

"Gray Weathersby," I say, shaking his hand. He has a weak grip and even softer fingers.

"Well, that is what we are about to confirm. That you are indeed Gray Weathersby." He smiles again, waving an arm in a sweeping motion. "Shall we?"

He leads me from the table and down yet another darkened passageway as Bree and her friends stare on with interest.

# TWENTY-FIVE

**IN A WINDOWLESS ROOM, HIDDEN** among Crevice Valley's innu-merable folds, Harvey hooks me up to an odd-looking machine. He tells me to not worry, that nothing will hurt, but it's hard to believe him. The machine has needles and levers and knobs that he twists to his liking after attaching various cords to my arms and temples. I'm certain pain is going to jolt through me at any moment, but when Harvey says we are ready to begin, the pain never comes.

"State your name," he says.

"Gray Weathersby."

Harvey makes a mark on a piece of paper feeding through the unit.

"Your age."

"Eighteen. Only . . . I thought I was seventeen until a few weeks ago."

Harvey looks up at me over the rim of his glasses as he marks the paper again.

"And why's that?"

"My family lied to me. Told me I was a year younger—told everyone, actually—to see if I would be Heisted with Blaine."

"I see." Another mark. "And who is Blaine?"

"My brother."

"Where is he now?"

"To the best of my knowledge, he's in your hospital. They tell me he's in a coma."

It goes on like this for far too long. Question after question about my past, my time in Taem, my journey through the Great Forest and into Crevice Valley. Eventually, when Harvey seems to be wrapping up, a voice cuts into the room, amplified through an unseen device.

"Ask him something more personal," it demands. Fallyn.

"He's done well enough," Harvey says, giving me a reassuring smile before whispering, "She likes to overdo things."

"I mean it, Harvey. Ask something the Order wouldn't know."

Harvey looks at a mirror lining the wall and I get the feeling Fallyn is somehow watching from behind it.

"Just humor her," a second voice says. This one belongs to Ryder.

"I'll need a little help with the questions." Harvey sighs in frustration.

My father speaks next. "What toy did I leave you and your brother before my Heist?"

"A wooden duck on wheels."

"How many paces is it to the top of the Council stairs?"

"Thirty-six."

"Why did Emma follow you over the Wall?"

I pause for a second. This question is harder. "She wanted answers. Like I did."

"Who on earth is Emma and why does she matter?" Fallyn asks irritably.

I'm annoyed by this comment. Furious, even. "She matters because I am responsible for her being in Frank's jail right now. She is amazing and sweet and strong willed, and I ran from her. I love her and yet I ran so that I could live."

Harvey smirks at the mirror. "Well, there's really no point asking anything else," he announces. "We all know Forgeries are incapable of love. Not to mention he passed every question with flying colors, not even a smidgeon of deceit in his answers."

"Well, one more question then," Fallyn says. "What was the goal of that Order troop? Why was Evan looking to approach Mount Martyr?"

"It was called Operation Ferret," I say. "The mission was to infiltrate Rebel Headquarters and bring Harvey back at all costs. Alive."

"Now I wonder why they'd want to do that," Harvey muses aloud, a playful note of humor in his voice.

"It's quite obvious why, isn't it, Harvey?" Fallyn jeers. "You've given us too much of an edge since you joined. The Order can't deal with your revealing their secrets anymore."

"Wait, what?" I ask.

"The Order's greatest weapon is near useless against us now," Fallyn continues. "Harvey knows all the secrets, the ticks, the signs. And Frank can't have that. He can't have someone revealing how all his technologies work, preparing for how to defend against them. Plus, he wants Harvey to finish the job he started."

I stare at the mirror in the back of the room. "I'm not following any of this."

Fallyn sighs heavily. "They want him back. They want back the man who engineered the Forgeries."

This is how another truth is revealed to me, ironed out before my eyes. My father said that it was impossible for Harvey to have started the Laicos Project because he would have been too young. And this is true. But Harvey was utilized at a young age. He was somewhat of a child prodigy, a genius with technology and genetics. After Frank's workers failed to create the tools he had hoped from the Heisted boys, Harvey was recruited at sixteen years old.

He worked in the Order's defense and weaponry units in Union Central. He spent months, bent over operating tables, extracting what he needed from Heisted boys. Many terms that I do not understand are mentioned, but through his technological ingenuity, Harvey created what no other scientist or lab worker could. Harvey produced the first Forgery. It was identical to the Heisted boy, both in appearance and personality, opening its eyes with the same skills and mannerisms as its source. The Forgery was strong and healthy, but it was still only one soldier.

Despite Frank's wishes, Harvey couldn't create multiple Forgeries from a single test subject. Each further replica was a weaker, fuzzier, less perfect version of the first, growing ill and perishing quickly. Frank urged Harvey to stay focused, and in the meantime, put the first generation of Forgeries to work on the front lines. They were effective in the field against AmWest, stealthy and powerful.

"A few years ago, things fell apart," Harvey says, as my father, Ryder, and Fallyn join us in the room. "I had been working to create limitless Forgeries for many years, and still couldn't crack it. One day, the subject I was running a test on died during the procedure. Even though it was a Forgery of a Forgery, I realized it was still a real, living, breathing person.

He had thoughts and a heart and a pulse. It was as if a veil of ignorance shattered then. For the first time in years I saw what I was doing. I was cutting up children and trying to make weapons for a man whose tactics I didn't fully support.

"Things had gone from bad to worse in Taem since I started working for Frank. Sure, the city was orderly and he protected the people from AmWest, but everything was regulated to an extreme. For me, water was plentiful and there was a library always at my disposal for research. Frank even let me play old records of Mozart while I worked because I said it helped me focus. But all around me, people were being arrested for those very same acts.

"So the next day when I was supposed to report for work, I got on the trolley, went the other direction, and didn't look back. I found a poor town beyond the dome willing to take me in. I stayed there for a few months, until the Order came looking for me. I took to the next town, and then the next. But they kept coming. They never stopped.

"I ran into Elijah in the Great Forest about three months ago. He told me that all across AmEast people had started to leave cities under Order control. Backlash in Taem was the worst. They knew the threat from AmWest was as present as ever, but they didn't believe Frank's way of life was their only option. Even former subjects of his project were slipping free when they could, running while on missions, or being snatched up by Elijah's troops when intersected in the forest. Elijah told me about a hideout he'd recently established, burrowed inside the mountains. He said I was welcome there.

"I had no intention of joining him until he mentioned the look-alikes, the familiar faces that had begun showing up, only to murder people in their sleep. I knew immediately that Frank must have realized his Forgeries had an in. I doubt he liked the idea of people gathering in opposition to him, was probably terrified that they would poison his city with the idea that he was unjust. Or maybe he feared these Rebels would leak information to AmWest about water resources and access points to the domed cities. Regardless, he was using the Forgeries in an attempt to squash the Rebels, and I knew I could help.

"Now, when anyone new enters Crevice Valley, I immediately run him through my test and determine if he can be trusted. You and your brother are a unique case, of course. You came here together, one on the verge of death. That would have taken quite some planning had you been Forgeries. Not to mention you were captured. Most Forgeries walk right to us, claiming to be seeking shelter when they are truly spies.

"My arrival in Crevice Valley has made it hard for Frank. Forgeries used to be his way inside, and that weapon has become nearly ineffective. I know it's nothing in comparison to all I've done in Frank's labs, but I hope that my work here is a step in the right direction. I hope that one day someone like you, a victim of the Laicos Project, will be thankful for at least some of my work."

Harvey's story ends here. He smiles at me, but my stomach is so unsettled I can't respond.

At first I hate him. How could he have *ever* thought his work for Frank was justified? But if I am unable to accept his change of heart, I'm no better than Hal or Polly, who disregarded me because I was brought into Crevice Valley by force. People have all sorts of pasts, sometimes dark or dreary, but perhaps the actions they choose in the present are the ones that carry the most weight. And Harvey is here, making changes, looking to undo the wrongs he has created. Maybe Harvey is okay.

"So what now?" my father asks, addressing no one in particular.

"Evan's group has retreated back to Taem," Ryder says. "And our scouts say the city has nearly recovered from the recent attack by AmWest. Regardless, if Frank wants Harvey, he will not rest until he has him."

"Right, so what now?" my father urges again.

"We are well fortified here. We wait for them to approach again, and this time, we take out the entire unit. If they try again, we repeat. Harvey, I'm afraid for the time being you'll be limited to Crevice Valley. It is far too risky for you to set foot outside."

"Fair enough." Harvey nods.

"That's it?" I ask. "We just sit and wait? I thought you guys were all for fighting?"

"We are, Gray," Ryder says, "but these things take time. When we are ready for that strike, it will be well planned and meticulously executed. For now, we wait and counter each advance as needed."

"I don't do well waiting," I admit.

"That works out perfectly," my father chimes in. "You start training tomorrow, and standards in Crevice Valley are no picnic."

"How's that?"

"They are brutal. Intense," Fallyn says with a wicked smile.

I believe her instantly. When I am dismissed from the room, I head back to my quarters with slow, deliberate steps, dreading the training that awaits me and the weary muscles I will certainly have by the following evening.

# TWENTY-SIX

**I WAKE EARLY. OR MAYBE** in the middle of the night. It is impossible to tell. I wonder if there is a moon tonight, if it is casting a silver-blue glow on the land beyond the mountain. On nights in Claysoot when Blaine was snoring too loudly for me to sleep, I used to walk out to the livestock fields and stare at the sky. There were evenings when the stars shone so brightly and the sky stretched so wide that I feared I might slip from the grass and float away into nothing. Now I have only four stone walls.

I try to return to my dreams, but my cot feels increasingly stiff. I sit up eventually and pull on my boots. If I can't sleep, I should do something useful, and I have gone too long without seeing my brother.

Crevice Valley's hospital is far more advanced than Claysoot's. Illuminated screens blink. Strange units hum. The place is deserted when I arrive, with the exception of the patients who sleep soundly in the dim room. I find Blaine in the back, on the very last bed.

The arrow has been removed and he sleeps in shorts, a bandage wrapped around his thigh. The bandage looks silly, as if his leg snapped in two and they tried to tie it back together with a piece of string. His hair is growing back, like mine, and his chest rises and falls softly as he sleeps. He's hooked up to some sort of machine, tubes from it burrowing into his arm.

I reach a hand out to hold his. It is heavy, stiff like a statue.

"He's doing better. Even if he doesn't look it." A young nurse stands behind me. I hadn't realized there was anyone else awake.

"Do you know how much longer? When he'll wake up?"

She shakes her head. "It could be a day. It could be months. There's no way to be sure."

Months? What if he's like this forever? What if he never wakes up? I drop his hand. I can't look at him. It's like watching Emma get carted off to Frank's prison. I don't want to see another situation I am powerless to change.

I hurry toward the exit and the nurse calls out to me.

"You should come back and talk to him sometime. I think he'd like that."

I look at Blaine one last time, and then leave without another word. I manage to sleep a little after that, although I'm not sure how. The thought of losing Blaine again, of being just half of myself for the rest of my life, terrifies me. My palms sweat throughout a dreamless sleep.

Morning brings a regime that I can scarcely complete. After a breakfast of gruel, Bree leads me to the Conditioning Room, which is an enclosed and sizeable training space located at the end of a tunnel housing the captains' quarters. There's a rock wall for scaling, targets that hang overhead, and a series of stairs and platforms I have no desire to climb.

Bree leaves me with Elijah for introductory training and heads to a more advanced conditioning session led by my father. He waves at me reassuringly, but then, as if he feels foolish or uncomfortable showing affection, turns his attention back to his troops.

Elijah has us start with a ridiculously lengthy run, following a path on the ground that creates an oblong loop through the room. A stitch forms in my side after the second lap, but I fight through it. I focus my thoughts on Emma. I promise myself, right then as I run and struggle to ignore the cramp in my abdomen, that I will return for her at any and all costs.

A dozen laps later, my legs are jelly, but Elijah is far from through with us. After a series of exercises called pushups, squats, and lunges, we take to scaling the rock wall. He orders us to climb in all directions: top to bottom, side to side, diagonally. Each pass takes more effort and concentration than the previous, muscles growing weak and footholds becoming harder to find. When we move on to a drill Elijah refers to as suicides—sprinting at varying lengths—I have lost all feeling in my legs. By the time Elijah passes out bows and arrows, I can barely stand without my knees knocking.

Shooting is at least enjoyable. The moving targets that zip by overhead create a near-realistic effect. My arms are tired from climbing, but I manage to hit nine out of my ten targets. For once, I easily outshine the others in my group. No matter how long I am away from it, shooting an arrow straight will always be second nature. My hands are incapable of forgetting the exact tautness to achieve before a release, the way to set my shot and exhale on followthrough.

We finish the session with a final lap around the room, and I collapse onto the floor upon completion. When my lungs stop screaming, when I can finally breathe without panting, I sit up to discover that the others in my group have already left.

"You did well today," Elijah says as he stacks bows back into a storage cabinet. He looks too young to have started a rebellion. "You kept up, and on your first session, which is more than most can say." I thank him, and he excuses himself, mumbling about a status meeting he is late for.

I stay on the ground, stretching my already tightening muscles. Bree's group is wrapping up their session in the distance. My father has them climbing ropes that hang from hooks anchored in the ceiling, and Bree floats up and down as though the rope were doing the work for her.

Their final drill is to find passage from one raised platform in the back of the room to another, which seems impossible. The space between the platforms is wide, and a fall would certainly result in some broken bones. The largest boy in the group, who looks something like a bear, simply jumps across, but his legs are so long he has an unfair advantage. Most of the others drop out completely, unable to complete the task. Bree, on the other hand, takes a spear in hand and runs full speed toward the gap. As her feet near the edge, she burrows the tip of the spear against the lip of the platform and propels herself into the air. The spear bows gracefully and projects her as fluidly as a bird in flight. She releases the spear at the peak of her arc and lands safely on the other platform, her knees bending and her hands finding ground before pushing to right herself. My father claps in approval, but the others stare on. I do, too. She's completely crazy— wild and ruthless. I scowl in disapproval until I realize this doesn't sound much unlike myself. As soon as their session ends, my father hurries off, mentioning how he needs to join Elijah.

"The captains have daily status meetings," Bree says, striding over to me. There is a ring of sweat on the neckline of her shirt. "Updates on the war, planning, tactics, that sort of stuff."

I stand and stretch my arms. Every muscle in my body argues with fatigue. I can already feel the soreness settling in.

"Library?" she asks.

"Definitely. Assuming you're still willing to take me."

She half smiles. "It's not on the top of my wish list, but I know how badly you're craving the truth. And, besides, there are so many details your father left out. Like the scale of the project, for instance."

"Scale?"

Bree's lips press into a smirk. "Makes you hate Frank even more when you know it wasn't just one test group, but five."

"Five? Like five different Claysoots?"

"Well, where do you think I came from, brainless? You didn't think I was one of those mundane Order folk turned Rebel, did you?"

"Aren't you?"

"Oh please, Gray," she says. "Even you admitted I was good—quiet, stealthy, quick. It shouldn't be so surprising that some places Heisted girls."

It makes sense. Her fluid and swift movements, her utmost

silence while tracking. She is tough. Raw, and powerful. Bree is like me, only from another Claysoot.

And suddenly, she is twice as interesting.

As we are leaving the Conditioning Room, the large boy who had leaped the width of the platforms brushes past us. He's a good head taller than me, with hands the size of a hornet's nest.

"That was some display back there, Bree," he says, running his hand over her shoulder in a way that comes across more condescending than sincere. "You know, there's nothing more sexy than a strong, aggressive woman."

"I'm not interested, Drake," she says, slapping his hand away.

Drake reaches for her again. "Aw, come on, Bree, you know you want to."

"She said she's not interested," I snap.

"No one asked your opinion." He pushes me in the chest firmly with both hands, and I nearly fall over from the force.

"No, but you asked hers, and she turned you down, so move on." His fist hits my jaw before I even see it coming. I stagger backward.

"See you tomorrow, gorgeous," Drake says to Bree, and then stalks away with cumbersome steps.

Bree folds her arms across her chest and looks at me. "You didn't have to do that. I can take care of myself."

"I know," I say. I lick my lips and taste blood. "You should really report him."

She pulls her shoulders into a shrug, and I'm surprised to see in her what Drake obviously had. Even covered in sweat, she *is* pretty. Stunning, really. Her limbs are long and lean, her curves itching to be touched. And her eyes, which usually look so harsh and stubborn, are suddenly soft. I'm terrified by how she's snuck up on me.

"Well, are you going to report him or not?" I ask.

"There's no point," she says. "People have more important things to worry about. We're at war, after all. And, besides, the things you fight alone make you stronger."

I'm fairly certain this is untrue, but I don't argue.

# TWENTY-SEVEN

**BREE PULLS A SERIES OF** thin white journals from the over-crowded library shelves.

"Most of the stuff in this room is documentation of the Rebel formation," she explains. "Forces aligning, plans of attack, defensive strategies. But these"—she raises the pale journals overhead before plopping them on the desk before me—"these are the goods."

"Proof of the Laicos Project?"

"Proof and then some," she says. "Notes and commentary written by Frank himself."

I run my hand over the cover of the top journal. The material is soft, like worn leather, and the corners curl toward the ceiling. A single, handwritten *1* sits on its center. This is the first of many. I take a deep breath and flip open the cover.

The words inside are too uniform to be written by hand. They remind me of the records Emma and I had found in Taem, each letter evenly spaced, each line precisely parallel. I lean over the bound pages and read.

Five test groups have been set up across AmEast, labeled, for now, from A to E. As the nature of this project is to create durable and tough soldiers, we need a range of subjects for experimentation. Each test group will be presented with a different scenario, ranging from most desirable (in A) to least desirable (in E). My initial prediction is that the most successful soldiers will be created from those groups in the most challenging of environments, but only time will tell.

Each group will be enclosed by a wall and supplied with basic tools for survival (axes, saws, knives, etc.). Some groups will even have existing shelters in place—with so many communities deserted or left in ruin after the Second Civil War, it seems foolish to waste these resources. We will raise walls strategically, so that our

cameras and monitoring systems can ensure
observation from Taem's control room.

Test subjects will be a mixture of boys and
girls—all fifteen or younger—acquired
from institutions overcrowded in the wake
of the war. Decisions are still to be made
regarding when test subjects should be
removed and transferred to Taem for further
research.

There is a blank page before the documentation picks up
again. I look to Bree, but her nose is buried deep in a book,
and so I continue.

Test Group Breakdown:
Group A, Western Territory. Most ideal
of living situations. Functioning farms,
factories, and food supplies already in
existence. Fruitful soil, fair weather.
Civilian houses in existence and supplied
with electricity.
Group B, Southern Sector. Comfortable
living conditions. Existing homes. Large
freshwater lake, plowable fields, warm
weather.
Group C, Capital Region. Base-level

conditions. Fair weather and terrain. Collapsing but salvageable cabins. Water resources: small lake and rivers.

Group D, Seacoast. Rough living conditions. Limited freshwater; rocky, dry land surrounded by salt water. No prebuilt structures, harsh sun, exposed to wind and other elements. Cold winters.

Group E, Northern Realm. Survival-of-the-fittest conditions. Cold, long winters. Short, cool summers. Heavily forested. No prebuilt structures.

The next several pages talk about the project's early days and Frank's initial observations. All five groups go through a phase he refers to as *hysteria*, where, regardless of the conditions of their environment, the children panic. They know their own identities, as well as basic knowledge acquired through schooling, but are completely unaware of an outside world, nor do they remember people from it. This convenient situation is the result of memory work conducted in Frank's labs prior to placing the subjects behind the Wall. When the hysteria passes, the real show begins, and the next phase takes up a handful of Frank's journals.

Interesting developments in groups B and C. A leader has emerged from each and attempted to divvy up roles and responsibilities. Each leader has named their land, Group B going by Dextern (the last name of the leader there) and Group C by Claysoot (selected because of the appearance of the location's soil). Group A is in a state of constant bickering and chaos. E struggles due to weather exposure. . . .

Group D, finally named Saltwater, has followed suit by producing a leader—surprising twist: a female. Group A remains unnamed and in conflict. Group E has nearly died out. Perhaps conditions there were simply too extreme. . . .

At six months, all groups have now discovered the Wall. Only some have climbed. All deem it unsafe due to the bodies we return, and have been successfully educated to stay within their confines. This is crucial, for if we want our experiments to continue beyond the first generation of test subjects, we cannot have them scaling the Wall freely. . . .

Group A has transitioned from chaos to war. Subjects are split and fighting one another over resources and control of the best living complexes. . . .

Group C has built a surprisingly stable town. In just over a year they now have livestock fields and markets. They have rebuilt all the cabins and their leader has formed a council, where representatives are elected from the group and lead lifestyle decisions for the greater community. Talks of something similar have sprung up in B. . . .

Group D is remarkably ingenious. Freshwater springs have been found and guided into reservoirs. Shelters from sun and wind have been created. Women have a surprising amount of power in this group when compared to other test groups and

share in many of the otherwise masculine
roles. . . .

Group E is extinct. Research here has been
halted. Group A continues to battle. Much
blood has been shed and I fear they will
eliminate themselves completely. . . .

The first of the extractions are
approaching. It has been agreed that
removing test subjects from Group A would
be foolish. The children have gone mad,
and any technologies created from them
will likely be unstable and volatile. For
Group A, the Laicos Project is over. I am
cutting the electricity to everything but
the cameras. They will remain on so that
we can confirm what we hope for: that the
savages die out completely. Extractions will
instead be performed in Groups B, C, and D.
Eighteen seems to be a fitting year for
boys. They are well matured and physically
in their prime. In Group D, however, many
of the girls are as strong and tough as the
males, partaking in very similar roles and

careers. Given this revelation, I believe
it may be beneficial to have several test
subjects of the female gender and Group D
will be the provider. We will pull girls
at sixteen and we will do so selectively,
ensuring we remove only the best candidates
to undergo experimentation.

All extracted subjects will be shipped to
Taem, where continued research will take
place. They will be kept in separate wings
and labs. There will be no crossover between
test subjects from different locations. . . .

I move on to the next set of books, which are full of notes
regarding the Heists: how they are performed, how each
group reacts to them. The shaking earth and general feeling
of discomfort during our Claysoot Heists now make sense.
The Order flew in by helicopter—a steel bird that sounds
similar to the objects I witnessed AmWest manning during
their attack on Taem—and dropped odorless drugs to subdue
the town while the boy was removed.

There are hundreds of pages covering experimentation
in the next several journals, but I skim through them. The
scenes Frank's words depict are too grim, and I don't want

to read about the people who died on his tables. I flip frantically through the documentation, and before I know it, I've
worked my way to the final journal.

I've recruited a new addition for our labs
today, a boy by the name of Harvey Maldoon.
He is young but brilliant, a genius at the
mere age of sixteen. The blessed child is
already hard at work, confident that he can
create a Forgery as skilled and mature as
its source. He promises me it will remain
healthy and strong, rather than faltering
after a day like the replicas my other lab
workers have created.

"Heists" (a term coined in Group C that we
have adopted internally) will continue, and
I keep my fingers crossed that Harvey will
be successful. I need him to be successful.
Only then can I set up a production
compound closer to the borderlines. AmWest
continues to attempt infiltration. They are
persistent, and while I must protect our
people from their wrath and our freshwater
from their greed, I cannot keep losing the
lives of Order members at their hands. These

**Forgeries, these lives without family or history or homes, will be an invaluable resource.**

The journal ends here, but I know where the story is headed. Experimentation would carry on for many years, and while Harvey would eventually create a successful Forgery, he would never manage to create the limitless variety that Frank still craves today. All along, things would steadily fall apart in Taem. Laws would become overbearing and people would begin to flee, Elijah among the first. The Rebels would become another nuisance in Frank's efforts, and when Harvey finally ran, Frank would do everything in his power to get him back.

I flip the final journal closed and push it toward the others. It's hard to take in so much so quickly, and yet it's oddly relieving to see the truth so plainly before my eyes. Reading it like that makes it feel so definite, concrete.

"So you were Group D then. Saltwater," I say to Bree. She looks up from her book and nods. "And Fallyn, as well?"

"You got it. There's a representative from each test group in Crevice Valley, serving as a captain under Ryder's command."

I do the math quickly. It's wrong. "But there's four captains, and only three groups faced Heists."

"Raid's from Group B, Dextern; Fallyn's Saltwater; your

father's Claysoot. And then there's Elijah. He represents the citizens of Taem. And there's a lot of them. In fact, they make up the majority of the Rebels."

So maybe Frank's records were right after all. "Did Elijah start the Rebellion?"

"Yes and no. He *was* one of the first to go in search of people sharing his viewpoint outside the city, but I think his act of running meant nothing until he met Ryder. They crossed paths somewhere past the Hairpin and started gathering supporters. That was when the Rebellion *really* began."

"What about Ryder? I mean, I know he was from Claysoot, but how'd he end up here?"

"I only know so much. You and I were lucky, Gray. When we got to Taem, Harvey had already run and, because of that, Frank's experiments were on hold. But Ryder didn't have that luxury. He was fed the lie that Frank was trying to free Claysoot and then underwent constant operations, thinking the lab workers would find something within his blood that could save his people from the Wall.

"From what I've pieced together, Ryder struck up a strong friendship with one of the other boys from Claysoot. They discussed how Frank never got any closer to solving things and agreed that their only chance of leading a somewhat normal life existed far away from Taem. They started talking about running for it, and eventually Ryder did."

"And the other boy?"

"The two of them broke into Frank's office during their escape instead of running straight for the hills. Stupid move, if you ask me, but at least Ryder managed to grab the journals you just read. They were caught on camera, though, which alerted the Order. Only Ryder made it out."

"And then he hid in the woods until Elijah found him years later?"

"Yup. And by then, Ryder didn't want to fight Frank anymore. He was old and more or less happy. But after Elijah told him everything Frank had done to the city and its people, Ryder was convinced it was never too late to fight back."

All the pieces are joining: the records in Union Central merging with the journals in this library, which are further stitched together by Bree's stories. My brain hurts, but in the best way possible. The truth is addictive.

"And you?" I ask her. "What's your story?"

"I got Heisted, although we called it being Snatched back on the island. I watched a video where Frank told me Harvey was behind it all, that he needed my patience and assistance until he could free Saltwater. I was out on a scouting mission when I realized I didn't want to go back. I trusted Frank at the time but didn't want to spend my whole life searching for Harvey. I guess this makes me sound pretty selfish, actually, not wanting to save the rest of my people, but I was alone and scared. So while everyone was sleeping, before I even contemplated if it was a smart idea, I took off. A few days later, I stumbled into a rough Rebel camp."

"So you're, what, sixteen, seventeen?"

"Almost seventeen," she answers.

"You don't seem that old."

"Why's that? Because I'm so mature and levelheaded?" She grins proudly.

"More the opposite. Because you're so wild and impulsive."

"Oh screw you." Her tone is half-serious, half-playful. "You're as impulsive as me—maybe even more so."

"I think we are both more alike than we'd care to admit."

Her face morphs into a scowl. "I've served more responsibly for the Rebels' cause than you can say. I've delivered on missions and promises and then some. That alone makes us very different."

"I just need the chance, Bree. I can shine under pressure, too." I flash her a smile and she rolls her eyes.

"Yeah? Well, I need a drink."

She stuffs Frank's journals back on the shelf and we leave the library in search of some alcohol.

# TWENTY-EIGHT

**IN THE BASIN, SQUISHED BETWEEN** the Eatery and some storage warehouses, is a damp, dusty building that the Rebels refer to as the Tap Room. When we enter, Clipper is weaving between the men at the bar, snatching near-empty mugs when drinkers aren't looking. I tell him he's too young to be drinking, but when he asks me how old I was when I had my first, I admit I was around his age and am forced to let it go.

The place is a combination of soldiers and civilians. Women cling to the shoulders of various men, dancing to the banjo and guitar being strummed in a corner. I look for my father among the faces, but he's nowhere to be found. Bree and I fight our way through the crowded space and up to a waist-high bar.

"Hey, Saul!" Bree shouts, leaning over the counter so far that her feet leave the ground. It causes her shirt to rise and a sliver of bare skin becomes visible above her pants. "We'll take two shots down here," she says. The bartender, an older, portly man, slides the drinks our way and Bree shouts her thanks.

"On getting through a full day without wanting to kill each other," I say, holding my drink before her.

"Speak for yourself." She smirks but clinks her drink against mine and we throw back the shot.

"Another round?" she asks.

"They don't ration this stuff?"

"Nah, but it's okay for alcohol to run out. Can't say the same about food."

We share another few rounds before moving to the far end of the bar where we watch a group of young men playing an odd game with miniature spears. They take turns throwing them at a small target that hangs from the wall.

"We've got the next game," Bree announces to them. The better of the men in the group, who has hit the bull's-eye several times over, turns to face us.

He has hair the color of mud that curls behind his ears and a square head, too angular and sharp for me to miss it. This is Xavier Piltess—taller, wider, and far more filled out than the fifteen-year-old who taught me to hunt in the forests of

Claysoot—but it is him. "Oh, you're going down, Bree," he says. "No way can you take me and Sammy."

"Xavier?" I venture.

He pauses for a second and stares at me. I watch as his gaze halts on my eyes, noting their color: gray, not blue. Recognition breaks across his face.

"Gray!" he exclaims. We clasp arms and he slaps me on the back the way an older sibling might. "How the heck are you? Where's your brother?"

We catch up for a few minutes while he finishes his game, never missing a shot. He was taken hostage by the Rebels over a year ago when an Order mission he was on failed. After hearing Frank's lies unravel, he switched allegiances.

I tell him my story, a shortened version, which is speckled with white lies, but for him it doesn't really matter: Blaine and I got Heisted. We're both here now, me in training and Blaine in the hospital. I feel guilty when I mention Blaine. I should visit him again.

Xavier then introduces me to Sammy, a twenty-year-old from Taem who joined the Rebels when his father was executed for counterfeiting ration cards. He'd been using them to acquire extra water that he often brought to struggling villages beyond the dome. Apparently Frank didn't consider this type of charity work acceptable.

Bree and I play the two of them in a game called darts. We

lose spectacularly. I can't seem to throw the darts with the right force or angle. They are like toothpick spears and my hands are clumsy with them. Xavier tries to correct my form and give me pointers, but I only improve by the smallest margin. I blame it on the alcohol.

We end up abandoning the game and taking a tall table hostage. Hal and Polly find the four of us, and we all sit on rickety stools, throwing back drinks too quickly and playing Bullshit. The game turns out to be identical to Claysoot's Little Lie, only with a fouler name. Bree is the best bullshitter of us all. She fools us again and again, her lie always blending in with the rest. Even when she starts slurring her words and leaning more on me than the table for support, she's still stumping us.

I learn that she found herself utterly alone when she was shipped to Taem after her Heist. She has no siblings; her mother died young; and, after being unable to locate her father in Crevice Valley, she assumes he's dead. I learn a few other things, trivial really, but for some reason, they fascinate me more than her historical details. Bree's elbows are double jointed. She has a birthmark in the shape of a crescent moon on her hip. Her favorite color is deep, rugged purple, the shade of silhouetted clouds against an evening sky. She hasn't yet adjusted to sleeping without the sound of waves crashing on the shore.

As the game continues, the laughter in the Tap Room becomes an infectious disease. Everyone is doing it. I can't remember the last time I laughed so freely.

Sometime much, much later, when we are all thoroughly giddy and a bit too gone, Bree attempts to visit the bar in search of another drink and instead falls off her stool. Polly shrieks with delight, as if this is the funniest thing, and the rest of us chuckle along in amusement.

"I'm gonna take her back," I tell the others. She's had enough, and no one argues with me. It takes us longer than it should to get to her quarters. I'm dizzy myself, not terribly, but Bree keeps directing me down incorrect passageways and we have to double back with uneven steps. She clings to my neck the entire time, her weight mostly supported by my arms, and mumbles incoherent things that I know she wouldn't be saying if it weren't for the alcohol: how nice I am, how she's thankful I stuck up for her with Drake, how she wishes she could go back and not be so cruel to me when I was first brought in.

"It's really hard discovering the truth," she mumbles as we get to her place. "And it was probably terrifying . . . you know? How we treated you like a prisoner . . . a Forgery." She pauses for a second and adds, "I'm sorry I wasn't nicer."

"No, you're not," I tell her. I let go of her cautiously as I fumble to open the door. She stands wavering on the spot, like tall grass in a breeze.

"Yes, I am. I'm sorry," she says stubbornly. Her shirt is hanging lazily off one of her shoulders and her eyes look confused, soft blue seas. She steps very close to me, so close that her eyelashes brush my chin, and leans in, pressing her hands into my chest. I know what she wants and I pull my head away.

"Why won't you kiss me?" she asks simply. Her voice sounds like a child's.

"You don't want me to kiss you."

"Yes, I do."

"No. You don't." We stand frozen in the doorway and she drops her hands to her sides.

"You don't think I'm pretty."

"That's not it," I admit.

"Then why? You got a girl already? You married?"

"What's *married*?"

"You know—two people, with rings. Together forever." She's swaying again, blowing ever so gently. I think of Emma. Two people. Together, like the birds.

"No, I'm not married," I say.

"Then kiss me." Her hands press onto my chest and she leans into me again, but I pull away. It's harder to resist her this time. There's this urge inside me, tugging, telling me that I should follow my feelings. It's what I always do. But this isn't really Bree, and this isn't really me, either. We are in cloudy bodies, foggy reflections of ourselves. We are feeling things that we might not tomorrow. And I love Emma. Emma, not Bree.

"I can't," I say, taking her hands in mine and squeezing them. Her skin is warm, on fire in my palms, and the words escape me before I can reflect on them. "But if you wake up tomorrow and you still want me to kiss you, I will."

Bree smiles, and then bends over to throw up on my boots.

# TWENTY-NINE

**THE NEXT MORNING, WHEN I** report to the Conditioning Room for training, Bree is nowhere to be found. Elijah runs us through another session of torturous hell. Every muscle in my body is stiff, pulled taut like an overstretched bow. I think I may snap in two, but as the drills continue, I slowly loosen up.

When the session finally ends, Elijah congratulates me on another strong performance, and then disappears with my father for a status meeting. I head to the Eatery for lunch but halfway there change directions and visit the hospital instead.

Blaine is on the same bed, wearing clean bandages. He still sleeps. I stand in the doorway and stare at him. A nurse urges me on, but she doesn't realize I'm terrified. Spending time with a person you may lose is the worst kind of torture. Blaine and I went through it with our mother. We sat by her side and held her hand and told her we loved her, and it only made it that much worse the day she failed to wake up.

I find the courage eventually, force my feet to move. I sit on the edge of Blaine's bed and hold his hand. I talk to him, as the night-shift nurse suggested. I tell him everything. I recount our trip through the forest, the waterfall behind the rocks. I tell him about Bree and the Rebels and our father. I tell him the truth that I had so long searched for, about the Laicos Project and the Heist, about Frank and Harvey. It's exhausting and it makes me realize how completely lost I feel, even now that I have the answers. Without Blaine, I am only half of myself.

"Wake up, Blaine. Please. I can't do this alone."

I squeeze his hand. He's still sleeping, but I swear he returns the pressure. It is so soft, I'm not positive it even happened.

I squeeze his hand a second time. This time I know I'm not imagining it. He squeezes back.

"Blaine? Can you hear me?"

He squeezes my hand again.

And then I'm yelling for the nurse and she's standing behind me as I tell her to watch, but she doesn't need to look at Blaine's hand, because this time, when I squeeze his palm, his eyes flutter open.

"Blaine!"

An older nurse pulls me away. "Careful, son. We don't want to startle him. He's opening his eyes for the first time in days."

I push her off. "You guys are the ones that will startle him. He's my brother. Seeing me will help."

But then I can hear his labored breathing, and there's a flurry of women around Blaine's bed. They wheel him from the room hurriedly, and all I can think is that he's not going to make it and they didn't even let me be the last thing he saw.

They bring him back in eventually, but the wait feels like an eternity. He is alive, intact, awake. Blaine rolls his head to the side, and when his eyes connect with mine, he is forcing a smile.

"Gray." It's all Blaine says, and it sounds dry and brittle.

"Hey."

He swallows heavily. "I heard you."

"I'm glad. 'Bout time you listened and came back."

"Not just that. I heard all of it . . . every last word."

He doesn't look angry or confused the way I did after discovering the truth, but maybe painting those expressions onto his face right now requires more energy than he has. Blaine places his palms against the bed and attempts to sit up. He fails.

"I need to get better." He forces the words out, his voice strained. "I need to get out of this bed and we need to stop him, Gray. Think of Kale."

I hadn't and I instantly feel terrible. There is a long pause where I hear nothing but the humming of a nurse and then Blaine finally says, "Everything was dark and I didn't know which way was up. Then I heard you. It was easy after that."

That feeling I get when he is gone, that pang in my chest— he must get it, too. We are linked, bound, reliant on the other even when we try so hard to appear independent. He needed me. This whole time, all he needed was to hear my voice.

"I'm so glad you're all right. I just . . . I thought . . . I don't know what to say."

"Don't say anything."

And I don't. We sit there together, comfortable in our silence. When my stomach growls audibly, he tells me to go eat.

"Come visit soon," he says.

"Only if you promise to stay here, with us."

"I have to, don't I? You wouldn't last a day without me."

I laugh. "Blaine . . . you made a joke."

He smiles, but it looks pained. "I'm shooting for a fast recovery."

Back in the Eatery, I get some food and sit alone. The fruit on my plate is mushy and I nibble at it cautiously. A couple of tables over I can make out Harvey, who is showing an odd contraption to Clipper. The boy holds it in his hands, turning it over in awe and amazement. I can't hear what they are saying, but I can tell Clipper is locked on every word escaping Harvey's lips.

I am just finishing my meal when a shadow falls across my plate. I look up to find an exhausted Bree, pale and somber, standing before me. Her hair is kinked from sleeping and fresh lines produced by bedsheets are strewn across her arms. She still smells like alcohol.

"Don't. Say. Anything," she commands as she sits.

"Wasn't planning on it." I can't help smiling, though. It's amusing to see her embarrassed.

"You're a jerk," she snaps. "I take back anything and everything I said last night."

"Do you even remember last night?"

"Some of it." She examines the fruit but ends up drinking some water instead.

"What's Clipper doing with Harvey?" I ask, changing the subject.

Bree rubs her temples. "He's in training. Next in line for head of tech operations."

"Really? He's the most qualified?"

"Do you have a thing against young talent or something?" she snaps. "Clipper invented the clipping machine on his own and was responsible for a lot of our basic technology.

None of it was as advanced as what we have now, but it got the job done when there was no Harvey."

"He just seems so young."

"What were you doing at twelve, Gray? Were you hunting for your village? Did people rely on you for things?"

I nod.

"Well, it's no different here. We rely on people with talent regardless of their age."

"Okay, okay, I'm sorry. Don't get all worked up."

She snorts and blows a stray hair from her eyes. "Oh please. As if you could do anything to get me worked up."

"I seemed to be able to last night."

She glares at me. "Yeah, well, sobriety changes things."

She looks pretty even in her wrecked and hungover state, but she's hot and unpredictable, a wild forest fire. What had we been thinking last night? Why had we gotten confused, even if only for a second? We are not a suitable match. We are better at each other's throats, better when we challenge the other. We are deadly. But one thing is for certain: We are back to normal.

# THIRTY

**MY FIRST TWO MONTHS IN** Crevice Valley pass quickly.

Training takes up most of my time, and I eventually graduate from Elijah's group into my father's. The work is harder, but my body has strengthened. I gain weight in ways I never had in Claysoot, muscles growing strong from repetitive workouts. My shooting lessons shift to include guns. I master them eventually, but only the long, slender ones. Rifles. I need a long barrel so that I feel I am holding a bow, and then my aim rings true.

Training with Owen is enjoyable, although I still don't feel like he's my father. If anything, he is an aged version of myself, with similar ideals and as stubborn a personality. We grow close, over the occasional drink at the Tap Room or an extra one-on-one training session, but not in the traditional way a parent and child might. The only time he ever feels like a father is when I catch him staring at me as I train, some look of utmost confusion on his face, as if he is uncertain I am really his.

The two of us visit Blaine often. Despite the fast recovery he wished for, his progress is slow but steady.

"The steady is the important part," our father says, "not the speed."

Most of our trips to the hospital consist of watching Blaine walk with crutches and telling him he's doing fantastic even when he's not. He knows we are lying and will change the subject of the conversation, asking questions about the Laicos Project or Crevice Valley. Most of the details my father spills are ones I've already heard, but I learn a few new gems during these visits, including the fact that our father joined the Rebels the way I did, after being captured and dragged through the door, and that Crevice Valley is such a fabulous and well-supplied site because it was once a military facility.

"When Elijah found it, all the hallways and rooms were already in place, the Conditioning Room sat there like it was waiting to be used, and the Basin was filled with dead crops. People had been here before us. And the fact that much of this place has electricity, plus a few underground bomb shelters that would be protected during a major attack—well, that proves this is more than a nifty hideout in the woods."

"If it's such a great military asset, why isn't the Order crawling all over it?" Blaine asks.

"We've often wondered that ourselves," Owen says. "Ryder thinks knowledge of this place died long before Frank and the Order came into power. He wagers its location was top secret and known only by a few key officials, all of whom likely were killed during the war."

"Lucky break," I say.

"Extremely. If Frank is so hungry to breach Mount Martyr for Harvey, imagine how rabid he'd be if he knew Crevice Valley was actually a functional military facility."

"Well, what *does* he think?" Blaine asks, wobbling on his crutches. "That you guys are sleeping out under the stars with nothing more than tents and campfires for company?"

"Who knows? He has a lot on his hands," our father says. "And we are a small threat in comparison to AmWest. The poor man is extremely overextended. If he doesn't watch it, everything is going to go crashing out of control on him."

I laugh. "Wouldn't that be tragic."

It is sometimes hard to believe that Crevice Valley flourished into its current state so quickly, but then I remember how Claysoot sprung from those dirt streets in under twelve months. When there was a need, the Rebels found a way, and the military officials that had previously engineered Crevice Valley had provided extremely sturdy building blocks.

Since replanting the crop fields, the land thrives. Sunlight and rain make their way into the Basin, giving way to corn and grain and endless rows of fruits and vegetables. The livestock fields are busy and dairy products always available. The hospital is all too often filled with injured or disabled soldiers, but a sizable field beside it houses much play, people joining together to kick a ball or host friendly archery matches. The laughter of their games drowns out cries of the injured.

There's also a school system for the youngest ones. I see one girl often, with curls so vibrant she reminds me of Kale. I imagine at some point later in their lives, this girl and all the children of Crevice Valley will look back and understand what took place here. They will come to see they were not just living, they were resisting. They burrowed into the earth by way of their parents and grew up amid a revolution. People here chose this life. Kale, however, will never have that luxury. Her life will always be a part of someone else's plan.

My absolute favorite place in Crevice Valley is the Technology Center. It is a mess of buildings, testing grounds, and storage facilities that begin in the Basin and roll their way into a set of tunnels piercing the mountain's depths. There is a weapons unit—where workers clean, repair, and improve upon any firearm, bow, arrow, spear, or ax that walks its way through the Crevice—and a monitoring room, where Harvey can not only survey the areas surrounding Mount Martyr but also keep tabs on all the motion sensors.

I like to walk through the center on my more quiet evenings and admire the various screens, the glowing dials. Sometimes I watch from afar, noting Harvey's patience as he works on the intricate equipment. He sits with poor posture, his shoulders arched awkwardly and his glasses resting on the tip of his crooked nose. When he catches me looking, he always smiles and gives me a feeble wave.

On one of those calm nights, I approach Harvey and ask him a question that has been swimming in my head since he first told me about Frank's labs.

"If a Forgery is just a copy—a physical and mental duplicate of a Heisted boy—why is it so loyal to Frank?"

Harvey pulls his glasses off and lays them on the table. "That, Gray, is a fantastic question, and not one that many people think to ask. It is, after all, the reason that none of Frank's lab workers could create a stable Forgery before me. If they managed to create one at all, its mind was too free. It would question Frank, and he disposed of those replicas swiftly. But I, on the other hand, had a passion for technology—a love for code, a way with software—and that is what made the difference."

"I'm missing something."

"A Forgery is similar to you and me," he continues. "It contains all the same organs, pumps the same type of blood, is built of the same bones. But you and I have free thought, Gray. A Forgery runs off software, data implanted in its brain that tells it how to act and who to listen to."

Harvey's smile, the one that exists when he talks about his passions, has faded. "This was really phenomenal when I created it. Now it mostly scares me that I was responsible for something so powerful."

"So why'd you do it, Harvey? Why work for him?"

He thinks about that for a moment. "I was young and impressionable, I suppose. Frank plucked me from my child-hood orphanage and brought me to Union Central, where there were state-of-the-art labs and technology and more water than I could ever drink. He treated me so well, and for the first time in my life I felt like I had family. Someone was caring for me. Someone was acting like my father. I wanted to please him, wanted to show him I could do anything, that I was smarter than every other grown man he had working in those labs. Guess I really did it, huh?"

I don't say anything, but I understand. I felt that same way with Frank, if only for a few days.

"And the limitless part," I prompt. "If you were able to make one successful Forgery, why can't you make a second or third off that same person? I don't get what's stopping you."

"It is a very complicated process," Harvey says. "If I tried to make too many replicas off you, Gray, it would kill you. I'm not just duplicating your physical attributes, but your mind as well. Your personality, your memories. The human brain can only be stretched so far before it breaks. So I shifted efforts to creating a Forgery of a Forgery, but that is an even messier process. Each generation is less like the first. Certain portions of the software don't mesh right, and the duplicate Forgeries end up disobedient. They malfunction. I probably could have solved it in time." He puts his glasses back on and winks at me. "Luckily, I've outgrown wanting to please Frank."

On select days, when scouting reports are positive and the Order nowhere nearby, I am allowed outside. One day a crisp gust of autumn air ruffles my hair. It has grown back, surpassing the stage of stiff stubble and reaching a point where it is soft again, falling into my eyes and curling behind my ears.

When I walk through the woods, it feels as if I am back in Claysoot. There are days that I wish I were truly there, that life was simple again. But Claysoot can never again be a comforting home to me, because even with its structure and rules and security, it is a fraud. Things in Crevice Valley are complicated; but here, what happens is by design of its people. Nothing greater has locked or imprisoned them.

Sometimes, when Bree is sent out on a scouting mission or water run, I venture to the grassy graveyard set in the hillsides beyond Mount Martyr's rear entrance. It seems every time I am there a new mound of fresh dirt has sprung up from the grass, like a daisy searching for sunlight. My father says this is just the beginning, that the real battle has not even started. I keep company with the deceased when Bree is away, taking refuge among the nameless bodies that lie beneath the ground; but even then I feel oddly alone, like a ghost among a sea of people.

I don't know what caused me to latch on to Bree the way I have, but whenever she leaves, I am slightly lost. I miss her fire, her scowling face and wild nature, her snide remarks. Each time she returns, I think of telling her this, but I never do. I sometimes even think of asking her if she still wants that kiss. But then Emma will creep into my mind—Emma who has been a pain in my chest for months, an ache I pray to extinguish in reunion every single day. And so I always let the feelings for Bree—the ones that creep up on me when she flashes me a smile or playfully punches my arm—fade away.

In the thick of autumn, when the days have grown much shorter and the evenings cool, I reach a point in my training where I am deemed fit for combat. My father puts me on an active list, and the excitement in me builds. Blaine frets in his big brother way, but since he is still recovering, he can't offer to take my place. He may be walking without his crutches now, but he has a solid two months of training before him. He has to put in his time, just like everyone else.

My first mission is a basic one, a scouting operation that will be led by Raid. The Order has reattempted Operation Ferret several times over since my arrival in Crevice Valley; and our mission is to cover ground west of Mount Martyr, deem it clear or, if the Order is spotted, report back with coordinates so a counterstrike team can be sent to disband them.

I never get to go on the mission.

On its eve, a sweaty Xavier bursts into a status meeting. The meeting is about the scouting mission itself, and for this reason I am among the shocked faces. The captains are there, along with Ryder, sitting around a circular table, while Bree and I stand with our backs to the wall. Even Harvey is in the room, but only because improved night-vision goggles are to be used on the excursion and he wants to be sure we understand the upgrades.

"Not now, Xavier," Ryder says as the doors are thrown open.

"But it's important, sir." Xavier gasps, nearly choking on his words. "I ran here straight from the interrogation cen-ter."

Something in this revelation has caught Ryder's attention and he nods at Xavier to continue.

"It's the new prisoner, the one Fallyn's team brought in the other day."

"What of him?" Ryder asks.

"Luke cracked him. We know how the Order plans to infiltrate Crevice Valley. It's a virus, sir. They've engineered a virus."

# THIRTY-ONE

IT'S QUIET, BUT ONLY FOR a second.

Fallyn throws her hands up first, and Elijah moans in defeat. The others begin talking frantically among themselves, wondering how Frank has confirmed our location, worrying about the threat of the virus. Xavier stands there helplessly, eyeing the group for some plan of action, until finally Ryder raises a hand and the room falls silent.

"You have more details, I assume?" he asks. His voice is still calm and steady, but his hands twist in small knots before him.

"They engineered it in the labs. The prisoner said it's airborne. It's apparently a mutated version of the original virus AmWest dropped on the East back during the war. Once we've been exposed, people will be sick within a day or two. He said we'd all be dead in a matter of weeks."

Fallyn frowns. "How can they be sure they won't infect themselves?"

"Vaccines," Xavier explains. "It's been mandatory for all serving in the Order and anyone wanting to stay within city limits. And it's being supplied to all Taem's domed sister cities across AmEast as well."

"And outlying towns?" Ryder prompts.

"I don't think Frank cares much. He doesn't need everyone to survive, just himself, the Order, and Harvey. Luke thinks the release of the virus depends on the success of this approaching Order team. Their mission is still Harvey, so they can't release it before they are in a position to retrieve him, otherwise they'll be risking the health of their target."

"Wait a minute," my father interjects. "How do they even know where we are? Sure, Mount Martyr's a well-known landmark, but we've been careful about our activity during daylight hours. They shouldn't know we are operating out of here, not unless . . . Do we have a leak?"

Raid shakes his head. "No one has been taken captive in recent weeks. I don't think information was snitched. But we need a plan, and we need it fast."

"Frank might have his suspicions about our location," Ryder says calmly, "but I doubt he truly knows where we are.

If he did, a virus would not be necessary. He'd simply fly over and drop bombs.

"So this can mean only one thing: The virus is coming on foot. I believe the Order will look to capture one of our soldiers in the field. Since they don't know how to find us, they will simply infect that prisoner and let him wander home. They'll want us to infect ourselves."

Ryder's logic makes perfect sense, and it sends another wave of panic through the room. I look at Bree, but her face is stern, her eyes focused.

"So we need the vaccine," she says to the worried captains.

Ryder nods in agreement. "Yes. The vaccine is the failsafe. We barricade our entrances, tighten security, and we do all we can to keep the virus from ever finding us. But if it does, we need the vaccine as a backup."

"Hold on," Fallyn says. "We're really going on the words of this one prisoner?"

"Fallyn, if you could see what Luke's done to him, you'd believe him," Xavier says. "He only wants the pain to stop. And you know how Luke is, the kind of agony he can inflict."

Elijah sighs. "It's a lost cause. The spies we have in Taem didn't see this coming, and if they are out of the loop, there's no way they can get us the vaccine in time. They probably don't even know where to start looking."

"I do," Harvey chimes in. It's the first words he's spoken

since the meeting began.

"Out of the question," Ryder states. "They want you too badly."

"Clearly not badly enough to keep me alive," he counters. "They are risking my death by sending a virus our way. I can die here with you, or we can attempt to get our hands on this fail-safe."

Ryder rubs his thumb and forefinger together. "You know where to look?"

"I spent countless days in both the technology wing and medical research center when I worked there. If the virus was born in those labs, so was the vaccine."

"There's no way they'll let you waltz back in," Elijah says.

And then I see it, a path forming before my eyes. This is my chance, the opportunity I've been praying for.

"They'll let us waltz in if I bring him back," I say. Everyone turns to stare. "It's simple. I march Harvey back to Taem, turn him in, and create a diversion allowing us to grab the vaccine. Then we sneak back to the woods before the Order even realizes what's happened."

*And I grab Emma along the way*, I think to myself. Exactly how, I am not sure, but at the moment, those details aren't slowing me.

Fallyn chortles. "Anyone can create a diversion. Why would you walking Harvey in be any more believable than someone else? What could you possibly tell them that would prevent them from shooting you both on sight?"

"First of all, the goal of Operation Ferret was always to bring Harvey back alive, so no one will be shot on sight. And then there's the fact that I'm a twin."

"Why would that matter?" she sneers.

"Because I won't be returning as myself. I'll be returning as Blaine. We are identical, and in the Order's eyes, Blaine never turned on them as I did. I can tell them I've been held captive since the Rebels attacked Evan's mission team. I'll say that you guys cut out my tracking device so I couldn't be traced, that I pretended to change sides. I'll say I gained your trust and then, when the opportunity presented itself, I took Harvey hostage and returned to Taem. If I tell them that story, I will be welcomed back with open arms. It will certainly get us back into Union Central, and from there, we can get the vaccine."

Harvey smiles, but the rest of the room is uncommonly still.

"It might work," Ryder admits finally. "It could go wrong a million different ways, but it's the best chance we have. Harvey, you're okay with this?"

"More than okay."

"Well I'm not," my father interrupts. "Gray's not prepared for something of this magnitude." I can see the terror in his eyes. For once he looks like a father.

"He's proven himself ready," Ryder says. "And he is on the active list. Gray, are you sure you want to do this?"

"Yes, but we'll need a guide. Neither Harvey or I know the forest well beyond Mount Martyr."

"I volunteer," my father says.

Ryder shakes his head. "Absolutely not. It can't be any of the captains. You are all too recognizable. It needs to be someone senior and yet someone who is not on their radar, someone who has proven themselves several times over and will not crack under pressure." I think Ryder is calling for a volunteer, but I find his eyes already locked on the blond figure to my left.

"I accept," Bree says, no waver or worry in her voice.

"Excellent," Ryder says. "The scouting mission is off. We have bigger missions to plan."


We spend the next several days in the status room with forest maps and city grids spread before us. We go over various routes and infiltration plans: how to break into the research facility, when to execute the diversion, how to make our escape. My father avoids the planning altogether, cursing under his breath and swearing he wants no part in coordinating his own son's death. Blaine seems to share his sentiments.

There is a day where Harvey and Bree are called to planning alone and I am not needed. They talk with the captains behind closed doors and I spend my time wondering what plans must be kept from me, and why. Bree tells me later it was nothing—housekeeping items that applied to technology and transportation only—but I suspect she's lying. She looks tired, though, taxed from the day, and I don't press her. Instead, I rifle through various scenarios of how and when I can sneak to the prison and pull Emma from her jail cell. If they can keep details from me, I can keep details from them.

The night before our departure, we pack our bags and go undercover. The Rebels dye Bree's hair dark brown and put thin disks in her eyes, which turn their depths the color of wet dirt. They call the disks "contacts" and give me similar ones, so that my eyes, the one feature different from Blaine's, appear blue.

I am laying my old Order uniform out across my cot when Bree stops by.

"You ready?" she asks.

"Yes. Are you?"

"Of course." She looks like a different person, but her voice is the same, and the way her brow ruffles in annoyance, unmistakable.

"You can still back out if you want," I tell her. "I won't take offense."

"No way, Gray. Someone has to make sure you come home in one piece." She stares at me for a moment, like she's expecting me to claim I don't need her help. "I'll see you in the morning, then," she says, and is gone as abruptly as she arrived.

I finish packing and sit at the end of my cot. I try to think about something, anything. Perhaps there is too much looming in the near future, so much that I am incapable of thinking of anything concrete. In need of a distraction, I head to the hospital to see Blaine.

He is hard at work in a physical therapy session with a nurse, and hops down from the steps she has him climbing when I arrive.

"Look at you, running stairs," I say.

He grins. "Getting stronger by the day. I just might have my full strength back when you return."

"You're dreaming."

He winds up for what I expect to be a playful punch, but ends up grabbing me instead.

"Be careful," he says. "Twin or not, you're still my kid brother and you don't know what it would do to me if something bad happened to you."

"Actually, I do know because I already went through it with you. When you were Heisted. When you were shot. When you slept in this hospital for days on end."

We break from our hug and he laughs. "Okay, okay. You win. I've put you through hell. Please don't try to make things even."

I leave Blaine to his therapy and head back to my room. I want to go to bed early so that I am well rested in the morning, but my father is waiting for me. He leans against my dresser, arms crossed.

"I want you to know I am proud of you," he says simply. "And I'm sorry I haven't been very supportive these last few days. I just don't want to lose you again."

I nod. I never thought his avoiding me was a malicious act. It was his way of dealing, of coming to terms with the uncertain future that steadily approaches.

"Trust your gut out there," he says. "It's kept you alive so far."

"I will." I almost call him Pa, but he says good night and leaves the room before I can work up the courage.

That night I sleep poorly. In my dreams, I am trying to get Harvey to Taem, but he keeps morphing into a black crow and flying in the opposite direction. Eventually I shoot him from the sky. When he hits the ground, he is no longer a crow but Bree, naked, her newly dark hair matted and bloody behind her head. I carry her in my arms, wandering aimlessly until she bleeds dry.

When I wake, it is still early, but my body is too anxious. I climb from the cot, pull on my Order uniform, and wait for it to begin.

# PART FOUR
# OF DIVERSIONS

# THIRTY-TWO

IT TAKES US FOUR DAYS to get to the city's outer limits. It is odd to be in open space again. I've seen nothing but the small radius surrounding Mount Martyr since my arrival, and to move through the land, to cover mountains and hillsides and valleys, is liberating. Harvey slows us a bit, his body not conditioned for the trek, but he doesn't complain once.

I hunt, setting traps during the night so we can fill our bellies each morning. Harvey keeps the Rebels informed every step of the way. He has a small earpiece and miniature microphone and whispers into it constantly. Bree gives him a hard time.

"They don't need to know that we rested for three minutes or that Gray went to take a piss or that I commented on the color of the sky."

"Of course they don't," Harvey says. "But small details are nice when dark clouds are on the horizon."

The morning that Taem's protective dome appears before us, we stop and rest for the final time. We pass a canteen of water around in silence, staring ahead at the looming city. No one mentions how getting in will be easy. It's leaving, vaccine in hand, that will be the real struggle.

"We should rough Harvey up before we head in," Bree says. "He needs to look convincing. If he was really your hostage, he'd show up with more than a sweaty shirt and dirty cheeks."

I look to Harvey. He is so frail and harmless. I don't think I can bring myself to even strike him across the cheek.

"If you must," Harvey says. He actually smiles at the idea.

I shake my head. "I'm not doing it."

Bree lets out a heavy sigh and then marches over to Harvey and punches him without warning. She shakes her fist out while Harvey tends to his now bloody nose.

"More," he insists.

Bree dislocates his shoulder and says, "You're no good to us if you're a completely broken mess. At least a dislocated shoulder is easy to right when needed."

With that, Bree picks up her bag and slings it over her shoulder. "I'll see you guys on the other side. Good luck."

She plants a kiss on my cheek, before sprinting off. While Harvey's and my arrival draws eyes elsewhere, she plans to hop an inbound trolley. I watch her run, my hand pressed to the place her lips had touched.

We begin our trek toward the glinting dome. Harvey walks in front of me, his dislocated arm cradled against his chest, while I point my rifle at his back. As we draw closer, I swear I can feel his eyes. From somewhere deep inside his fortress, Frank is watching the cameras as his prized possession appears from the woods.

The barrier opens, wide and gleaming, and we walk into the city's claws.

Waiting for us beside a car, with the door already open, is Marco. Order members stand at his side, their weapons following our movements as we approach. I can see the fear starting to take over Harvey now. I feel it, too.

"Well, if it isn't a Weathersby twin, back from the dead. And with Mr. Maldoon, no less," Marco comments. He bends forward and stares into my eyes, noting their color before righting himself. "Well done, Blaine. Well done indeed."

The guards grab us, and we are forced into the car.

Frank's office is as I remember it, a gleaming spectacle of decor and ornamentation. Marco shoves us into the chairs facing the desk and we wait. A moment later the doors behind us slide open, but there are no footsteps. I crane my neck around. Frank stands in the doorway. He examines his fingernails, cracks his knuckles methodically, and then enters the room.

He looks us over, first Harvey, then me, then Harvey again. His eyes gleam. As he examines us, he presses his fingers together in his quintessential wave, but today, the motion is not thoughtful and calm. It's menacing. They are pale and knobby, his fingers, like dead tree branches.

"Welcome home, Blaine," Frank says finally. His voice is as soft and buttery as ever. He smiles, a wide and mischievous grin. I shift in my seat.

Frank puts a spidery hand on my chin and pushes my face to the side. With another finger, he traces the faint scar on my neck. "My, what happened here?"

"I don't know," I lie. "The Rebels tortured me for information. I passed out and woke up with a bandage on my neck."

Frank squints at me. "How fortunate you are alive. We feared the worst." He folds his arms across his chest, not once alluding to the fact that there had been a tracker under my skin. "How did you escape?"

Frank flashes his teeth in another ominous smile and I feel like throwing up. Why hadn't I spent less time analyzing escape routes and more time practicing answers to these types of questions? I swallow and pray my voice remains steady.

"I went undercover. Pretended to understand their angle. Became sympathetic. I was under constant surveillance, but when I saw an opportunity, I acted on it. I jumped my guards during a rotation switch, took Harvey hostage, and hiked back." I motion toward Harvey when I say his name and he flinches.

"That right, Harvey?" Frank asks. "Is that how it happened?"

"Y-yes, sir," Harvey stammers. He looks terrified, and I don't think he's acting.

"You had a good thing here, Harvey, a real good thing," Frank coos. "I don't know why you made it come to this."

The blood from Harvey's nosebleed is now dry against his shirt, and with his bravery lost and his arm hanging limply, he really does look like a hostage.

Frank turns his attention back to me. "I'm so sorry about your brother." His voice doesn't sound sorry at all. "We received reports that he was lost during the fight that broke out beyond the Hairpin. You must be devastated."

I'm not sure what reaction to play here: surprise, as if I hadn't known the news, or grief, as if I am in mourning. Before I can make up my mind, Frank bends down so that his face is right before mine. I stare straight ahead, praying he can't see the edges of the blue contacts in my eyes.

"So, Blaine," Frank says. "You come back here, after disappearing for over two months, and because you have single-handedly completed Operation Ferret, you think I'm going to believe you."

"Don't you?" I ask.

"No, Blaine. I don't. Not one bit." The softness of his voice is gone, a bitter edge breaking through. "But you can make me believe you. Harvey is going to be executed tomorrow morning. Publicly. And you, my dear boy, will do the honors." He smiles, a gleaming evil thing, like a pale moon breaking from behind a rugged mountain range.

"But . . . you said to bring him back alive. That was the mission. How can you free Claysoot if you just kill him?"

Frank keeps smiling. "There has been some progress since you left. We no longer need his answers." A blatant, obvious lie. "But we do need Harvey alive so we can dispose of him ourselves and relish it. Do you know how happy the people of Taem will be to see this traitorous, murderous, deceitful man meet his end? Justice will finally be served, and you will be the bearer, Blaine. You will execute Harvey and prove to me your loyalty."

Things start swimming in my head: timelines, plans, diversions. This changes everything, puts a giant gash in our strategy. We now have less than a day, until nightfall, to get what we need and run. I have only hours to find Emma. And, as if Frank has read my mind, he throws another gem at me.

"Oh," he adds, grinning viciously. "Your brother seemed to have a strong liking for a girl named Emma."

I stare through him, focusing on the fall leaves outside his window. *Please don't tell me Emma is dead.* I say it over and over to myself. I won't be able to hold it together if she is.

Frank moves his fingers in delicate waves. "She's been working in our hospitals. Perhaps you'd like to pay her a visit? She's awfully pretty, and since Gray's gone, maybe a near look-alike will be enough to satiate her."

My fists clench and Frank sees it. He smiles wickedly, and then adds, in that soft, flowing voice, "Now if you'll excuse me, Gray—I'm sorry, Blaine—I have prior obligations to attend to."

I sit there, wondering if he honestly mixed up the names or if he knows.

I have an uneasy feeling he can see right through me.


Harvey gets put in lockdown, not in the prisons but in a lone room on a busy corridor where three Order members guard him. A few workers in white lab coats are ushered into his room, bags in hand. Medics, maybe. I bet Frank is twisted enough to want Harvey in tip-top shape when he executes him.

I am allowed to roam the grounds of Union Central freely, but it takes only a few minutes to notice the guard tailing me, always staying far enough away to not be perceived as a threat but close enough to keep tabs. I sneak into a bathroom and bolt the door. After double-checking the place and confirming it's empty, I attempt to contact Bree. I have a small earpiece, hidden from view, and a tiny microphone that Harvey has wired to the inside of my shirt.

"Bree?" I ask into it. "What's your status?" There is nothing but static for several seconds, followed by a crackle, and then finally, Bree's voice.

"Inside city limits. Got on the trolley no problem, and just had to ditch a few overfriendly Order folk."

"What about the diversion? Where are you with that?"

"What am I, lightning? Look, I've got to find a way to get into Union Central without drawing too much attention."

"You're wearing your old uniform. Just walk in."

"Gray, we've been over this. I need to be invisible; no one can know I'm there. What's the rush, anyway? We agreed the diversion would take place first thing in the morning."

"About that . . . there's been a change of plans." I tell her of Harvey's scheduled execution, and my supposed role.

She says nothing other than, "Don't worry. I'll make it happen today."

"How?"

"I don't know yet," she says. "But I'll trigger the diversion by late afternoon. I promise."

"It's already noon."

"Then you better stop distracting me. Just be ready for the signal."

With that, she cuts out and I am left sitting in the bathroom, staring at my dazed reflection in the mirror. I try to focus on the approaching diversion, but even when I close my eyes, Emma is the only thing I see. I'm sure Frank did it purposely, filled my head with thoughts of her simply to distract me, to torture me. Knowing there is nothing I can do until I get Bree's signal, I leave the bathroom. I look for the guard who was shadowing me, but seem to have lost him. My wrist access no longer works, and so at each door, I have to wait for someone in the Order to walk by and unlock it first.

The hospital is busy, but Emma is nowhere to be found. Perhaps she has the morning off or is working evening shifts instead. I let my feet take me by memory toward her quarters. I wait for what feels like hours before an Order member exits her hallway, and as he does, I slip through. Emma's door is closed, but light trickles from beneath it.

Why am I not excited? Why am I not bursting with joy? This is what I wanted, my ulterior motive since the beginning. This is Emma. Emma who I've loved and still love and thought I might never see again. Is that why it's hard? Because part of me never believed we'd be reunited? I raise my hand to knock, but pause. What will I even say?

Before I can lose my nerve, I let my knuckles rap on the wood. I hear the footsteps coming, bare feet shuffling across the carpet. Hands work the latch, and then the door opens, but the face before me does not belong to Emma.

"Blaine! You're alive." Craw beams. I can see Emma behind him. Her hair is a mess, sleepy waves coaxed out by the pillows. She holds bedsheets over her chest.

I punch Craw in the face before storming down the hallway.

# THIRTY-THREE

**CRAW CURSES.**

"Blaine, wait!" Emma is shouting, running after me, the bedsheets still clutched about her. I don't stop.

"Blaine!" she shouts again. She catches up to me and grabs my arm. "What on earth has gotten into you?"

I turn to face her. I'm angry, so very angry, but I need to stay in character. I clench my teeth.

"Why did you do that?" she asks. "I've never seen you hit someone. Ever. Did . . ." But then she trails off. Her eyes are locked on mine, searching for something. They work their way over my face, beginning with my eyebrows and moving down toward my jaw. She reaches out one hand and places it against my cheek. Her eyes grow wide as she lets a finger slide over my nose, trace the contours of my chin.

"Oh my gosh," she gasps, pulling her hand back. "Gray."

I have no idea how she knows, but she does. I'm about to lose it, explode right in the hallway, and so I turn and start walking.

Emma grabs my arm. "Gray, please. It's not like that."

"Like what, Emma?" I shout, spinning to face her. She backs away from me, almost fearfully.

"We . . . we thought you were dead. Everyone did," she says. "They said you were there when the Rebels attacked, that you and Blaine were killed."

"Well, we weren't!"

"You think it was easy for me?" Water builds in her eyes and a small tear rolls its way over the beauty mark on her cheek. Even when I'm furious it hurts to see her cry.

"Do you think it was for *me*? You have no clue what I've been through to get back here, Emma. And how do you repay me? You go sleep with Craw."

"That's not fair," she says.

"Fair? *I'm* the one being unfair? I never stopped thinking about you and you moved on in a matter of days."

She stands there helpless, clutching the pale sheets to the front of her chest and covering skin that Craw, but not I, has seen. She was supposed to be mine. I hers. We were supposed to be like the birds. She reaches up and brushes the tears from her face with the back of her hand.

"I never moved on, Gray," she says. "Physically maybe, because I was lost and heartbroken, but never truly. Please don't run from me. Don't leave again." She reaches for me, but I pull away.

"Did Craw give you my message at least?"

She looks down at the carpet. "Yes."

I'm thinking about how this makes it even worse, when there is a crackle in my ear.

"Soon," Bree whispers. "Get ready."

"I have to go," I say.

"Don't," Emma begs. "I'm so sorry that you had to see me like this, that I even did this, but please don't go."

"I need some time."

"For what?"

"To decide if you deserve a second chance."

All those times that I felt things for Bree, anytime there was even the slightest feeling of affection growing, I'd brushed it aside for Emma, told myself it wasn't real. I'd done nothing but think of her, attempt to get back to her, and she'd forgotten me almost instantly.

"Everyone deserves a second chance, Gray," she says, the tears still streaming down her face.

"Maybe," I say, and then I turn away from her. The diversion is coming and I need to be ready.

I head back to the room where Harvey is being held and watch the guards pace outside it. I stand around a corner, waiting. I feel oddly vulnerable, weak from my encounter with Emma and defenseless since I've been stripped of my rifle.

Suddenly there's a large *crack* that cuts through Union Central, a screeching static on the intercom. Bree's signal. My cue.

"What was that?" one of the guards asks. The others shake their heads. And then it starts, softly at first, like the pitter-patter of an evening rainstorm. It is delicate and patient, and then it builds, the notes getting louder, the melody stronger.

"Is that . . . music?"

"It sounds like it."

"I haven't heard music since I was a kid. It's beautiful."

Even I am in awe. It is like nothing I have ever witnessed, so much more powerful than the few drums or flutes played about Claysoot campfires. It cuts into my soul, stops my breathing. I am suspended in time. The music courses through the Union. It fills the hallways, projects into the training field outside. I look out the window behind me, and find everyone frozen as they look into the sky for the source of the music.

"It's playing everywhere. Even outside," a guard says.

"Frank is going to be furious," says another, and as he does, the internal alarm system goes off. Red lights flash. Sirens blare. They sound identical to the ones I heard from the rooftop during AmWest's attack.

There is a voice this time though, audible in the hallways. "Code Red Lockdown," it declares without an ounce of emotion. "Order members report for duty. Code Red Lockdown." The voice continues, along with the blaring alarm, but neither can fully drown out the music.

Order members begin to flood the hallways, racing left and right, scrambling into action. Harvey's guards abandon their post and as they race by, I trip one. I grab his handgun and then use the weapon to strike his head. He crumples to the ground and the others, swept up in the panicked hallway, don't even notice their fallen companion. I drag the unconscious guard to Harvey's room and use his wrist to open the door.

Harvey stands before me, looking phenomenally better than when I'd last seen him. His nose is still swollen, but the medics have fixed his shoulder and given him a clean shirt. "Mozart," he exclaims. "Used to listen to this overture all the time when I worked in the labs."

"How long do you think we have 'til they override the system?"

"Twenty minutes, maybe? Thirty, tops."

"Then let's get going."

Union Central has descended into utter chaos. Workers tear through the corridors, filing into elevators that will drop them into the lockdown safe chambers. Order members attempt to report for duty as the intercom voice demands. No one notices us cutting down staircases and into rooms we should not be entering.

Harvey leads, turning down now-empty hallways and waving his wrist before panels that have not had their access codes changed. We end up in a windowless corridor far underground. It is pristine, though, with glass panels and shiny floors. We pass a section Harvey refers to as his old station. It has been abandoned in the uproar, workers seeking refuge in the underground shelters, but various weapons and machinery can be seen lying on metal tables, illuminated screens lit up with numbers and graphics.

"This one," Harvey says, approaching a door with another silver access box. He waves his wrist but the unit flashes red. He tries again, but to no avail.

"You boys need assistance?" a voice asks from behind us. A tall, thin woman in a white lab coat stands in the hallway. There is a red triangle atop her chest. I instantly point the gun at her, and she raises her hands.

"I'm Christie. Ryder contacted me, said you might need some help?"

Harvey nods, and I lower my weapon.

Christie swipes us into the medical research facility and tells us she's been working undercover for the Rebels for over a year now, reporting findings, news, and supply shipment information back to Mount Martyr.

"We had no clue about the virus," she says as Harvey examines computer files. "It was explained to citizens as a generic shot, a precautionary measure against the winter flu season. When Ryder got the message to us that you were coming, we made sure someone gained access to this room. I wish we could offer you better information."

"You've done more than enough," I say.

Harvey finds the data he's looking for and then locates the supposed vaccine in a steel cabinet. He takes numerous bottles while Christie packs a canvas bag with syringes and other supplies.

"So you can cultivate more when you return," she says, handing the bag to Harvey.

"Much obliged," he says.

The music cuts off abruptly, and then starts back up, looping from the beginning. Harvey tosses the bag to me. "We should go. You hang on to that for safekeeping."

Something has changed in Harvey. He is confident, the nervousness gone from his face. I wonder if he is positive we will succeed, that with the vaccine acquired and the diversion still strong, we can escape Union Central easily. I hope he's right.

"Thanks, Christie," I shout over my shoulder as we race from the room. She waves an arm overhead and we disappear around a corner.

"Bree, we've got it!" I call into my mic. "Where are you?

Let's meet up and get out of here."

"Well that's going to be a problem, isn't it?" My heart drops. "They've got Union Central in lockdown, trying to figure out who started the music. I can't get out. You won't be able to either. I'm guessing they think AmWest infiltrated the Union somehow. This music was supposed to create a little panic, distract them for a while, not scare them into a full blown Code Red."

"So what do we do?" I ask as Harvey and I reach the main floors again.

"I don't know," she says. "Try to get out to the training field. It's chaos outside, but if we can at least meet up, maybe we'll figure something out."

Harvey and I make a quick turn, heading back down the hallway where he was being held. The music finally cuts out, but the sirens continue blaring, the red lights flashing off the walls. As we near Harvey's room, I see a figure moving beyond the corner of his doorframe. I recognize it, know who it is before his face even appears. I'm prepared to shoot him if I have to, but then a team of Order members spill into the hallway, and I realize we're trapped. I do the only thing I can think of that might preserve our cover.

"Freeze," I yell at Harvey, aiming the gun at his back. He looks at me in horror, but then, as Marco steps from the room, he understands.

"I caught him trying to escape in the panic," I tell Marco.

"We wouldn't want that to happen, now would we? Not after all you've done to get him back to us." Marco smiles savagely. "I think Harvey is a bit more troublesome than we give him credit for, wouldn't you agree, Blaine?"

"Definitely."

"I'll speak to Frank," he says. "Seems best to move the execution up to tonight, take care of things before anything else happens."

I feel my mouth fall open. "Move it up? But why? I still don't understand why we are so quick to dispose of him. Didn't Frank need Harvey's help?"

I know the answer is yes. Frank wants his limitless Forgeries and he needs Harvey to get them. Unless . . .

My grip slackens on the gun. Maybe Frank solved it. Maybe in the time I've been away, someone in his labs wrote the right code and now Frank can make Forgery after Forgery after Forgery. Endless replications of the replicas. His voice echoes in my mind. *There has been some progress since you left. We no longer need his answers.*

Marco sneers at my question. "Frank doesn't want the help of traitors. The only thing he wants from Harvey's kind is to see them die."

And with that, he walks up to Harvey and yanks his shoulder back out of place. Harvey cries out in pain and slumps to the ground. All I can do is stand there, helpless, knowing we've failed.

# THIRTY-FOUR

**WE GET LOCKED IN A** room together. It has no windows and the ceiling panels refuse to give way when I push on them. There is no escape. Harvey keeps telling me it's fine, that things will work out.

"How is this fine?" I snap at him. "It wasn't supposed to happen like this. We were supposed to get out. We were supposed to be successful."

"You still can," he says. "I never planned on making it back, even from the beginning."

My eyes go wide as I understand. "This is what you were talking about in those private meetings. The fact that you might have to die in order for Bree and me to escape."

He nods.

"Why did I have to be kept out of those conversations?"

"Because you would have argued," he admits, "as you are right now."

"Of course I'm arguing, because it shouldn't be like this. If I had been included in those meetings, maybe we could have thought up another plan, a strategy for if we got into this predicament. Plus, the Rebels need you. Badly."

"Clayton is wise beyond his years. I've taught him everything I know. The Rebels will be fine. And what makes you think we didn't try to come up with other strategies?"

"Because you're willingly walking to your death!"

"Maybe that's the plan."

"Well, that's as dumb a plan as any."

"Gray," he says simply, "it is a worthwhile sacrifice, one life for many, and you will be a fool to waste it. Don't do anything stupid when the time comes. I will not be angry with you. This is the way for you and Bree to make it back. Do this final deed, and then, as they celebrate my demise, when they trust you, bring the vaccine back to Crevice Valley so this battle can continue."

I sit there and shake my head in disbelief. Before I can find peace in my thoughts, the guards are leading us from the room.

Union Central is quiet again. The alarms have been turned off, the Code Red cleared. Harvey and I are pushed into a car, which drives us downtown to the same public square where Emma and I witnessed the water thief's execution. Here, it is busy, citizens and Order members alike buzzing through the space. Frank stands on the raised platform and quiets the crowd. He speaks into a tall narrow contraption that amplifies his voice through the square.

"This is Harvey Maldoon," Frank says. The wall behind Frank illuminates with the visuals from Harvey's wanted posters as the guards drag him onto the platform. They secure him to a wooden post. He doesn't struggle. In fact, he willingly participates, arranging his arms so the Order can more easily bind him.

"This man is no stranger to us," Frank continues. "We have seen his face strung up around the city, but I think it is worth reiterating the evils he has committed. This is a man who has no desire to live by laws that are just and fair. He is a snake and a coward, a murderer and a traitor, a filthy disease that Taem will be cleansed of tonight. Harvey has traded information and knowledge to AmWest, and in doing so he has betrayed us all. He has clearly proven that he wishes every one of us dead, and so tonight, this man will die!"

The spectators erupt in cheers, lifting arms above their heads and urging on the execution. Frank continues talking, working the people into a frenzied rally, but I am not listening. Where is Bree? I whisper to her through my mic, but she doesn't respond. I look around, but we are surrounded, trapped. City towers bear down on us from all angles, and the crowd is a swarming sea of anger around the platform.

"Blaine Weathersby has brought Mr. Maldoon back to us," Frank continues. Suddenly I fill the wall behind Frank, and not just a static image but a moving one. Wall me blinks when I blink, moves as I move. Video. It must be. "Blaine has shown honesty and faithfulness to Taem. He has shown us respect for law and order. He has returned Harvey to our city, and now, before you all, Blaine will eliminate this threat forever."

The crowd proceeds to cheer. I search the angry faces, looking for Emma, but she's nowhere to be found. I never should have walked away from her. A guard leads me onto the stage and positions me across the platform from Harvey. The wall shows it all, both Harvey and myself now filling its surface. The guard hands me a rifle and Frank presses a finger to his lip, smiling.

The weapon feels heavy in the approaching twilight. I could kill Frank. This is my chance if I want it. He is standing right there, but then what? I would certainly be shot dead by the Order or trampled by the crowd and the vaccine would never make it back to the Rebels. Frank would be dead, but would his Laicos Project? Would Marco step in and fill Frank's shoes? Continue Heisting for Forgeries? Send the virus to Mount Martyr? Would killing Frank now even matter?

I look down at the gun and then back to Harvey.

*Don't do anything stupid when the time comes.*

Those were his words, and maybe he is right. Maybe this really is the only way. Harvey is sacrificed for the greater good, the survival of the Rebels and the hope that the Rebellion can continue after the vaccine is administered. Tonight is not the night to defeat Frank. That battle waits but in a much different future.

As I ready myself for the actions I am still hesitant to take, I see a flash out of the corner of my eye, movement on a nearby roof. I look up and there she is, Bree, crouched behind a chimney of an adjacent building with her rifle in hand. She nearly blends into the dark stone structure, her hair disguising her. I can't quite tell, but I think she nods at me, urges me on. This is the path she and Harvey agreed upon behind closed doors. This is the path that I have had no say in. I am part of a plan already set in motion. I can refuse to play by the rules and everyone will lose.

Or I can pull the trigger.

I raise the rifle, position the butt against my shoulder, and look down the barrel at Harvey. His face is peaceful when he mouths, *I'm ready*. He closes his eyes, and I take aim.

My blood rushes; my hair stands on end; and, as my finger reaches toward the trigger, as I am about to pull it, I hear a gunshot.

This is when Bree shoots me. This is when I fall to the ground. And this is when the world around me goes up in flames.

# THIRTY-FIVE

FEET RACE ABOUT MY BODY. I can hear the gunfire erupting, but in a distant way, my ears ringing so intensely that everything simply hangs in space. I clutch my stomach, the place where I felt the bullet strike. I ache. I burn. I squint through the smoke. Harvey is gone. Flames lick across the platform, racing up the stake that held him just moments earlier. Someone has started a fire in the madness—as a distraction to help Frank escape the now violent square, perhaps. Or maybe it was Bree. But why?

The crowd is a slew of panicked shouts.

"Rebels are here! Undercover!"

"No, it's AmWest!"

"They're trying to kill the boy."

"They're trying to save Harvey."

Not a single accusation is true. And there are certainly no Rebels in the square. None other than Bree and myself, although perhaps it is possible she was trying to take me out. But why? Was *this* the plan devised behind closed doors? That *I* should die so Harvey and Bree could return? Or maybe it is just another diversion, Bree making things up as she goes.

I continue to hold my stomach, but the heat is intensifying quickly. I'm pretty sure my arm is on fire, but I am too stiff to shed my shirt. The platform is empty. I am alone, burning. I'm trying to come to peace with it, trying to accept that this is where I will die, when a pair of arms hook beneath my shoulders and drag me from the flaming stage. I can't see who they belong to, and I don't care. I let them pull me down a deserted alley and to safety. Hands rip the canvas bag holding the vaccine from my back and strip me of my shirt. Strong feet stamp out the flames that eat the material. I lie there, my back slumped against a stone wall until my senses return to me. The stinging in my eyes fades, my lungs cease screaming for air. And then my rescuer comes into view.

"You?" I mumble. "Why are you helping me?"

"You think you're the only one who's in on what's happening here? You don't think there have been others helping your crazy mission?" Bozo stands before me, his body hunched at an awkward angle as if he's forgotten how to stand up straight.

"What are you talking about?"

"There's a lot of people on the Rebels' side in Taem. Just because we didn't know about the virus doesn't mean we weren't ready to help when Ryder made the calls." He seems stronger out of his cell, his voice more steady, his limbs looser. His fingers still race in odd, twitching patterns, tapping at the wall he leans against, but without his tattered prison garb, he could almost pass for a civilized member of society.

"But . . . why would Ryder call on a crazy prisoner for help?"

"Ryder and I grew up together. We tried to run from Frank together once, too. I was stupid and got myself hurt. Had to tell Ryder to go on without me."

"You!" It's suddenly so clear. He knew about the test groups the first day I met him, I'd just thought he was talking about something else. How had I not seen it? He's not crazy, not Bozo at all.

"You're Bo Chilton!" I declare.

He shoots me a wild grin. "Guilty."

"How did you get out of the prison?"

"Bree had her own set of orders from Ryder, and she paid me a visit while Mozart was playing, broke me out on the spot."

I should be happy about this. This plan helped me avoid shooting Harvey. This plan led to my being saved from the fire and yet I am furious. Livid.

"She kept me in the dark. That lying, back-stabbing, stubborn . . . And she shot me!"

"Oh, quit your whining," Bo says. "She shot you with a rubber bullet and it was necessary. The others Ryder called on are fighting right now, keeping the Order busy so that you can get out of here. It's a cover, don't you see? A fight breaks out, the square goes up in flames, and you guys run in the thick of it."

I look down at my stomach, the place I had been clutching in pain. There is blood, but not nearly as much as I expect. Beneath my sweaty palm is a nasty welt, red and raised and already blossoming into a bruise. Painful, yes, but not deadly. If anything, the wound I should worry about is my burned left arm, blistering from the shirt I have since shed.

"Nothing is more convincing than authentic shock, and you wouldn't have acted the same if you knew the true plan," Bo continues. "We only get one shot at this, and Ryder thought this was the best chance at getting all three of you out alive."

"Harvey!" I exclaim, looking back toward the square. "Where is he?"

"He got hit by some crossfire—I saw that much. And then someone dragged him off the stage. I was told to get you both, if I could, but I think we've lost him. And if you and Bree want to get out of here, we have to move. Now."

And right then, when her name is not included, I know I

can't leave without her.

"We have to go back for someone," I say.

"Yes. Bree," Bo agrees. "She is meeting us back at Union Central. We'll hop a car from there."

"Of course Bree. But Emma, too. I have to go back for Emma."

He smiles a crooked grin. "Emma. She spoke about you."

I pause, confused. "You know her?"

"We were cell mates for a few days, until they discovered that she was handy with a scalpel."

"And she talked about me?"

"Wouldn't shut up. I had to launch into real dark stories to keep her quiet. Stories about the Laicos Project and Claysoot and Frank's Heists."

So she knows. Emma knows everything. I picture her now, somewhere in Union Central, walking around with that burden of knowledge. Knowledge she can't share with anyone. Her only proof is the word of a crazy man; if she spoke up, she'd be deemed as insane as him. Emma is free of her cell but still locked in a prison. I may not be ready to forgive her, but I love her too much to leave her stuck in that state.

"We have to get her. After we meet up with Bree."

Bo taps his fingers frantically against the wall. "We can try."

And in that moment, trying is enough.

I am on my feet quickly, ripping an undamaged section

from my discarded shirt and wrapping it around my burned arm. I sling the bag holding the vaccine on my back, Bo hands me his rifle, and we take off down the deserted alley.

Union Central is once again in an uproar, the alarm jarring people into action. Workers who had vacated the shelters since the previous Code Red now scurry to get back in them. Order members race to organize troops and head downtown. It is not hard for Bo and me to blend in among them. People are too panicked to really look at anyone's face.

We meet up with Bree near the dining halls. When I see her, a million thoughts fly through my head: relief, hatred, betrayal. It's confusing, and not knowing which one to act upon, I simply glare at her. She, on the other hand, runs to me and throws her arms around my neck with such force that I stumble backward.

"You're okay," she gasps, as if she doesn't believe it's possible. Her mouth hangs open, as though there is something important she wants to say, but she settles on an emotionless command in the end. "Let's go. The garage is this way."

But I can't. Not yet. "I have to make a detour first."

"We don't have the time," she argues.

"There is time for this."

Not waiting for her answer, I take off down the hallway. I hear Bo and Bree fall in line behind me. Given the panicked state of Union Central, someone has overridden the access panels so that workers can run freely between corridors and rooms. Taking the stairs, I sprint until I get to Emma's quarters. Her door is already open. She runs from the room, and I collide with her.

"Gray!" Emma exclaims. "I was just heading to the hospital. What are you doing here?" She holds a medic bag in her arms. My eyes connect with hers and I lose myself in their color. I forget what I had wanted to say.

"Who is this?" Bree erupts behind me. "And why does she know who you are?"

"It's okay," I say, without turning around. "I know her. She's from Claysoot. I left her here when I ran to the Rebels."

Bree steps between us. "Was this your motive when you volunteered for the mission?" she asks. "Are you risking all our hides right now for some girl none of us have ever heard of?"

"I can't leave Emma again. I've been waiting for an opportunity to get her out of Taem, and I wasn't going to ignore my chance when it finally arrived."

"Please, I want to come," Emma says. "Take me with you. I can't stay here any longer."

Bree snorts and steps closer to me, so close I can feel the warmth of her breath as she exhales. She presses a finger into my chest. "She can come if she's that important to you, but we are not spending another moment bickering in this hallway."

I look over Bree's head at Emma. "She's coming."

Bree scowls, but then motions for us to follow her. "This way."

Bo tails Bree, and as I move to do the same, Emma grabs my arm. "Thank you," she says. "For my second chance."

For a split second I contemplate kissing her, grabbing her face and pulling it to mine. But then I think that the last hands holding her face were likely Craw's, that his lips were the last to press against hers. Something hardens in the pit of my stomach.

"Second chances are not the same as forgiveness, Emma." I shake her hand from mine. "Don't slow us down."

We race on, following Bree down a stairwell. On the bottom floor, we find ourselves in what must be Frank's surveillance quarters. Screens split the room into a variety of aisles, each display showing a different corner of Union Central: corridors, bedrooms, fields, the dining hall. It's eerie, the visuals flickering solemnly as we watch Order members sprint through the frames. Some even show select areas of downtown Taem. Fighting and smoke fill the ones focused on the public square. As we pause to catch our breath, I see a dark flash move beyond a series of screens.

"Someone's here," I whisper. We steal silently down the

row, moving away from our pursuer. From behind us, another pattering of feet. We cut down a different aisle. Soon we are so deep in the rows that Bree becomes uncertain which way we came from and which way leads to the garage. The feet keep trailing us, flicking around corners and tracking our moves.

"Here," I whisper, pointing to a room off one of the corridors. We step in quickly and bolt the door behind us. It flattens the alarm into a duller echo. Emma leans against the wall in relief and lights click on.

The room becomes visible, bluish lighting flickering overhead. It is a lengthy room, much like the aisles we've left, but its contents are far more important. It doesn't take long for us to know what we are looking at. There must be hundreds of screens, but their visuals are unmistakable. Dirty streets. Island sand. Huts and livestock fields and town squares.

"This is the control room," Bree says, her hand running over a screen that shows two young boys playing along a sandy shoreline.

I step up to a screen that houses familiar visuals: the steps leading to the Council building in Claysoot. Kale is hopping up and down them, pulling her wooden duck behind her. There is no sound coming from the screen, and she could be a memory, a daydream, something not even happening. It has been just three months, and yet I feel I've been gone for decades longer. So much has changed since I called those clay streets my home. Kale hears something, and hops down the steps and out of the frame.

Another screen is eerily labeled Group C: Maude. Within its borders I can see the inside of her home: the simple wooden table, the faucet that could be pumped for running water. But what's most unsettling is that these things are in the background, visible beyond her bedroom doorframe. The bulk of the image is focused on Maude's bed, on the place I saw her standing the night I ran from Claysoot, the place she had discussed things with a voice I'm now certain belonged to Frank. If she was talking to him that night, does that mean she was in on it all along?

Bo moves to my side and taps at the corner of Maude's visuals. I think it is his customary twitch until I notice the objects beneath his fingers: five strawberries, lined up with precision on the nightstand beside Maude's bed. He's not tapping. He is counting.

My voice comes out a whisper. "Five red berries in a row."

"Sown with love so that they'll grow," Bo sings. But this time doesn't stop.

> *"The first for when your throat is dry*
> *The next for under rainless skies*
> *If suns are strong, eat the third*

*Need one more? Just say the word*
*When water's scarce, please have the last*
*Drink its juice and drink it fast*
*And when the thirst has stricken me*
*Please sow five new berry seeds*
*With luck and faith we'll watch them bloom*
*Else thirst will drive us to our tomb"*

He breaks into tapping again, fingers dancing over Maude's video.

"We both knew that song when we woke up in Claysoot," he says. "Maude said our mother must have sung it to us, even though neither of us could remember her. Or a home that we shared with her, even."

"She knows there's more out here, doesn't she?" I ask.

"Yes, and it's my fault." He sinks to the floor and leans against the wall, knees pulled in toward his chest. "When the Order caught me running with Ryder, I told them I'd found a way to alert Maude of life beyond the Wall. It was a lie and a foolish one. I thought that if the Order believed Claysoot knew about the project, it all might stop. But that's not what happened. Someone in the Order made contact with Maude. They discovered she knew nothing, but after revealing themselves, they had to ensure she'd keep quiet. Frank told her I was in his custody and promised to kill me if she let the truth slip.

"She demanded to see me first. I remember the video session. We saw each other for no more than ten seconds, and she started crying in half that time. After that, they used her as a resource, asked her all sorts of questions, still do I think. She is their eyes behind the Wall. And she goes along with everything, all because of me. She'd do anything for me; it's her greatest weakness."

I'm now positive Maude is the reason I was saved from the Outer Ring. She likely worried Bo would be hurt if Frank believed her responsible for my beating the Heist, for keeping my birth date secret. She must have told him the truth as soon as I admitted it to her.

"And the berries?" I ask.

He shrugs. "I'm guessing she leaves them there in case I were to reappear, to show that she's never forgotten me."

"We should go," Emma says.

I nod and move for the door, but something catches me off guard. Something odd in one of the topmost screens labeled Group A. "Wait! Did you see that?"

"See what?" Bree asks, looking at the screen I point to. We wait, and again there is movement, a shadow darting through the frame.

"That, just there. Did you see that?" Bree nods. So does Emma.

We spread out in the control room, locating the other

screens labeled Group A and wait. While each screen shows havoc—charred buildings and trampled livestock fields—we begin to see life among them: the faintest of silhouettes, darting through the frames. You would miss them if you weren't deliberately looking for life, which would be easy to do when the screens sit beside the lively pictures of groups B, C, and D.

"I thought Group A was gone," I say.

Bree shrugs. "Our journals are incomplete, so I'm not sure."

"No, they killed each other off," Bo says. "I heard it reported. Occasionally, in the early weeks after I was captured, I became Frank's favorite test subject. He hated Ryder for escaping and he took that anger out on me. I spent hours on his workers' tables. Each time I prayed that I would die, but I never got quite that lucky.

"I remember the day Frank received the report that Group A had died off. They thought I was unconscious, but I heard the whole thing. Dead. Extinct. Gone. Every last one of them."

"Maybe Frank's wrong, though," Bree says, looking back to the images. "Maybe a few of them made it."

"And maybe our eyes are playing tricks on us," Bo says. "Whatever is left of that ruined place, it is not an area that could easily foster life."

"True," I say. "But even if they were fighting at one point, all it would have taken was a handful of people who had hope, who wanted to keep going. Claysoot formed out of nearly nothing. So did Saltwater and Dextern. These people in Group A had electricity and shelter. If they decided they wanted to live, they did."

Bree and Bo nod in agreement, but Emma has grown distracted by a display that shows Carter hunched over medical scrolls in the Clinic.

"Come on," Bo says. "We need to keep moving."

He checks the door, and after deeming it safe, we open it. The alarm is still blaring and we skirt through the rows of screens, red light dancing over our faces. Up ahead, the hallway opens into the garage.

And then there is a voice behind us. "Freeze."

Bo, Emma, and I do, but Bree reacts so instinctively I don't have time to stop her. She spins on her heels, brings her rifle up to her chest. She aims and fires.

But I hear two shots.

And then I hear two bodies crumpling to the ground.

# THIRTY-SIX

**THE BLOOD COMES SLOWLY AT** first, soft and delicate, and then spreads over the fabric of her shirt like fire swallowing dry leaves. Bree lies on her back, eyes looking up at the ceiling, and draws short, panicked breaths. I drop beside her, not bothering to check if the threat has been eliminated.

"Bree?"

"I'm okay. I'm okay," she gasps. Her hand finds mine and grips it tightly. The bullet has hit her upper arm, and as she lies there, panting violently, I realize how much she means to me. My chest starts pounding. I stand up quickly, my hands moving of their own accord. I aim my rifle down the hallway, but it is empty.

There is a body lying on the concrete floor. Bo has gone into self-preservation mode at my side, rocking and tapping and humming his song about berries. Emma stoops to examine Bree, and I leave them, cautiously approaching the fallen Order member.

He is young and his breathing rapid and shallow. Bree's bullet hit him square in the chest.

"You won't . . . get out . . . of here . . . alive," he pants.

I look down at his chest, damp with blood. "Are you alone?" He keeps panting. I move my rifle before his eyes. "Answer me. Are you alone?"

He nods, and then forces out more words. "You won't . . . make it . . . back," he gasps. "Frank . . . will kill . . . you all . . . All the Rebels."

I clench my teeth, push the rifle against his cheek. My finger reaches for the trigger.

"Do it," he begs. "Please."

I don't.

"Please?"

I sling the rifle across my back and run the other way. I drop to my knees beside Emma. "Will she live?"

"I don't know," she says. "It only hit her arm, but there's a lot of blood. And she's going into shock from the pain."

I scoop Bree into my arms and nudge Bo with my boot. "Come on, let's go."

He keeps rocking back and forth, his hands covering his head, humming.

"Bo, please," Emma urges.

He snaps from his panicked trance at Emma's touch, and again we are moving. We duck into the garage and stay out of view, our backs pressed against the rear wall. The place is racing with activity. Vehicles maneuver about the troops, making their way toward the exit and the riot downtown.

"Bree's not going to be able to drive us," I say to Bo. She has grown heavy in my arms, and her blood is sticky on my skin. I look at the various cars before us. "Which ones do you know how to operate?"

"I don't," he says. "But how hard can it be? Your hands steer and your feet handle the stop and go. I'll figure the rest out as I need to."

I'm skeptical but in no position to argue. We slink toward a deep green car. Bo pulls the back door open and I lay Bree across the bench seat. She shudders as I transfer her to the leather.

Bo finds keys under the front seat and Emma and I climb into the back. I look at Bree. Her chest is still heaving.

"Can you fix her?" I ask Emma. She looks so unsure it nearly breaks me. "Please, Emma. I need you to fix her."

The car lunges forward. No one stops us. We are just another vehicle heading to the riot. As we break into the now dark evening, Emma bends over Bree, and opens her bag.

～∽～

By the time the last ounce of light has been leeched from the night sky, we enter the woods.

Bo's driving is turbulent at best, and Emma fights the lurching and abrupt movements of the car as she works on Bree. She fishes out the bullet—a skill she must have learned during her time working in Union Central's hospital—and makes a bloody mess of both Bree's arm and the car seat in the process. Bree loses consciousness along the way, but Emma stitches her up, dresses the wound, and tells me she's done the best she can. Bo takes us as far as possible, following a dirt road that weaves through the trees, which grow thicker and thicker, until we finally have to abandon our vehicle.

I gather Bree in my arms, and lead the way, hiking in what I believe to be the right direction. I'm slow, carrying her like that, and it gives me too much time to think about Harvey. We left him. We didn't know if he was dead or alive or taken captive and we left without him.

Eventually, Bo claims we should rest. "Only Bree knows how to get back," he points out. "We should make camp for the night."

Taem's dome is barely visible in the distance, and the occasional explosion or gunfire can be heard. It makes me uncomfortable, being so close.

"What if someone's following us?" I ask.

"They're not," Bo says. "They are fighting a bigger battle right now."

Bo makes a fire and Emma and I sit on opposite sides, staring at each other through the flames. Bree sleeps, her head in my lap. I say nothing to Emma. I don't even know where to begin. I want her beside me, and yet I want her far, far away, hurting as I do.

"Gray?"

I look down to see Bree's eyes flickering open. They are blue again. She must have ditched her contacts at some point.

"Hey, Bree."

She tries to sit up, but winces. "What happened?"

"You got shot."

"I know that, stupid. What happened *after* I got shot?" She speaks slowly, but I can tell it's meant to have fire in it. Her stubbornness makes me grin.

"We got to a car. Bo drove us to safety. And Emma fixed you. We're camping in the woods now."

"Emma? The Emma you never told me about? The girl you risked all our lives attempting to save?"

"Yeah, that one."

She frowns. "She means a lot to you, doesn't she?"

"Yes. But so do you." It's a complicated response, but an honest one.

Bree lies there for a second, looking up at me. "Your eyes

are still blue. I like them better when they're gray."

"Why?" I ask, thinking of how gray is so dull, and not even a color at all.

"They remind me of cloudy skies over Saltwater. And morning waves. That color is familiar. Comforting."

I fish the contacts from my eyes and flick them aside. "Better?"

She smiles. I return my attention to the fire, admiring an especially hot patch of blue flames.

"Gray?" Bree whispers again.

"Yeah?"

"Do you remember that night in the Tap Room, when I drank too much?"

"I remember you threw up on my boots."

"No, not that." She shakes her head slowly. "Before that. Do you remember what I asked you?"

I nod. I've never forgotten.

"If I asked you that again, right now, would you turn me down?"

"No," I tell her honestly. I've been fighting anything I felt toward her because of Emma—Emma, who didn't fight a thing herself.

Bree tries to sit again, and grimaces. She won't give up, though; she's far too stubborn. She locks her good arm behind my neck and pulls until she's upright in my lap. Her face is dangerously close to mine. I'm positive Emma is staring at us, watching my every move through the fire, but I am bitter and hurt and angry. A part of me wants her to hurt, too.

Bree leans in a little, her arms still behind my neck. "Kiss me?" she asks.

And I do.

As Bree's lips meet mine, as her arms latch more tightly behind my neck, something washes over me. Guilt, maybe? Confusion? I try to stifle it, because even with it stirring in my gut, Bree tastes so good. I let it go from one kiss to many. I kiss her several times over, then her nose, her neck.

Bree is warm. She is soft. She clings to me as though her life depends on it. I am hungry for her, but I am also hungry for revenge. And the more of it I get, the worse I feel, because I can't pull away. I am crashing, tumbling, gathering speed and unable to stop. I don't know how far it would have gone, the two of us—even with Emma and Bo sitting on the other side of the camp—if the celebration hadn't started.

There is one at first, a whiz of noise followed by a burst of blue light overhead. The second is red, a third yellow.

"Fireworks," Bo says.

The battle in Taem is over. We watch the show in silence. It is beautiful, an explosion of colors against a blanket of black. And then a projection lights up the sky. It is an image, as dark and dismal as any.

Harvey, dead.

He is tied to the wooden pole in the public square. They've stripped him naked and painted a red triangle atop his chest. His head hangs toward it, as though he were trying to kiss its peak.

The fireworks continue in the distance, covering Harvey's projection until he fades out completely. In the midst of Harvey's sacrifice, my revenge on Emma suddenly feels juvenile and foolish, completely unwarranted. I am focused on all the wrong things. Getting even with Emma doesn't matter. Not in the slightest. It's not even making me feel any better.

What matters is that while we have succeeded in one mission, we are far from finished. If Frank is not overthrown, Harvey's death will be for nothing. The battle with Frank and his Forgeries—*limitless* Forgeries, given what I've learned in Taem—trumps all. Only then will Harvey's death have been worth it. Only then will Claysoot and the other test groups be free. And only then will the people of this odd country be able to decide their own fate, their own rules.

Later, when the fire dies out and Bo and Emma have fallen asleep, Bree curls up at my side. She kisses me long and hard, so confidently that I know she means it, that she wants to be with me, and I am overwhelmed with another wave of guilt. She drifts to sleep as I run my hand along her back.

Halfway through the night Bo wakes and takes over watch,

but I still can't sleep. The best I do is nod in and out of consciousness, my arms always hugging Bree, but my eyes lingering on Emma, who shivers while she dreams.

Morning breaks and no one has tracked us. Bo claims it's because they got what they really wanted. "Harvey's dead, and that, at the moment, is enough. But they'll come eventually, especially once they discover we've broken in and stolen from their medical center."

As the sun rises between the tightly packed trees, Bree radios Ryder and shares the news. We walk in silence the first day. I look over my shoulder occasionally and find Emma in conversation with Bo. Her lips are pursed and her eyes, sleepy. Bo seems to do most of the talking. He taps on his skull with twitching fingers and tries to coax conversation from her. Emma just gazes at the medic bag in her arms.

That night, after catching rabbit and cooking the meat over a small fire, Bo approaches me. "You should really talk to her," he says. "She's sorry. And confused."

"I don't have anything to say." But as soon as the words leave my mouth I know it's not that I don't want to talk to her but that I'm afraid to. I'm terrified because I do feel something for Bree, and what I did with her makes me no different from Emma, who acted on her feelings for Craw. I want to apologize and tell Emma the birds still exist, and, yes, some people really do live that way, but I don't know how to put it into words.

It doesn't make sense, this mess of emotions. I always follow my gut, find my path with such little deliberation. But this, with Emma, is crippling. How is it possible that I can feel so much and still not know what to do?

Just past noon a few days later, Mount Martyr emerges from between a dense throng of trees. We climb to the base of the Crevice, and find Elijah waiting with his back against the stony facade. He is drinking from a standard water canteen, but when he congratulates us on a job well done, hugging us each in turn, he smells like alcohol.

"I still can't believe you guys pulled it off," he says, beaming. "We've been celebrating since Bree called with the news."

He jiggles the canteen at us in offering and when no one takes it, he continues. "We owe Harvey so much." At that, we stand in silence for a moment; there are no words that could possibly do Harvey justice. Elijah lowers his drink, eyes the bloodied state of Bree's uniform, and adds, "We should get moving, I suppose. There's still a vaccine to administer."

# THIRTY-SEVEN

**EVERYONE IS WAITING FOR US** in the Technology Center. Clipper and a few doctors look anxious to get to work; but, true to Elijah's words, most people are in merry, boisterous spirits. Ryder and the other captains are laughing as we enter, a half dozen empty mugs scattered across the table before them. Clipper takes the canvas bag from me and he's barely stepped aside before my father is pulling me into his arms and hugging me so tightly I'm afraid my ribs might crack.

"That is the last time I let Ryder decide what missions you're fit for," he says, his breath hot with ale. "It was too risky."

"I heard that," Ryder says.

"It's the truth and I won't lie about it. And this is *not* the alcohol talking."

Ryder laughs. "I never suspected it was. Regardless, the boy did well—you should be proud."

"I am." He turns, rests a hand on my shoulder, and puts on a stern fatherlike face before repeating it to me. "I am very proud."

He gives me this smile that is full of both relief and joy, and I know that while love was rarely spoken of in Claysoot, it certainly existed. In glances like this. In small moments exchanged. Raid pours a new round of drinks, and my father moves to join the captains.

"Hey, Pa?" He starts at the fatherly endearment. "It's really good to see you again."

His smile is too wide, like it might split the corners of his mouth. I'm wondering if this is the result of his drinking or my words, when he nods and says, "Likewise."

And then he's back with the others, laughing, cheering, shouting. They raise their mugs and bring them together in a clatter of glass. I frown. I can admit this moment truly is a cause for celebration, but even still it feels wrong. Like we are callous to be happy in the wake of Harvey's death.

Bree points at Fallyn—who has discovered she is capable of smiling—and asks, "Should they really be drinking when they're about to get a vaccination?"

"Probably not," Emma says.

"Definitely not." Clipper glances at Emma's medical bag

and adds, "But I'll still put in a good word for you at the hospital. Won't tell them you were *probably* okay with treating intoxicated patients."

Bree is so busy looking smug at this comment that she fails to notice Clipper's wink.

"You ready?" he asks me.

The syringe he holds looks terrifying, but I nod anyway. He pulls me aside, cleans an area of my upper arm, and then pushes the needle in without warning. "Owen was a mess while you were gone," he says. "I doubt he slept more than five minutes until Bree radioed and said you were safe."

Drinks clink behind us, and Clipper finishes administering the shot without another word. When he's done, I can't help but notice that he looks older than I remember, and taller.

"I'm sorry about Harvey," I say. "I know he was sort of a father to you."

"He was, wasn't he?" The boy forces a smile, and moves on to Bree.


I visit Blaine that afternoon. He has moved from the hospital to his own room and while he is much healthier, he is still not fully recovered.

"I can't run for more than a few minutes," he admits. "Too much weight on my leg and the pain is worse than that time you hooked my lip when we went fishing. Remember that?"

I do and the image makes me smile. My first one since returning.

"I feel really guilty," I say. I shouldn't be smiling.

"About my lip? Forget it. We were kids."

"No, about Harvey. We left him there. Bo said there wasn't time, that we needed to keep moving, but I still can't get over the fact that we didn't even look for him. After everything he sacrificed, we just ran the other way."

Blaine drags a hand through his hair which, like mine, has grown back out.

"Look, it was horrible when you were gone," he says. "I hated it. I was positive you weren't going to make it back. Pa was, too. And this sounds so terrible, like I don't care at all about Harvey, but I'm glad it was him and not you. If some-one had sat me down and made me pick, this is what I'd have chosen."

I frown. "No one should have to pick, Blaine. Not over stuff like this."

"I know. But still."

He leaves to attend a physical therapy session, and I wander off to find some food. It's a bit early for dinner, but my stomach is unsettled. I'm not sure if it's from nerves or guilt or actual hunger, but I make my way to the Eatery and collect a small meal from the kitchen. I end up sitting with Bree, who looks like she visited the hospital to get her wound cleaned up. She's wearing a blood-free shirt and is filling Polly and Hal in on our mission.

"So we can't be certain, but including Christie, it seems like the Rebels lost another hundred or so after we left."

"What?"

Bree looks at me like I'm an idiot and then says, "Oh, I forgot. You went to see Blaine during the debriefing meeting." I stare at her until she realizes I want the details. "Right, so a bunch of Rebels fell in the public square—there just weren't enough of them once the Order sent reinforcements—and that woman Christie? I guess they had footage of her helping you into the labs. One of our spies said she was executed the following morning. Publicly, just like Harvey."

My stomach seizes. Christie must have known the consequences if Frank's cameras caught her actions, but I still feel sick. I am alive because of her. All of Crevice Valley has the vaccine because of her. The number of people who have died for the Rebels is steadily growing and it's not right. Why them? Why not me? Or Bree? Or Bo? How did we manage to get so lucky?

Suddenly, I need to be alone.

"Gray?" Bree asks as I get up from the table. "You okay?"

I leave without answering.

In the Basin, people have erected a memorial for Harvey

and those lost during the battle in Taem. It's nothing more than a circle drawn in the dirt, but people step into its center to lay down notes and flowers and candles. My pockets are empty and I have nothing to add to the tribute, but I step into the ring anyway. I close my eyes and I thank Harvey and Christie and all the other nameless Rebels who fell for a greater good. I tell them that I still stand by the promise I made the other night by the fire. The fight is not over, and while some may need a few days of revelry to celebrate this small victory, the Rebels have a steep climb ahead. I will climb alongside them. I'll even lead if I have to.

When I turn to exit the ring, Emma waits behind me, a small candle cupped in her palm. The flame throws shadows across her face; and even though I know I should say something, I walk by her without a single word.

My room is as I left it, plain and uninviting. Sitting on the edge of my cot, I try to remember what life was like before all this. I don't feel like the same person anymore. Maybe I'm not. There was a time when all I wanted was Emma and now even that confuses me.

I stare at the painting on my wall and wish it were a window. I need to see blue sky and clouds and birds flying in twos. I need to know that somewhere in this world, things are fair.

# THIRTY-EIGHT

**LIFE CONTINUES IN CREVICE VALLEY.** Even amid all the darkness and death, babies are born, people are married. When you don't have to worry about Heists and losing your society's ability to reproduce, people really do settle down like the birds.

Emma transitions into a nursing job and I avoid her. I am alone with her only once, when I visit the hospital to have my burned arm treated. She dresses the burn with salve and bandages. I'd forgotten how gentle her hands are, how their touch makes my chest ache. I'm thinking of kissing her, of grabbing her chin and saying, "Let's start over," when she turns her back on me to retrieve more salve. The impulse vanishes with her. The burns on my arm heal, turning to rippled and uneven skin over time, but the tension between us does not.

Bree washes the dye from her hair, visits the hospital several times to tend to her bullet wound, and in a matter of days it's as if she never set foot in Taem at all. We fall back into our regular banter. When we train, we egg each other on. In conversations she interjects ridicule and I tease her endlessly. We avoid repeating our display around the fire on the eve of Harvey's death, at least publicly. But on quiet nights, when she knocks on my door and stands before me with her blond hair framing that perfect face, I never turn her away.

There is little sleep on those evenings. We become a flurry of hands and lips and skin, but she always stops me when things get too heated. She doesn't want a baby, and neither do I, but deep down it's like I know sleeping with her will make it impossible to repair things with Emma. I find myself oddly relieved each time Bree presses her palms against my chest, whispering, "Not now. Not tonight." If it weren't for her words, I know I wouldn't stop.

One day, as we sit bundled outside in the graveyard, I ask Bree how she deals with all the death, how she was able to spin and so quickly shoot the guard in the Union Central's surveillance corridor.

"Gray, have you ever killed a man?" she asks, staring me

down with those blue eyes of hers. I think it over, and amazingly, even with all I've been through, I haven't. I couldn't even kill an Order member, begging to be shot.

"I've only been hunting," I say.

"Well it's different from hunting. It's so very different. When I had my first kill, on a mission here with the Rebels, I cried. Imagine that—me, crying. And then, after time, as the numbers added up, it grew easier. I'm not saying I like it, or ever want to do it, but you come to a point where, if your life is on the line and you see your path of escape closing before your eyes, you don't think about morals or right and wrong. You think about life and death. You think about survival. In Taem, I did what I thought would keep us alive, and that included pulling the trigger. There will come a day, as this battle continues, that you will face that same decision, and believe me when I say that you will choose your own life over sparing another."

"It just seems so heartless, the way we are killing each other. And you act like it's necessary. You're proud to do it."

"I'm not proud of killing, but I am proud to be a part of the Rebellion. I'm proud to fight for our people, and that's never going to change."

I smile at her certainty. "Are you always going to be so blunt?" I jest.

She misses my playful tone and frowns. "No one said I was easy to love, Gray."

"Is that was this is, then? You and me?"

"I guess that depends on how you feel. I've made myself clear. You're the one who has to make up his mind."

She leaves me there, in the graveyard beyond Mount Martyr, and as she walks away, my thoughts fall on Emma.

Winter approaches and on a blustery day when the first snowflakes have started to fall into the Basin, Ryder calls an impromptu status meeting. When I arrive, the captains are sitting about the table, while Bree, Xavier, and even Clipper stand with their backs against the wall. Bo is there, too, and he winks at me as I enter.

The two of us have talked often since our return to Crevice Valley, discussing what we'd seen in the control room and how those visuals might give the Rebels an extra edge. This wink from Bo can only mean that he finally spoke to Ryder about our ideas.

"We need to talk about next steps," Ryder says, calling the meeting to order. "I believe our time of hiding, of fighting only in defense, has passed. It is time to fight for everything that first brought us together. It is time for offense, for strategy. It is time to attack."

"But even if everyone in Crevice Valley were to fight, our numbers aren't enough," Elijah says.

"Precisely why Bo's suggestion is so valid," Ryder replies.

Fallyn looks at Bo. "What suggestion?"

"We're going to Group A," Bo announces, beaming. I'm smiling with him, but everyone else looks shocked.

"There's nothing left of Group A," Raid states, and several of the others around him nod in agreement.

"No, there is," I chime in. "Well, there might be. It warrants checking out."

"We are going to trek halfway across the country?" Fallyn shoots back. "Leave the safety of Crevice Valley and go on some wild-goose chase, all on the hunch that there might be a few survivors in Group A?"

"Not everyone will go," Ryder says. "Just a few, a select team."

"Fine, so this select team gets all the way out to Group A, assuming we even know where it is, which we don't, and brings back what? Savages? Wild animals? How does this help us?"

"First of all, I know exactly where it is," Bo says, tapping the side of his skull with a fidgeting forefinger. "Well, not exactly, but I overheard enough conversations in Taem to have a more than rough idea. Furthermore, if anyone is left in Group A, I doubt they are savages."

"And why would you think that?" Fallyn asks, but I start speaking before Bo does.

"Because we saw them. In the control room, in Union

Central. There are dozens of screens still watching Group A. If you looked carefully, you could see them moving about the shadows, ducking out of view. I think they know they are being watched and I think they are undercover purposefully. They are staying out of sight and under the illusion of a wrecked society in the hopes of something. I'm not sure what. Escape, maybe? If we can get in there, break them out, we will have willing participants for our fight against Frank."

"Sounds an awful lot like a Heist to me," Bree says.

"Yes, but a very different Heist," I say. "A Heist they want. A Heist they are waiting for."

"Precisely." Ryder smiles, and then pushes a list of team members before us.

There is a mere dusting of snow on the ground when we pack our bags for the Western Territory. We leave today to begin a journey that will take many weeks; and with luck, we will secure the numbers to beat Frank for good.

Saying good-bye to Blaine is so difficult it hurts. He wants to come, begs to even, but Ryder refuses. While Blaine is stronger, he's still not strong enough. It's his stamina. I worry he'll never be quite the same. He puts on his best big brother face and tells me to be careful. Even though it is a vow larger than life, I promise him I'll keep myself in one piece.

I head outside and wait for the group in the cemetery. There is a new headstone in the forefront, carved with Harvey's name even though the Rebels had no body to bury beneath it. I stop beside it and watch my breath smoke through the late November air. A black crow joins me and takes to pecking at the stone.

"Go on. Get." I swat at the bird. He caws at me viciously, black feathers gleaming in the white landscape. Footsteps approach, and annoyed by them, the bird flies off.

"You ready?" Emma asks. She wears a thick coat and is loaded up with gear, our medic for the journey.

I nod.

"I hope we can put things right on this mission, Gray," she says simply, her dark eyes darting between me and her palms. "I don't like when we are like this, so distant."

"Me neither," I confess. I should say a million other things, but I can't find the words.

"It's a long trip," she adds. "Maybe we could talk a little."

"Yeah. We should."

She smiles and it is the first one I've ever been able to truly read. Her lips are wistful, pinched to one side and upturned, full of promise. It makes me hopeful, which is the clearest emotion I've felt in weeks.

I hear voices and turn my attention to the rest of the team that is appearing behind her. My father is first—he'll be heading up the expedition—along with Xavier, Bo, and even Clipper, who will be our technical edge. Bo looks surprisingly ready. After several weeks of conditioning he has abandoned his usual hunched-over state for a limber, upright one. This alone made Blaine furious, but of course, Bo was never in a coma. A few other faces join us, additional team members. The rest of the captains are staying behind. There will be scouting missions and other things to attend to while we are gone.

And then Bree appears, stepping from the safety of Crevice Valley last, a pack on her back, rifle in her arms, and a scowl on her face as stubborn as ever. There is a thick hat pulled down over her ears, but her blond hair spills from beneath it.

"You ready to perform your first Heist?" she jokes.

"You know it."

We shift the weight of our bags on our shoulders and start moving, following the team before us.

I hear the crow before I see him. He appears overhead, a dark silhouette against a pallid sky. He tails us for a while, overseeing our hopeful caravan and our boot prints, which leave soft impressions in the shallow snow as we head west.

# ACKNOWLEDGMENTS

Numerous people made this book possible. I'm near positive my gratitude could fill a second novel and then some, so I'll attempt to restrain myself. Many thanks, in no particular order:

To my fearless agent, Sara Crowe. This has been one heck of a journey and I'd have lost my way a long time ago had it not been for you. Thank you for taking a chance on me. And for answering all my emails. Especially the ones that started with *"This is probably a silly question, but . . ."* You are a godsend.

To my brilliant editor, Erica Sussman, for getting it and loving it and making it better. Until your purple pen started scrawling questions in the margins, Gray's story was only a fraction of what it is now. I can't thank you enough.

To the folks at HarperTeen / HarperCollins Children's for welcoming me to the family and being nothing short of awesome. Erin Fitzsimmons for a cover that still makes me giddy with happiness, plus gorgeous interior pages to boot. Alison Donalty, Alisdair Miller, and Howard Huang, who were also instrumental in the creation of *Taken*'s artwork. Tyler Infinger for the smile-inducing emails (and packages!). And to everyone else at Harper who worked on this book, championed for it, and helped see it into the world, please know I am terribly appreciative of all you do.

April Tucholke, for reading this novel countless times and always providing insightful feedback. You're the best critique partner a girl could ask for.

All my writer friends in the Twittersphere and beyond: You've kept me sane. Particularly Sarah Maas and Susan Dennard. Thank you for squeeing with me at the high points and holding my hand at the lows. I owe you both a cupcake. Or four.

Every teacher who has touched and inspired, but especially Lynn McMullin. That creative writing class my senior year of high school changed everything.

Michelle Sinclair, for being a positive, radiant, inspirational force in my life. I adore you. Alanna and Tammy, for cheering me on and promising to buy a million copies. (I'm half-tempted to hold you to that.) Dave, for always brainstorming with me. And to the rest of my old coworkers who put up with my weird part-time schedule that allowed me to chase a dream, thank you. (Carin, I can't tell you how grateful I am that I had such flexibility.) You guys all rock.

Kara, Katie, Kristen, and Nikki, because friendship is priceless.

Ava, Becca, and Dave (see above).

My extended family, large and sprawling: It is a blessing to be surrounded by such wonderful people.

An endless thank-you to my parents, John and Maureen Snyder, for being the very best teachers around. For filling my childhood with books and adventures and travels. For encouraging me to dream big. And for not having cable television. I may have hated it when I was younger, but it was because of the mere two-channel reception that I spent so much time with my nose deep in books. Years later, I am eternally grateful.

My sister, Kelsy, for being my first reader, best friend, and number-one fan. This novel would still be a mere handful of chapters on my laptop had you not begged to know what happens next.

My husband, Rob, for being patient. And supportive. And believing in me all the times I stopped believing in myself. You are my bird and I'll fly with you anywhere.

And above all, to you, dear reader: Thank you for picking up this novel. Thank you for loving stories and words and *Once upon a time*. Thank you for giving books a home. The world needs more people like you.

# THE TIME HAS COME FOR THE REBELS TO FIGHT BACK.

Turn the page for a sneak peek at
the next chapter in Gray's story

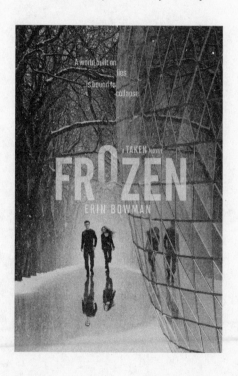

# ONE

WE HAVE BEEN WALKING FOR two weeks. Nothing tails us but snow and crows and dark shadows of doubt. The days grow shorter, the evenings frigid. I thought I'd be able to handle the cold.

I was wrong.

Back in Claysoot, our winters were hard, but while our homes were drafty and crude, we still had shelter. Even if I had to bundle up and head into the woods for a day of hunting, I could always return to a house. I could light a fire and put on clean socks and cling to a cup of hot tea as though my life depended on it.

Now it is just endless walking. Endless cold. At night we have only tents. And exposed fires. And blankets and jackets and countless additional layers that are never enough to chase the chill from our bones.

It's funny how Claysoot actually looks good on some days. When it's freezing and no amount of blowing on my hands seems to warm them, I can't help but think of the comforts of my old home. I have to remind myself that Claysoot was never a home. A home is a place you are safe, at ease, able to let down your guard. Claysoot is none of these things. It will never be these things. The Laicos Project made sure of that, starting the day Frank locked children away to serve his own needs, corralling them like cattle, raising them to create the perfect soldiers: Forgeries. Human machines to do his bidding. Perfect replicas of the people he imprisoned.

And now we march to one of those prisons, a forgotten group in the Western Territory of AmEast's vast countryside. We'll look for survivors at Group A, invite them to join us in the fight against Frank. See what secrets they've learned in all their years of hiding. Ryder's holding out hope that Group A might make a decent secondary base, help us extend our reach to the opposite end of the country.

I look at my hands, dry and chapped. Snow is falling again, drifting through the early-morning light as delicate, gray flakes. I'm supposed to be doing something. What am I supposed to be doing?

I see the footprints, and I remember. Clipper.

He's been drifting from our team lately. We'll settle down for the night, or pause for a water break, and then someone will notice that he's missing. I always get saddled with the honor of retrieving him.

I stand and pull my gloves back on, return my focus to tracking him. I crest a small rise and there he is, leaning against a pale birch tree.

"We need to keep moving. You ready?"

"Gray," he says, turning to face me. "I didn't hear you."

I force a smile. "You never do."

"True." There's an unmistakable heaviness to Clipper's voice. He sounds older. Looks it, too. After Harvey died—was murdered by Frank—the boy took over as the Rebels' head of technology. All the added responsibility seems to have aged him.

"I miss her," Clipper says, touching a twine bracelet I watched his mother give him when they said their good-byes two weeks earlier. "And Harvey." He kicks at a snow-dusted rock at his feet. "He was . . . I don't know how to put it. I just feel lost without him."

Harvey was like a father to Clipper. That's what he means to say. I know it, and so does the rest of our team. It's painfully obvious.

"You've got me, at least," I offer. "I'm the one who races after you every time you take off. That has to count for something, right?"

He laughs. It's a short, quick noise. More of a snort than anything.

"Come on. Everyone's waiting."

Clipper straightens and takes one last look into the endless forest of tree trunks. "You know I'll never actually leave you guys, right? Sometimes I just need some space."

"I understand."

"But you always come after me."

"It makes my father feel better. We'd be lost without you, and as our captain, he sleeps better knowing you're not running away."

Clipper frowns. "I might get scared, but I'm not a coward." He folds his arms around the location device, clutching it to his chest as we head for camp. Clipper's spent so much time staring at the thing lately, I've started to think he believes Harvey is out here somewhere, waiting in a snow-filled gully that Clipper can get to if he only plugs in the right coordinates.

Even though my father has been pressing us at a grueling pace lately, the camp is still not broken down when it comes into view. Tents as bright as grass speckle the snow, and a fire sends a thin line of smoke through the tree branches.

Xavier and Sammy are pulling their tent stakes from the frozen earth, but everyone else is huddled around September, a mean-looking girl in her early twenties who is actually far sweeter than her angled features let on. She's dishing out a breakfast of grits. This has been our fare since we set out. Grits in the morning. Whatever meat we manage to catch throughout the day for dinner. And little rest in between.

Bree spots Clipper and me first. She shoots me a smile, wide and shameless. It's a good look on her. Refreshing, even, since she seems bent on scowling most of the time. She elbows Emma, who stands beside her, a wool hat pulled over wavy hair. Even from a distance I can hear Bree's energetic words. "They're back. I told you not to worry."

Emma looks up and raises a hand in a shy sort of greeting. I don't return the wave. I wish I could forgive her. For replacing me so quickly when we were separated earlier this year—me on the run from Frank, her stuck under his watch in Taem. For moving on as if what we had was meaningless, as if we never talked about birds and pairs and settling into something that feels right. I know it's foolish to hold a grudge, but I've never been the forgiving type. I've never been able to look past people's faults or bite my tongue or be generally decent. I am not my brother.

Clipper runs ahead to retrieve a cup of grits from

September and my father shouts to me from across camp. "Took you long enough!"

"The wind covered his footprints," I lie. I don't want to mention that like Clipper, I experienced a moment of weakness alone in the woods. That I stopped to ponder it all: the grimness of what we face, the bleakness of our journey so far.

My father swallows a spoonful of his breakfast before narrowing his eyes at Clipper. "I won't have this anymore, Clayton." Hearing Clipper's true name makes the entire team freeze. "We waste time whenever you take off. Gray has to find you. We all have to wait. And we can't afford delays like that—not when our mission's details could be spilled at any moment."

Just three days after we left Crevice Valley, Rebel headquarters, Ryder radioed to tell us one of our own fell into enemy hands. We're now well out of communication range, with no way of knowing how much information, if any, the Order acquired. Still, we spend a lot of time glancing over our shoulders as we hike. Fear is an ugly thing to have chasing you.

"I need you to start acting like a soldier," my father adds, jerking his chin toward Clipper. "You hear me?"

"Oh, go easy on him, Owen," Xavier calls out, securing his broken-down tent to the underside of his pack. The act reminds me of when he taught me to hunt in Claysoot, him loading up his gear and signaling for me to follow him into the woods. "He's just a kid."

Clipper frowns at this, obviously disagreeing that a boy of almost thirteen is nothing but a child.

Sammy stops wrestling with his pack. "Yeah, he's just an immature, no-good, brainless computer whiz who can take any piece of equipment and make it do his bidding. Actually, on that note: Clipper, can you fabricate a time machine so we can get to Group A already? My toes are about to fall off, and I could really benefit from an accelerated schedule."

This gets a light chuckle from the group. I met Sammy over a game of darts back in Crevice Valley, but it wasn't until this mission that I truly came to know him. He's good-natured, endlessly sarcastic, and has a quick-witted sense of humor that's been a welcome distraction.

"We all know you're cold, Sammy," my father says sternly.

"I'm not just cold, I'm freezing," he responds, wrestling a hat down farther over his pale hair. "And think of what this wind is doing to my face! How am I going to win over any girls when I have these windburned cheeks?" He pats them with his palms.

"The only girls you'll be seeing for the foreseeable future are the three in our group. And they're not interested."

Sammy raises his eyebrows as if he means to accept Owen's words as a challenge, and my father adds, "Don't get any ideas."

"Let's start moving," Bo says. "Standing still only chills a person further." His customary twitch surfaces—a forefinger tapping frantically against his mug of grits—and I decide he looks the coldest of us all. His aged frame appears thinner and paler with each day. He's younger than Frank, in his early sixties, but the years he spent cramped in Taem's prison weren't kind to his body. Sometimes I'm amazed Bo's made it this far without complications. I half expected him to turn back to Crevice Valley during the first few days of hiking. I'm pretty certain Blaine would have expected the same.

But of course Blaine isn't here to confirm or deny the theory, and sometimes, his absence hurts worse than the cold. I always feel slightly lost without my brother, my twin. Next time I see him, he'd better be back to his old self. I miss the brother that could keep up with me while hunting, and run without getting winded. I even miss his disapproving, judgmental looks, although I'll never tell him that.

September spreads out the coals and the team scatters to break down the rest of camp. We've all become so proficient at the process that in mere minutes, our bags are packed and we're falling into a thin line.

I tell my feet to move, one in front of the next. Bree joins me, assuming her usual place at my side.

"Think it's too late to turn back?" She says it like she's joking, but I can see the seriousness on her face.

"What? Why would you say that?"

"The more I think about it, the more I worry we won't find anything. I mean, the Order confirmed Group A extinct years ago. Maybe we saw what we wanted to in Frank's control room."

"No. There were people moving through those frames. We both saw it. Bo and Emma, too. We didn't *all* see something that wasn't there."

She lets out a long exhale.

"And it was the most advanced of the test groups," I add. "Even if we find it empty—which we *won't*—we're still going to see if there's anything we can salvage. Ryder thinks—"

"It could make a good secondary base. I know. He yapped about it enough before we left. There's just that small problem about it being without power."

"And that's why we've got Clipper. He'll work his magic."

She nudges me with her elbow. "When did you become so positive?"

"When I decided Sammy alone wasn't enough."

She grins at that and even though I know Emma is behind us, I throw an arm over Bree's shoulder and pull her closer.

It's late afternoon and we're staring at a town that shouldn't be nestled in the base of the valley before us, at least according to Clipper. He's been using his maps and location device to steer us down the least populated routes. Sometimes we'll cross an abandoned, deteriorating stretch of road, or spot a town so far away it looks like a minuscule set of children's building blocks on the horizon; but this community, practically at our feet, is a first. Surprising, too, since we left the Capital Region a few days back and have since entered the Wastes, a giant stretch of mostly unpopulated land that Clipper claims will take close to two weeks to cross. At least it's flatter. The mountain pass that filled the first week of our journey was so brutal I still have sore calves.

Owen pulls out a pair of binoculars. "No lights or movement that I can see. Deserted, probably."

"Maybe we should hike around it," Bo offers. "Just to be safe."

People this far west are likely harmless—average civilians trying to make a life for themselves beyond Frank's reach—but we've been extremely cautious about revealing our presence to *anyone*, especially since Ryder called about the captured Rebel.

I'm as surprised as anyone when my father stows the binoculars away and says, "We're cutting through. The town's abandoned, and we could all do well with a night inside four walls."

I'm thinking about sleeping in comfort—being *truly* warm for once—when I spot the crows. There are dozens of them, circling over the buildings waiting ahead. I don't like the way they hover, or how their shrill cries echo through the valley.

Owen pushes open the wooden gate that borders the community and waves Bree and me in first. We pass beneath a sign reading *Town of Stonewall*, weapons ready. The crows' shadows glide across the snow as we walk up the main street.

The homes are in rickety condition, but not because they've been long abandoned. There are signs of life everywhere: an evergreen wreath on a door, hung in recent weeks given how lush it still is. A wheelbarrow on its side, as though it was dropped in a hurry. Clothing, strung up on a warmer day, now frozen and stiff, that creaks on a line.

Something crunches beneath my boot. I look down.

Fingers, hidden beneath a thin layer of snow.

Fingers that attach to a hand, an arm, a torso. I step back quickly. Then I spot another. Human remains slouched alongside a well just ahead. And suddenly, they are everywhere. Mounds I thought to be snowdrifts are bodies, rotting and festering and rigid in death.

Bree uses her rifle to roll over the one at my feet. Two hollow eye sockets stare back. When she speaks, it is nothing but a whisper.

"What happened here?"

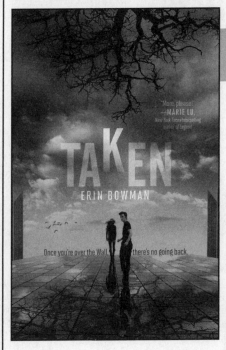